Praise for Ellen Hopkins's
New York Times bestselling books

Crank

"Powerful and unsettling." —*Kirkus Reviews*

"The poems are masterpieces of word, shape, and pacing . . .
a stunning portrayal of a teen's loss of direction."
—*School Library Journal*

"Hopkins delivers a gritty, fast-paced read." —*VOYA*

Identical

★ "Sharp and stunning, with a brilliant final page."
—*Kirkus Reviews*, starred review

★ "A harrowing ride. . . . Hopkins's verse is not only lean
and sinuous, it also demonstrates a mastery of technique."
—*Publishers Weekly*, starred review

"The tension builds slowly and subtly, erupting in a shattering
climax of psychological disintegration and breakthrough. . . .
Gritty and compelling. . . ."—*School Library Journal*

Also by Ellen Hopkins

Crank

Burned

Impulse

Glass

Tricks

Fallout

Margaret K. McElderry Books

IDENTICAL

Ellen Hopkins

Margaret K. McElderry Books
NEW YORK LONDON TORONTO SYDNEY

MARGARET K. McELDERRY BOOKS

An imprint of Simon & Schuster Children's Publishing Division

1230 Avenue of the Americas, New York, New York 10020

This book is a work of fiction. Any references to historical events, real people, or real locales are used fictitiously. Other names, characters, places, and incidents are products of the author's imagination, and any resemblance to actual events or locales or persons, living or dead, is entirely coincidental.

MARGARET K. McELDERRY BOOKS is a trademark of Simon & Schuster, Inc.

For information about special discounts for bulk purchases, please contact Simon & Schuster Special Sales at 1-866-506-1949 or business@simonandschuster.com.

The Simon & Schuster Speakers Bureau can bring authors to your live event. For more information or to book an event, contact the Simon & Schuster Speakers Bureau at 1-866-248-3049 or visit our website at www.simonspeakers.com.

Also available in a Margaret K. McElderry Books hardcover edition.

Book design by Mike Rosamilia

The text for this book is set in Trade Gothic Condensed Eighteen.

Manufactured in the United States of America

First paperback edition December 2010

10 9 8 7 6

The Library of Congress has cataloged the hardcover edition as follows:

Hopkins, Ellen.

Identical / Ellen Hopkins.—1st ed.

p. cm.

Summary: Sixteen-year-old identical twin daughters of a district-court judge and a candidate for the United States House of Representatives, Kaeleigh and Raeanne Gardella desperately struggle with secrets that have already torn them and their family apart.

ISBN 978-1-4169-5005-9 (hc)

[1. Novels in verse. 2. Family problems—Fiction. 3. Emotional problems—Fiction. 4. Secrets—Fiction. 5. Sexual abuse victims—Fiction. 6. Twins—Fiction. 7. Sisters—Fiction. 8. California—Fiction.] I. Title.

PZ7.5.H67 Ide 2008

[Fic]—dc22

2007032463

ISBN 978-1-4169-5006-6 (pbk)

ISBN 978-1-4169-8465-8 (eBook)

This book is dedicated to Dianne, Karen, and Tracy, dear friends and special women who rose to shine like stars above dark places in their lives.

With special thanks to Jude, who provided invaluable insight about the psychology of sexual abuse—its victims and victimizers.

IDENTICAL

Raeanne
Mirror, Mirror

When I look into a
mirror,
it is her face I see.
Her right is my left, double
moles, dimple and all.
My right is her left,
unblemished.

We are exact
opposites,
Kaeleigh and me.
Mirror-image identical
twins. One egg, one sperm,
one zygote, divided,
sharing one complete
set of genetic markers.

On the outside
we are the same. But not
inside. I think
she is the egg, so
much like our mother
it makes me want to scream.
Cold.
Controlled.
That makes me the sperm,
I guess. I take completely
after our father.

All Daddy, that's me.
Codependent.
Cowardly.

Good, bad. Left, right.
Kaeleigh and Raeanne.
One egg, one sperm.
One being, split in two.

And how many
souls?

Interesting Question

Don't you think?
I mean, if the Supreme
Being inserts a single soul
at the moment of conception,
does that essence divide
itself? Does each half then
strive to become whole
again, like a starfish
or an earthworm?

Or might the soul clone itself,
create a perfect imitation
of something yet to be
defined? In this way,
can a reflection be altered?

Or does the Maker,
in fact, choose
to place two
separate souls within
a single cell, to spark
the skirmish that ultimately
causes such an unlikely rift?

Do twins begin in the womb?
Or in a better place?

One Soul or Two

We live in a smug California
valley. Rolling ranch land, surrounded
by shrugs of oak-jeweled hills.
Green for two brilliant
months sometime around spring,
burnt-toast brown the rest of the year.

Just over an unremarkable mountain
stretches the endless Pacific.
Mornings here come wrapped
in droops of gray mist.
Most days it burns off by noon.
Other days it just hangs on
and on. Smothers like a wet blanket.

Three towns triangulate
the valley, three corners, each
with a unique flavor:
weathered Old West;
antiques and wine tasting;
just-off-the-freeway boring.

Smack in the center is the town
where we live, and it is the most
unique of all, with its windmills
and cobbled sidewalks, designed
to carry tourists to Denmark.
Denmark, California-style.

The houses line smooth black
streets, prim rows
of postcard-pretty dwellings,
coiffed and manicured from curb
to chimney. Like Kaeleigh
and me, they're perfect
on the outside. But behind
the Norman Rockwell facades,
each holds its secrets.

Like Kaeleigh's and mine,
some are dark. Untellable.
Practically unbelievable.

But Telling

Isn't an option.
If you tell

                              a secret

about someone
you don't really know,
other people might

                              listen,

but decide you're
making it up. Even if you
happen to know for a fact

                              it's true.

If you tell a secret
about a friend, other people

                              want to hear

all of it, prologue
to epilogue. But then they

                              think

you're totally messed
up for telling it
in the first place. They

                              think

they can't trust you.
And hey, they probably
can't. Once a nark,
always a nark, you

                              know?

Kaeleigh
I Wish I Could Tell

But to whom could
I possibly confess

a secret,

any secret? Not to my mom,
who's never around. A time
or two, I've begged her to

listen,

to give me just a few
precious minutes between
campaign swings. Of course

it's true

the wrong secret could take her
down, but you'd think she'd

want to hear

it. I mean, what if she had
to defend it? Really, you'd

think

she'd want to be forewarned,
in case the *International Inquisitor*
got hold of it. Does she

think

this family has no secrets?
The clues are everywhere, whether
or not she wants to

know.

There's Daddy

Who comes
home every
day, dives
straight into
a tall amber
bottle, falls
into a stone-
walled well
of silence, a
place where he can tread
the suffocating loneliness.
On the surface, he's a proud
man. But just beneath his not-
so-thick skin, is a broken soul.
In his courtroom, he's a tough
but evenhanded jurist, respected
if not particularly well liked. At
home, he doesn't try to disguise his
bad habits, has no friends, a tattered
family. A part of me despises him,
what he's done. What he continues
to do. Another part pities him and
will always be his little girl, his
devoted, copper-haired daughter.
His unfolding flower. But enough
about Daddy, who most definitely
has plenty of secrets. Secrets Mom
should want to know about. Secrets
I should tell, but instead tuck away.
Because if I tell on him, I'd have to . . .

Tell on Me

How I'm a total
        wreck. Afraid to
let anyone near.
        Afraid they'll see
the real me, not
        Kaeleigh at all.

                I do have friends,
        but they don't know
                me, only someone
        I've created to take
                my place. Someone
        sculpted from ice.

                I keep the melted
                        me bottled up
                inside. Where no
                        one can touch her,
                until, unbidden, she
                        comes pouring out.

        She puddles then,
upon fear-trodden
        ground. I am always
afraid, and I am vague
        about why. My life
isn't so awful. Is it?

We Live in a Fine Home

With lots of beautiful stuff—
fine leather sofas and oiled

teak tables and expensive
artwork on walls and shelves.

Of course, someone used to
such things might wonder

why there are no family
photos anywhere. It's almost

like we're afraid of ourselves.
And maybe we are, and not

only ourselves, but whatever
history created us. There are no

albums, with pictures of graying
grandparents, or pony rides

(never done one of those)
or memorable Gardella family parties.

(The Gardellas don't do parties,
not even on holidays.)

No first communions or christening
gowns. (We don't do church, either.)

Of course, no one ever comes
over, so no one has ever wondered

about these things, unless it's our
housekeeper, Manuela. Have to have

one of those, since Mom's never home
and Daddy often works late, and even

if he didn't, he wouldn't clean house
or go to the grocery store. Normal

parents do those things, right? I'm
not sure what normal is or isn't.

But It Really

Doesn't matter. Normal
is what's normal for me.
I've got nice clothes,

nicer than most. Pricey
things that other girls would
kill for, or shoplift, if they

could get away with it.
I have a room of my own,
decorated to my taste

(okay, with a lot of Daddy's
input) and most of the time
when I'm home, I hang out in

there, alone. Listen to music.
Read. Do my homework.
What more could a girl ask

for, right? I mean,
my life really isn't so bad.
Is it?

I Clearly Recall

Once upon a time, long
ago, when everything
was different. Mom

and Daddy were in love,
at least it sure looked
that way to Raeanne

and me. How we used
to giggle at them, kissing
and holding hands.

I remember how they used
to joke about their names.
Ray[mond] and Kay

How fate must have been
a bad poet and wrote them
into a poem together.

Then Raeanne or I would beg
them to tell—just one more time—
the story of how they met.

Mom Always Started

I was in college. UC Santa Barbara,
best university in California.
I had this really awful boyfriend.

I thought we'd run away
and live happily ever after.
Thank God he got arrested.

Then Daddy would *humph*
and *haw* and take over.
So there he was, in my court-

room, with a despicable
public defender failing
to come up with an even

halfway decent excuse for
why his client was driving
drunk. In one ear, out

the other. I'd heard it all
before, and anyway, the only
thing I could think about

was this creep's gorgeous
girl, sitting front and center,
hoping I'd go easy on him.

And Mom would interrupt.
Actually, I only hoped that
until I took a good, long look

at your father. Then I kind
of hoped he'd lock up my
boyfriend for a long time.

Then we'd laugh and my
parents would kiss and all
was perfect in our little world.

But That Was Before

Daddy fractured our world,
tilted it off its axis, sent it

careening out of control.
That was before the day

his own impairment
made him overcorrect, jerk

the Mercedes onto unpaved
shoulder, then back

across two lanes of traffic,
and over the double yellow

lines, head-on into traffic.
That was before the one-ton

truck sliced the passenger
side wide open. That was

before premature death, battered
bodies, and scars no plastic

surgeon could ever repair.
Yes, that was before.

Afterward

Mom didn't love Daddy
anymore, though he stayed
by her side until she healed,
begging forgiveness, promising
to somehow make everything right.

In fact, since the accident,
Mom doesn't love anyone.
She is marble. Beautiful.
Frigid. Easily stained
by her family. What's left
of us, anyway. We are corpses.

At first, we sought rebirth.
But resurrection devoid
of her love has made us zombies.
We get up every morning,
skip breakfast, hurry off
to work or school. For in
those other places,
we are more at home.

And sometimes, we stagger
beneath the weight of grief,
the immensity of aloneness.

No One Else Suspects

Not our neighbors.
Not our friends.
Not even our relatives.

                No one

suspects Mom's real
motive for running
for Congress is to run
away from us. No one

                suspects

the depth of her rejection,
or how drowning
in it has affected

                my father,

a powerful district
court judge, a man who
puts bad guys away,
slumped down

                on his knees,

unable to breathe,
unable to swim,
unable to stop

                begging

me to open my arms,

                let me stay,

and please, please love
him the way Mom used to.

Raeanne
Kaeleigh Closes Herself Off

From Daddy. And I think
she's completely insane.
I crave his affection.

No one,

no one normal, that is, will
understand. Yeah, yeah,
I'm all fucked up. My mantra.
But if anyone actually

suspects

how fucked up I am, they've
yet to let me know.
And, really, why would

my father

be so taken with her, but distance
himself from me? We're
identical. Except for the egg/
sperm thing. Would he fall

on his knees

in front of me, if I were
more like Mom and less
like him? Would he come,

begging,

to me, too,

let me stay,

if he realized I want to love
him the way Mom used to?

But Obsessions Are Personal, I Guess

Daddy's   obsession
with Kaeleigh   strikes at the
heart of me. But   looking at it real
objectively, I think I understand. She's
soft. Pliable. Gullible.   It's easy enough to
believe his declaration that should someone
root out his secrets, he'll swallow a bullet.

You know, he just might, though I see him
as much more likely to pick up that gun
and shoot Mom, especially if he's on
a bender. More and more of those
lately, both for him and for
me. My own obsession.
Falling into a state
of numb.

Numb

Sometimes that seems like a great
place to be. Closed off from it all,
in no need of love, no need of family.

To be honest, I've erected a huge,
huge wall between myself and Mom,
myself and Kaeleigh, who I avoid

whenever I can. Can't stand that hurt,
ever-present in her eyes. Eyes—
and hurt—that mirror my own.

Anyway, she makes me mad, mad
that she hides in her own mind so
well. Hides there from Daddy.

The only person I want to be close
to is Daddy, and he doesn't even see
me. It's like I'm not even here.

Most of the time I muddle through,
pretending I don't need to be held,
need to be touched, kissed.

But then need swells up, a thunderhead.
Storms down, sweeps over me
like a summer flash flood of need.

Numb Cannot Fight Such Need

So I turn to Mick, valley hardass
in more ways than one.

     Mom says, *That boy is trouble.*
     You steer clear, understand?

Like I give a rat's shiny pink
butt about what Mom thinks.

Actually, I'm amazed she even
noticed. Maybe she has spies

     who keep an eye on us when
     she can't be bothered. After

all, it wouldn't do for a daughter
of a United States congresswoman

to get pregnant, now would it?
Oh, she would shit, if she had

     any real idea of the things I do
     with Mick. So if she has spies,

they must be voyeurs. I know
it's ridiculous, but I glance around.

Nope, no discernable spies. Good
thing. Mick and I are taking off at lunch.

     We probably won't eat much.
     (No sandwiches, anyway.)

So if I do head back to class
afterward, it will be in an altered state.

Self-medication firmly at the top
of my agenda, I blow through
                    Lawler's history quiz, put my
                    pencil down, and sit staring out
the window, waiting for the bell.
A black shape materializes in the sky,

wings slowly through the mist. Buzzard?
No, as it nears, I see it's a condor.
                    Some kind of omen there. As I
                    consider exactly what kind,
someone taps my shoulder. I wheel
around. *Finished?* asks Mr. Lawler.

I nod and hand him my paper, and
when I look into his gold-flecked
                    green eyes, I think for about
                    the hundredth time what a fine
guy he is. As if I had said it out
loud, he smiles. *You may go, then.*

I smile right back. "Thanks. See you
tomorrow." I pick up my books, stand
                    with deliberate grace, and as
                    I walk toward the door I feel
eyes on my back, know at least one
pair belongs to him. Men are so easy.

I Stop in the Girls' Room

For a quick pee and to redo my makeup.
The bell finally rings. Within seconds,
the lunch rush madhouse erupts.

Hurry up!   *What the fuck?*
       Hey, you, come here!

It's the same every day. Same voices.
Same laughter. Same lame people
I've known most of my life.

Got a smoke?   *Got a Tic Tac?*
      Did you hear about . . . ?

I hustle along the walkway, mostly
ignoring the waves and hellos of
people I rarely give the time of day to.

. . . got the lead . . .   *. . . made honor roll . . .*
      Ian's looking for you.

Ah, see, they're confusing me with
Kaeleigh. Sometimes I think that's
funny. Other times, it just annoys

the living crap out of me. Guess that's
what comes of sharing a wardrobe,
not to mention a face. Oh, well.

At least Mick won't confuse me
with her. She wouldn't go near him.
He's much too much like Daddy.

Both of them are tough outside.
But dig down under the skin,
there's a soft, gooey core.

Auger into that core, like tapping
a maple, you'll get doused
with incredibly sweet sap.

It's a lot of work, work that
Kaeleigh could never appreciate,
because she doesn't like maple

syrup anyway. But I do. I love
it. And if Daddy would just stand
still for me, I'd happily tap his core.

Mick's Sexy

Chevy Avalanche, with slate gray
paint and silver leather seats, idles
in a far corner of the parking lot.
Two years out of school, he isn't
really supposed to be here.
But he generally comes running
when I call. He likes what I give him.

I like what he gives me, too,
and I'm mostly talking about
the bud. I pick up my pace because
right under his front seat I know
there's a fat, stinky joint
with my name on it.

Okay, Mick's name is there too.
It's his dope, after all.
But he's always happy to share.
Of course, he expects compensation,
and after smoking a big ol' doobie,
I'm generally willing to cooperate.

Life has gotten better—or at least
more bearable—since I was introduced
to my good friend, marijuana.
You couldn't have a more decent friend.
I love everything about it.

I love the way it smells—good green
bud, anyway, and that's the only
kind Mick gets. I guess his brother
knows a Humboldt grower. Okay,
the pot smells a lot like skunk juice.
But somehow, there's a difference.
A good one.

I love the way the thick smoke
tastes, curling across my tongue,
snaking down my throat. I love
holding it in. Coughing it out.
I love head rushes, the creeping
warmth that follows.

And I love the distant place
it takes me to. Everything feels
right there. Mellow. Easy.
Stress-free. I even love the munchies,
the perfect excuse for devouring a pint
of Häagen-Dazs. Of course, afterward
I have to go stick my finger down
my throat. Don't dare get fat.
Daddy would not like that.

Mick and Marijuana

Await me. I'm ready to pay
Mick's going rate for the pot.
(And I'm not talking money.)
Some people would balk
at the price tag.

Not me.

You might think, because
of the things I've seen
Daddy do, I'd be disgusted
by sex. No way.

I like it.

I like how it feels physically,
yes. Kisses, hot and prickly
as August. Hands, tan
and rough against my soft
white skin. And the last, extreme
punctuation.

I get off.

But getting off myself
isn't the best part. I do
everything in my power
to make sure

he gets off.

And that puts me indisputably
in control. (He thinks otherwise,
and I let him.) It's the only time
I am in control. And I like
how that feels

most of all.

Kaeleigh
Call Me Powerless

Yeah, I know on first glance
I have it all. Looks. Money.
Straight As. Leads. Popularity.
I'm a regular princess, right?

Not me.

The final bell rings and I dash
for my locker, hoping no one
offers me a ride home. Some
people despise the bus, but

I like it.

Yes, it's mostly freshmen
and losers, and I fit right in.
Anyway, no one bugs me
with questions or invitations.
I am practically anonymous.
Too soon, brakes screech and

I get off

a few blocks from home. The walk
is usually silent. But today Ian's
Yamaha rips around the corner.
It slows, stops, and I wait as

he gets off,

sheds his helmet, draws near.
                    Have you been avoiding me?
I have, and I struggle to meet
his eyes. When I finally do, I find
concern. Pain. Anger. And love,

most of all.

Ian Is My Best Friend

He has loved me since
fourth grade. I would trust
him with my life, and all
my secrets but one.

Soooo . . . have you?

I wish I were worthy
of his love. (Any love.)
I should tell him to run.
But I can't. I need him.

Ahem. Hello?

He deserves to be loved,
by someone really great.
He's gorgeous, in an artsy
way. No ego. All heart.

Earth to Kaeleigh . . .

All heart and waiting for me
to respond. "I . . . um . . . Sorry,
I'm a million miles away.
What did you say?"

*Ah, the old "million miles
away" excuse.*

His smile holds the warmth
of the sun, and when he
opens his arms, I plunge
deep between them. "Sorry."

*For what? Oh, you have
been avoiding me, huh?*

His body is toned, and he smells
yummy, like some kind of spice.
I look up into eyes, the turquoise
of the Caribbean. "Sort of."

*I always said I liked your
honesty. Still . . .*

"Not avoiding you in particular.
More like everyone, kind of.
Sometimes I get antisocial.
You know that, though."

*Yeah, I do, but I'm not
exactly sure why.*

"I must get it from my dad.
Can't be from Mom, the world-
class go-getter, hand shaker,
and baby kisser."

*I don't think a judge
should be antisocial.*

Can't talk about my father.
Too much to say that can't
be said. I pull away from Ian's
hug. "You're probably right."

*So, may I walk you home?
Or would you rather ride?*

"Two blocks? Think we can
walk it. But hey, if you be
really, really nice, I'll let
you give me a ride to work."

*Deal. Being nice to you is easy,
even when you try to avoid me.*

This Huge Part of Me

Is so happy Ian won't let me avoid
        him, won't let me push him away.
What I don't understand is why not.

I mean, girls hit on him all the time.
        Over the years he has gone out
with a few. But he never gets serious.

I know he wants to get serious.
        He's definitely not a player, not
a poser, not a loser, not a user.

Ian wants deep down forever love,
        love he knows he can count on.
And that so sets him up for hurt.

Last year he and Katie were an item
        for several months. After he broke
up with her, I asked what happened.

        We were on the hill behind
                his house, soaking up April sun.
        Katie's great, he said. *Pretty. Sweet.*

"So what, then?" I asked, knowing
        the answer but wanting to hear it.
(And realizing how selfish that was.)

He turned his face away from me,
            into the spring breeze. *She's great,*
he repeated. *But she'll never be you.*

Then he looked straight into my eyes.
            I love you, and I know you know how
much. I also know there's something

that keeps you from loving me back.
            What is it, Kaeleigh? Is it me?
Because I swear I'll change. . . .

"No! It's not you. Oh Ian, you're
            the absolute best. If I could love
anyone, it would be you. I want . . ."

The rest, the "to love you" stuck
            like a giant wad of gum in my throat.
Ian pulled me into him, held me close.

Please! he pleaded. And then he kissed
            me. Gently. And I kissed him back,
but only for a second because suddenly

all I could see was a featureless
            face, with a wide, sour mouth
coaxing, *Please, baby. I won't hurt you.*

Fear enveloped me, clasped itself
               around me. I couldn't shake
free, struggled to find breath.

Still seeking air, I jerked back.
               I will never forget the look on
Ian's face, contorted with my pain.

               What the fuck is it, Kaeleigh?
                              Whatever it is, don't leave it
               inside. Someday you'll implode.

Trembling, eyes burning, I reached
               for his hand. "I know. I only hope
you won't have to clean up the mess."

I Still Haven't Imploded

Though, I have to admit,
sometimes (maybe even often)

I wish

I would. Wish I could
just get it over with. But it's
not going to happen right

this moment

so I'll go to work instead.
Arms tight around Ian's waist,
cool October wind in my face,
I truly wish the power of his love

could eclipse

the overwhelming shame.
He deserves someone better
than me, someone pure. Worthy.

The shadows

bend long toward evening
as the Yamaha quiets to a stutter.
A cloud of regret boils up,
rains sadness down all

around me

and as I climb from the bike,
a strange desire grips me. I can
do this. Want to do this.
I steel myself against the specters

always haunting me,

gather all my inner strength,
softly kiss the promise of his lips.

Raeanne
Promises Are Meaningless

Mom: *I promise I'll be home soon.*
Mick: *I promise I want only you.*

I wish

they'd both take a one-way
elevator to hell! Okay, I'm used
to my mother's lies. Right at

this moment

it's Mick whose bullshit
is pissing me off. Yeah, I guess
I'm a total dumb-ass for believing
the thought of being with me

could eclipse

his testosterone-fueled flirtations.
I mean, at lunch, I could hardly
wait to be with him. I sprinted
toward his truck, out of

the shadows

and into the bright autumn
glare. And there, leaning into
his open window, was that bitch
Madison. Jealousy squeezed

around me,

choked off my scream. Too much
to let myself dwell on, like visions,

always haunting me,

of Kaeleigh and Daddy.

Madison Happens to Be

Mick's ex, the operative two
        letters being *e* and *x*. Why
             can't she just leave him
                   alone? She's totally
            wrong for him. Anyway,
        it was her decision for them
to break up. A very good decision.

                First of all, Mick's out of
            school. Graduated, bottom
        of his class, two years ago.
Madison is the type who needs
        a guy on her arm at school,
            someone to flaunt, someone
                cute she can order around.

More to the point, the only
        drugs Madison will likely
            ever do are steroids. She's
                a total mainstream jock.
            Softball team. Swim team.
        Golf team. If it means creaming
an opponent, she's all over it.

                Could be why she's hustling
            Mick now. When he was up
        for grabs, she couldn't care
less about scratching his

figurative itch. All it took
               was his hooking up with me,
                         and out came her stubby claws.

Well, mine are a whole
          lot sharper, though she
                    doesn't seem to realize it.
                              Just wait till I dig them
                    into that sun-toughened
          jockette hide. Then it won't
matter if I can't scream.

She'll Scream Loud Enough

For both of us, and I do look forward
to that. Ooh. Was that mean? Maybe.

But hey, I'm sick and tired of playing
passive. No, I'll leave that to Kaeleigh.

Kaeleigh, queen of passive, all the time
saying no, but not strong enough

to mean it. Not strong enough to fight.
Not anywhere near as strong as me.

I have to say I rather enjoyed verbally sparring
instead of retreating. Once I finally caught

my breath, I climbed up into the Avalanche,
slid across the seat, almost into Mick's lap.

He turned (not quite quick enough, but it
was what it was), grinning. *'Bout time you*

got here. I almost took off without you.
Unsaid words hung like a heavy curtain:

Without you. And with Madison. I pretended
not to hear them, not to get mad at them.

Ignoring Ms. Jock completely, I looked straight
into his eyes. "Really? And miss out on this?"

Then I kissed him. Hard. Wet. Sharp stabs
of tongue. My fingers drifted in between

his thighs, finding exactly what they expected.
Madison gave a little gasp. "Oh," I said. "Sorry,

didn't mean to offend you." I laughed. Mick
joined me, then said, *That's my cue. See ya, Mad.*

She Was Mad, Okay

Madison puffed up red, venomous
as an adder. Holy crud. I've never
seen anyone flip from flirt to viper
so quickly. Totally scary!

She didn't budge as we backed out
of the parking space. Just stood
there, boiling, not a word escaping
her lips. But her eyes said plenty:

I'll get you back. Wait and see.

I smiled, moved even closer to Mick,
making steering problematic. *Could
you give me an inch or two, please?*
he said. I gave him a lot more than that.

In fact, once we were well beyond
Madison's sight, I scooted clear over
by the opposite door, clamped my mouth
shut before I said something I'd regret.

C'mon. Not my fault she's still hot for me.

He reached across the seat, grabbed
hold of my arm. Pulled. When I resisted,
he yanked harder. Hard enough to hurt.
Hard enough to leave purple bruises.

Someone smart would have screamed.
Someone sane would have waited
for a stop sign, thrown themselves free.
Someone whole would have said no.

Get the fuck over here and don't give me shit.

I did as instructed. Worse, I liked that he told
me what to do. It meant he cared, really cared.
Right? Whatever. "Did you score some bud?"
I asked, more to change the subject than anything.

Under the seat. Twist one up, okay? We headed
out Happy Canyon Road, only horses and cattle
to mind our business. We could have gone home—
no one there—but I was still too mad for sex.

You know you want me. You'd take slimy seconds.

Gross. "Yeah, right. Like your pimply butt
is such a turn-on." It isn't too pimply, and it's
kind of a turn-on, but that was beside the point.
His hand brushed my left nipple. *You love it.*

"Not while wondering who you're thinking
about, Madison or me." I took a deep drag,
held it. Took another without passing the joint,
exhaling giant smoke puffs right in his face.

Bogart. Pass that fucking thing over here.

So I did, and once we were totally buzzed
he pulled off onto a dirt ranch road, parked.
No maid out here. Just birds and squirrels.
Defenses lowered by excellent bud, I said

okay to a quickie. Totally in control.

In Control

Out of control.
                        Sometimes they're

            the same thing.
                        The trick is knowing
that, realizing
                        it's okay to feel
                                    out of control
            once in a while,
as long as
                        you're sure
                                    you can regain
the upper hand
                        when you
            absolutely need to.
                                    And really, when
            it comes to my

reclaiming control,

it comes down to one

simple little thing,

something I sometimes

have difficulty with:

saying no.

I've Got to Learn

To say no, and not only say
it, but mean it. In some
situations, not always
the right ones, I know,

I'm strong.

Really strong. Tough,
even. I guess, in a very odd
way, I'm something of

a survivor.

But there are times when,
much as I want to assert
myself, know it's the right
thing to do,

I can't

find the inner fortitude
to follow through with a simple
two-letter word. NO. One of
the first words babies can

understand,

one of the first they learn
to repeat. No. No, Mick, I won't
let you treat me with disrespect. No,
Mick, and I don't have to explain

why I

won't let you touch me this time.
Okay, so maybe I'm a little
confused. Does being in control
mean I have to cave in, have to

crumble?

Kaeleigh
If Only

I could say yes, Ian, get close to me.
But it's a place no one should ever be,
and it would be cruel to let him think

I'm strong

enough to ever say yes, I need you.
I start toward the pink stucco building,
see Greta at the window. She's

a survivor,

having defied the Nazis in World
War II, smuggling Danish Jews into
Sweden. *They almost caught us twice,*
she remembers. *But we outwitted them.*

I can't

comprehend that kind of courage.
Funny thing. My friends (what few
real friends I have) don't

understand

why I work here at the Lutheran
home. They think old people
are lame. But they're not. They're
awesome, and I know exactly

why I

think so. It's because they've
lived entire lifetimes. Loved.
Laughed. Surrendered. Stumbled.
Weathered, beaten, still they don't

crumble,

not even as they inch toward death.

I Work Part-Time

Setting tables for dinner,
washing dishes afterward,
arranging flowers in vases,
reading to those whose
eyes no longer can. But
the absolute best is when
they share their stories.

There's Sam Lonnigan, who
as a liberal-leaning broad-
caster became snared by Joe
McCarthy's communist witch
hunt. Commie? No way,
not that his true ideology
ever came into play.

Miss High Fashion Spyre
lost her modeling career
when "skin-and-bones,
raccoon-eyes Twiggy" hit
the scene. *Till then, curves
were hip,* she complains.
Size subzero? Spare me!

Also sharing words of
wisdom are a fifties test
pilot, three retired doctors,
one author, one poet, two
politicians, one Olympic
medalist, four domestic
divas, and Greta Sorenson.

Greta Is My Faux Grandma

It's nice having her take on the grand-
        parent role, because I never see my own.
Mom's father was killed in Vietnam.

        Her mother, Grandma Betty, retired
to Florida. She used to visit, but not
        since the accident. I don't blame her.

Daddy's father and mother divorced
        when Daddy was still in grade school.
The reasons were so ugly no one

        will talk about them. Other than
a few creepy film noir–type scenes,
        I can hardly remember Grandma

Gardella, can barely conjure her
        face. Daddy says she only ever
came around looking for money.

        When I asked what for, he clammed
up completely, except to say he
        wasn't about to finance her binges.

Grandpa and Daddy haven't
        spoken in three decades. A few
years ago I tracked Grandpa down,

told him we were studying family
genealogy in school. He had no clue
        Daddy was married, let alone about

Raeanne and me. Sheesh. He
        sent us birthday cards for a year
or two, until Daddy found out.

        I'll never forget the fit he threw.
That sonofabitch better stay far,
            far away, or I swear I'll kill him.

When I asked him why, he had
        nothing substantial to say. I haven't
heard a word from Grandpa since.

        So I have a stranger for a grandma.
At least she was a stranger until
        we got to talking. And now it's like

we've known each other forever.
        Not that she knows everything,
a fact that she's quite aware of.

        Pretty young woman like you,
    spending so much time with an old
            lady like me, instead of out

with your friends? That can
        only add up to one thing—
you're hiding from something.

        Said with a sparkle in her ice
blue Scandinavian eyes. But her
        tone was 100 percent serious.

That's okay, honey. You know
        you're safe here with me. And if
you ever want to talk about

        it, I'm a hell of a good listener.
Meanwhile, why don't I teach
        you to crochet? It's a lost art.

Sometimes, mid–slip stitch,
        I'll catch those sharp blue eyes
poking at me, as if trying to pierce

        my armor. So far, they haven't
succeeded. But, to tell the truth,
        once in a while they come close.

Once in a While

I catch something
in her eyes, something
not meant for me to see.
Something very close
to what she sees in mine:

           fear.

Once, I gathered up
all my courage, asked,
"What are you afraid of?"
She sat very quietly
for several long minutes.

           Finally,

                she took a long, deep
                breath. Cleared her throat.
                Nothing. Now. But I used
                to be afraid all the time.
                I met evil when I was only a

        child.

It followed me for many
years, through adolescence,
into adulthood. I married
evil, but it was nothing new
and so I accepted it. It was the

wrong

thing to do. Never accept
evil as something you must
walk with, something you
deserve. Somehow. Do you
understand what I mean?

I nod, because I do
understand. I'm just not
sure how to go about
divorcing myself from
the evil I've already

accepted.

This Afternoon

Greta is in her room, napping.
Unusual. The pre-dinner hour
is generally noisy, busy with
afternoon activities designed
to keep older minds exercised.

Card games. Sing-alongs.
Classes on memoir and poetry.
I almost always find Greta
smack in the middle of it all.
Today she's under the weather.

I bustle around, doing assorted
duties, every so often poking
my head through her door. Shades
drawn, her room is dark as a coffin.
And why did I think that, exactly?

That pulls my thoughts toward
something she told me once, how
she never really rested until she saw
"that no-good son of a bitch"
laid down in the hard, cold ground.

I asked her who, but she was lost
in reverie, stuck in some horrible
memory, unable to extricate herself.
I saw something in her eyes, though.
Something that made me afraid for her.

Hello? Miss Gardella? Sam calls
from the confines of his wheelchair.
*Would you mind giving me a push
to the rec room? The arthritis
is acting up something awful today.*

I turn away from Greta's sleeping
form, softly close her door. "No
problem, Sam. Sorry about the
arthritis." I give the brakes a nudge.
"Hold on tight. Here we go."

One Problem About Caring

For someone, especially someone
who's getting on in years,
is the likelihood you'll lose them

          too soon.

The nurse says Greta has a flu
bug, nothing major, but just
the thought of her giving in to

          death

makes me indescribably sad.
I want to wake her, soothe
her fever, tell her how much
she means to me before it's

          too late.

Don't worry, says Psychic Sam.
*No damn flu gonna take Greta
down.* I nod, thinking about
going "down," no last shot at

          redemption.

That will likely be my fate.
Done in by some viral villain,
sent straight to the fiery pits,
shackled by my silence,

          sentenced to

spend eternity locked in
a hot red chamber, no way
to claim innocence and avoid
an eternal

          dance with the devil.

Raeanne
Mick Picked Me Up

And I made sure he kept
me out extremely late. It's always
desirable not to get home

too soon.

I can't always manage it, though.
Daddy doesn't always cooperate,
drink himself to a state resembling

death.

Tonight Kaeleigh and I are in luck.
The bitter perfume of bourbon
smacks me as I stumble in. It makes
me thirsty. It's late, but never

too late

for one last shot. I tiptoe past
Daddy's snoring, ease the Wild
Turkey from the table. Can't
really blame him for choosing

redemption

in a bottle. Two bottles, actually.
One holds 750 ml of amber liquid.
The other is small enough to fit
in a pocket. Daddy has been

sentenced to

pain abatement à la OxyContin.
The accident was eight years ago
and his doctor keeps refilling,
like he doesn't know about Daddy's

dance with the devil.

Like I Care

Truth is, I borrow a little Oxy
  every now and then too. Not
    often, though. It's expensive.

    Daddy would miss it, even if
      his dimwit doctor didn't. I
        have to admit it's tempting.

      It makes me feel like how
        you feel when you fall in
          a dream. Only you don't

          wake up. You just keep
            falling deeper and deeper
              into the darkest recesses

            of sleep. Especially when
              you help it out with a nip
                or two of Wild Turkey.

Of course, I have to be
  very careful not to do it
    when Daddy's not trapped

    in the snare of sleep too.
      Wouldn't do to be lying
        there unaware if he came

crawling to me. No, I'd
 want to be totally ready.
  But it won't be tonight.

  Fifth of whiskey beneath
   my arm, I slip noiselessly
    into the kitchen, pour two

     fingers, replace the bottle.
     Then I slither into Daddy's
      bathroom, help myself to a

      small green pill. Just one.
       Just enough for a free fall
        totally without a parachute.

My Bedroom Is Dark

Quiet as death, and I keep it exactly
that way. Even the bed cooperates,

as I slide like a whisper under
the cumbersome quilts, sit up in bed,

motionless. I feel like I'm in
a hollow black space. A cave.

Empty. I chance a sip of Turkey.

Have to wet my tongue before

letting the Oxy dissolve. Slowly.

Nasty. Another sip. Jet fuel, hot
and acrid against my taste buds.

Another time, another place, I'd let
myself cough. Not now. Not here.

Nothing to disturb the deep breaths
resonating throughout the house.

My tongue burns. My mouth
tastes like crap. The spinning

inside my head begins. Grins.

I lie flat, give myself up to the

Oxy/Turkey merry-go-round.

Eyes closed, I start the tumble.
Round. Round. Down. Down.

Outside, the wind rouses suddenly.
Branches scratch against the window

and the sound, like something wants me,
carries me where sleep will not follow.

It's Bone-Chilling Here

In this memory. Nothing
can thaw me. Not quilt. Not
whiskey. Not even opiate.
I'm frozen solidly in place,
just like I was that night,
the first time Daddy came.
A night Kaeleigh can't (or
won't) remember. But I do.

It was a year or so after
the accident. Kaeleigh
and I were nine, give
or take. Mom had gone
in for another round of
surgery. She was already
lost to us. Lost. Long gone.

I could barely remember
how her kisses felt. They
rode away on the bumper
of that fucking semi. How
we hungered for them!

Daddy smelled of Wild
Turkey. Each night, we knew,
he drank more and more.
That night, he had drunk
just enough. *Kaeleigh, girl.*

His voice was a soft hiss.
Are you awake? Talk to me.
Daddy ish-is sh-so lonely.

I'd never heard him sound
like that. Like a stranger.
A drunk, slurring stranger.
Where was my daddy?

Kaeleigh, all sweetness,
wanted to comfort Daddy,
who drew her onto his lap.
Stroked her hair. Kissed
her gently on the forehead.
Cheeks. Eyes. Finally, on
her lips, but not nasty
or mean or with tongue
or anything but misplaced
love. Love meant for Mom.

He just held her, kissed
her. Breathed Wild Turkey
all over her until they both
fell asleep, woven together.

Woven

Knitted together,

       threaded by pain-

sharpened needles.

       That one innocent

joining was only

       the beginning, but

neither realized it

       that night. And all

I could do was linger

       in a dark corner,

sharp jabs of envy

       tearing my eyes.

The Innocence

With which Kaeleigh
accepted that gesture
was to be corrupted,
but not immediately.
Maybe this is the place
she settles into, when
forced to escape the
reality of what came
later, what continues
still. See, she doesn't
really remember the
details. It's a defense
mechanism, a gift
from nature around
post-traumatic stress.
Remembering the ins
and outs, so to speak,
is left up to me. I am
almost always there,
or at least close by,
though I have never
interfered. Oh, I did
try to tell Mom once, but she closed up like an
oyster around that pearl of truth. I guess I could
have offered descriptions of Daddy's "privates"
(his word), the way he wears his scars. But hey,
if she didn't care, why the hell should I? Instead,
I stood by and watched father love turn to   L U S T.

What Came Later

Belies the purity of that first night.
Time crept by in slow motion,
and I felt a million miles away.

I watched

the two of them dozing, father
and mother/daughter, until
weariness weighted my eyes.

I slipped

into the river of their breathing,
floated in the current of Daddy's
all-encompassing need.

I fell

asleep, thinking about Daddy
kissing Kaeleigh, craving his kiss,
understanding its significance.

We unraveled

that night, and I don't think
things can ever be put right
again. Sad, that lives can be

shattered,

into so many pieces that they
can never be put back together,
by the relentless force of love.

Irreparable.

Kaeleigh
Can't Believe

I watched

I got the lead in *Grease,* the winter musical.
I'm a pretty good actress, but my
dance is rusty and my singing, well . . .

as Ms. Cavendish posted the cast
list. Everyone gathered around
the bulletin board, exhaling loudly.

I slipped

in between Ian and Shelby to get
a better look. *Sorry you didn't make
it*, poked Shelby. Stupid me,

I fell

for it, until she and Ian cracked up.
"You may be sorry I *did* make it."
I broke into an off-key rendition of "Fame."

We unraveled

into a giant fit of laughter. People
stared, including Madison, who got
a big part too. The look she gave me

shattered

any idea that this play might be fun
after all. The slim chance rehearsals
might go smoothly shredded.

Irreparable.

Drama Is Last Block

On Tuesdays and Thursdays. Today, however, being Friday,
last block is PE. I wish I would've opted for modern dance.

Instead I'm dressed out for volleyball. And lucky me, my
dear friend Madison is across the net, getting ready to serve.

Even better, I'm in front, where I can't miss the vile promise
in her eyes: *I'm gonna ram this ball right down your throat.*

Fortunately, her anger sends the ball clear out of bounds. We
rotate, and it's my turn to serve. Madison moves left one slot.

I swear, even from here, I can see the steam rising off her.
Whoo-ee, is she hot! I shouldn't let it bother me, but it does.

I serve into the net. *Side-out!* yells Madison, and my teammates
groan. "Sorry," I try. "It slipped." Okay, lame excuse.

Here comes the ball again. Long volley. On the far side
of the net, Serena sets up. Madison spikes. Damn! The sucker

slams right into my chest, bounces undeniably out of bounds.
Madison smiles. *Too bad you don't have much padding there.*

Everyone laughs. My face flashes, hot. But for once the perfect
retort comes to mind immediately. Love when that happens.

"Yeah, well, I guess you're right. I don't have much padding,
but at least what I've got is all mine, not Victoria's."

Victoria? Madison stops. Thinks. Gets a "duh" look on her face. Shakes her head and I've got her. *Who's Victoria?*

"I don't know. But she's got a secret. And you're wearing it. Oh, wait. Let me look again. Never mind. Can't be Victoria's

Secret. Anything that lumpy must have come from Wal-Mart. Wait, wait. Not even Wal-Mart. More like Salvation Army."

Wha . . . ? Hmph! You shut the fuck up, bitch! Madison storms off, intensely pissed. A chorus of howls follows her.

Not Sure Why

I felt the need to provoke her.
        She and her inner circle carry
a lot of weight around here.

        I'm just sick of that pissy look,
the off-the-wall snipes. I had
        nothing to do with her problems

with Mick. What wasn't her
        being a bitch was him, being
a creep. All I am is fallout.

        The bell rings. *Okay, girls!* yells
Ms. Petrie. *Hit the showers!*
        Showers. Oh, goody. Can't wait.

        Yeah, I'm dripping sweat. It's
not what you might call fragrant.
        Not good fragrant, anyway.

But public showering is
        my least favorite thing about
PE, and considering I hate PE,

        that says a lot. Ugh! Stripping
down to skin and hair, showing
        everything to everyone else.

That includes Ms. Petrie, our
            elderly PE teacher, who seems
more interested in our hygiene

            than in our physical fitness.
The one job she takes seriously
            is making sure we shower.

It's kind of creepy, although
            I suppose some people might
never de-sweat without a Ms. Petrie

            to check up on them. Anyway,
today I want to make sure Madison
            is scrubbed and dressed before

I even look at the shower. I help
            Ms. Petrie bring in the balls and nets.
By the time I shed my shorts

            and lather up, the locker room
is mostly empty. The final bell
            rings and I'm still under water.

            When I exit, hair dripping, out
the double doors, I'm mortified
            to find the bus has already gone.

I Need to Get My License

I've been old enough for months.
Problem is, you need a parent to sign
off for you. And I do not have
the luxury of parents who are able
or willing to do that for me.

Mom is always traveling. She only
drops by long enough to pick up
a change of clothes and maybe,
if we're very, very lucky, share
a meal. She has completely
forgotten what being a mother means.

Kitchen duty and housework fall
mostly on Manuela, who comes in
three times a week to do laundry, dust
and vacuum, cook and freeze meals.

As for Daddy, well, he pretty much
works from early morning until
the sun creeps toward the western
horizon. The closest DMV is in Lompoc,
a half hour from here. Closed Saturdays.

Not that Daddy is likely to let me
have my license anyway. A car means
escape. And I'm pretty sure he plans
to keep me his prisoner forever.

The More Immediate Problem

Is I need a ride home and the parking lot
is deserted. Everyone bails as soon as
       the last bell rings. Walking home

isn't impossible, but it's five miles away.
Who can I call? Ian, of course. But his cell
       rings four times, goes to voice mail.

I try Shelby. Katrina. Lisa. Danette. No luck.
Everyone's busy, grounded, unavailable,
       or simply not picking up.

Just as I think I'll have to walk after all,
a black Charger draws even, window lowering.
       Something wrong? It's Mr. Lawler.

"Kind of. I missed the bus. I've called everyone
I know but can't seem to find a ride home."
       Hop in. I'll take you. I'm going that way.

Does he know where I live? I give the parking
lot another scan. He smiles at my hesitation.
       What? Don't tell me you don't trust me?

Not at All

You can't trust a man,
any man,
any more than you can
put your
faith in a rabid dog, not
even your
own dog, one who would
never hurt
you, except he's rabid.

Not sure why I believe that.
But I solidly
do. I've seen guys act
like they
are just so in love with
their girl-
of-the-moment, only
to turn
around and dump her cold.

And as for adult men, men
who should
not look twice at someone
half their
age, well that rarely turns out
to be their MO.
No, their method of operation
is to hang
out their tongues and pant.

To Be Fair

I haven't seen Mr. Lawler
actually pant. And the only
time I've seen his tongue

is when I've bothered to look.
So I say, "Of course I trust
you. Thanks for offering."

And, mostly against my better
judgment, I open the door, slip
into the shelter of his car.

Promise not to tell, okay?
I could get into all kinds
of trouble, you know.

My turn to smile.
"What? For rescuing
a damsel in distress?"

For others' perceptions.
But I promise to be the
perfect gentleman.

He turns toward town,
drives cautiously, completely
the perfect gentleman.

Some Girls I Know

Talk about Mr. Lawler like he's
on their "available" list or something. He's not married, at least

                    I don't think

so. I guess he could be closet
married, but why bother?
Teachers and students?
Absolutely taboo! If

                    I could ever

get past my private taboo,
I'd have to call Mr. Lawler
"cute." But how could I

                    get beyond

the fact that he's almost
as old as Daddy? And yet,
as we drive along, I find myself
moving closer to him,

                    pretending

I can't quite hear what he's
saying with his frothy, smooth
cappuccino voice. One time
in class a couple of weeks ago,

                    he was

lecturing about immigration.
I was lost in reverie about the night
before, and when Mr. Lawler called
on me, I almost answered, "Yes,

                    Daddy?"

Raeanne
Kind of Funny

I don't think

> Watching Lawler and Kaeleigh
> pull up at the house together.

> I've ever seen her alone
> with a grown man (well, except
> for Daddy and he doesn't count).
> Maybe I need to miss the bus. If

I could ever

> find a good excuse to get Lawler
> alone, he would discover a different
> Gardella girl, one who could easily

get beyond

> not only his age, but also any
> stupid notion of impropriety.
> I would never act like Kaeleigh,
> craving his proximity, his touch, yet

pretending

> not to notice the cut of his silk
> trousers, the way his biceps fill
> his tailored shirtsleeves. Even
> from a distance, I could tell

he was

> interested in more than just giving
> her a ride home. She should
> consider it. After all, there happen
> to be better men out there than

Daddy.

Other Men, Anyway

A whole big, giant world,

full of men. Men with blue eyes.

Brown eyes. Green eyes. And indescribable

shades in between. Tall men. Short men. Skinny men.

Built men. And all combinations thereof. Nice men (so I've

heard, but never really seen). Mean men. Decent men, indecent.

And who knows which is the best kind to have, to hold, to love?

I'd say, with so many men in the world, it would pay to sample

a few. Scratch that. More than a few. Lots and lots. And then

a few more. And maybe, after years and years of research,

taste testing, and trying 'em on for size, just maybe,

you might find one worth not throwing back.

But hey, the fun is in the fishing.

Kaeleigh's Not into Fishing

Too much effort, too few rewards.
Watching her work Daddy now,
you'd think she reeled in the big one.

        Selective amnesia?
        Putting on a show?

She is a good little actress.
Daddy is already home but
hasn't yet waded into his bottle.

        "You're home early today,"
        she soothes. "Special occasion?"

                He's jonesing for a swig. Can't.
                Your mother will be here soon.
                Press conference on the lawn.

        "Oh, right. I forgot. Do you want
        me to iron a shirt for you?"

                Daddy shakes his head.
                A jacket will do. You should
                put on something pretty, though.

She nods and we go to change,
knowing where his eyes are.

No Doubt

He'll be watching the sway
of Kaeleigh's hips, craving her.

And a drink. Not sure which one
he craves more. But tonight

he'll have to play the good (sober)
husband and devoted father.

As I slip into a Vera Wang blouse,
Tommy Hilfiger jeans, I can hear

> Mom's well-staged entrance.
> *Hello, Raymond. You look well.*

The election is a few precious
weeks away. Before the final charge,

Mom needs to make her constituency
believe she actually cares about family.

> Her own family is the best place to start.
> *They're setting up the cameras.*

Being fairly cute and very well
dressed, we make a damn fine photo

op, too. Especially just as the sun
starts to sink behind our designer home.

Reporters and news crews have
gathered on the front lawn.

Mom herds us outside.
Don't forget to smile.

Yeah, Mom. Like what else would
we do? Stick out our tongues?

Flip them off? Drop our pants, bend
over, and tell them just what to kiss?

The thought makes me smile. Not only
that, but the grin stretches lobe to lobe.

Poor Mom only knows I'm smiling.
She smiles too. *That's my girl.*

Daddy Isn't Running

This time round, but he has before
and is intimately aware of campaign
protocol. Exactly as might be expected,

he drapes an arm (a ravenous arm, but
no one but his closest family members
knows that) around Mom's shoulder.

She stiffens, and her smile slips ever so
slightly, but I'm the only one who notices.
And she doesn't dare shrug him off.

> *Thank you all for coming*, she says.
> *It's good to be home with my family.*
> *The campaign trail is a lonely one.*

I wonder just how lonely. I wonder
if she's getting a little on the side.
Probably not. I can't imagine her

actually getting close enough to
someone—anyone—to invite them
into her bed, let alone her pants.

> I watch her, the ultimate politician,
> working the press like she was born
> for it. *I'll take questions now.*

Queries Fly

... universal health care

                       ... uranium enrichment

       ... trade deficit

                         ... right to choose

... gay marriage

         ... immigration reform

Mom is prepared,

                   knows every answer

        by heart, could

                     recite them in

    her sleep, in fact.

            Harder questions.

... balanced budget

               ... troop withdrawal

      ... raising taxes

                   ... torturing terrorists

... citizens' rights

        ... presidential authority

Cool under pressure,

                she words her responses

       carefully, no

                  missteps that might

    make dirty TV spots.

         She's twelve for twelve.

And then ...

Some Thirtyish Ditz

Tosses her long, dark-rooted
platinum hair. In a cheap tweed suit,
with a skirt much too short

to compliment the blocky legs
poking out from under it,

she clears her throat, squeaks,
What about judicial reform?
How do you feel about judges

who break the same laws
they are sworn to uphold?

All eyes latch onto Daddy,
whose face is the color of raw
cotton. His own eyes scream

panic, but the subtle shake of my
head reassures, "Nope, not a word."

Mom remains the stoic politician.
I'm sure such a thing is a rare
occurrence. No judge I know

holds him or herself above
the law. It is sacrosanct.

Ms. Tree-Trunk Legs refuses
to be so easily satisfied. She
hems and haws, checking her

notes. Finally, just as the others
seem ready to pack up and leave,

> she throws a bucket of verbal shit.
> *Isn't it true that while under*
> *the influence, your husband,*
>
> *Judge Raymond Leland Gardella,*
> *was involved in a fatal accident? And . . .*

If she thinks she can possibly
go one-on-one with my mother
and come out on top, she really

should think again. Like a wolf
on a duck (with incredibly fat legs!),

> Mom turns on the reporter.
> *Ray is the finest jurist I know.*
> *He does not hold himself above*
>
> *the law, but dispenses it with*
> *knowledge and forthrightness.*

Told you Mom had every
correct response right at her
fingertips. If there was ever

any doubt about where Kaeleigh
got her acting ability, this

afternoon smashed it to bits, and
Mom is not quite finished yet.
The incident to which you refer

was a great personal tragedy.
Should we apologize for not dying?

Castrated

Frustrated, the brittle
blonde shakes her head,
ignoring the buzz
all around her.

What she still doesn't
get, I'm betting,
is how connected
my parents are.

The others, still
buzzing like electric
lines in a storm,
understand, though.

My parents' connections
reach well beyond
political circles,
and some of those

connections might very
well disconnect one
mouthy young reporter
from her job.

Sound Bites Bitten

Mom actually cooks dinner
tonight, perhaps worried some
nosy journalist might peek

                through the window.

Of course, it's frozen lasagna
and bagged salad. But hey,
who's complaining?

                It's almost

like we used to be, once
upon a time. If I close my
eyes, I can almost pretend

                like we're

a normal family, gathered
round the table, discussing
stuff like plays and grades,

                not unusual

dinner-table topics like war
chests and fund-raisers. If
I keep my eyes closed, Mom is

                not indifferent,

not some cardboard cutout
in a lace apron. Eyes firmly
closed, Daddy is

                not famished

for affection, perverted or
otherwise. Eyes squeezed
tight, Kaeleigh and I are

                not irrelevant.

Kaeleigh
Having Mom Home

Makes things easier. Makes things
harder, like looking

through the window,

needing to see what's on the other
side, but your eyes have to work
too hard to reach beyond the grime.

It's almost

as hard as pretending I don't care
if she leaves again. Almost as hard as
sitting around the dinner table

like we're

a cohesive family unit. A little
pasta, little wine, little conversation.
Damn little, which is

not unusual

for the Gardella clan. What talk
there is, of course, is election talk.
I guess I should act like I'm

not indifferent

and, really, I'm not. I hope with
every ounce of hope I have left
that the voters snub her. No, I'm

not famished

for revenge. I'm starved for her
company and even more, for her
affection. I love her, and that's

not irrelevant.

Actually, I'm Hungry

For more than Mom's affection.
My body is screaming for food.
And tonight we get the
real deal (instead of
our usual fast

or flash-

frozen repast).
But any food is my
friend because it's under
my control, unlike most of the
rest of my life. I eat when I'm sad.

I eat when I'm lonely. I eat when
I hurt so much inside, it's
either eat or find an
easy way to die.
The only

time I

can't eat to
total contentment
is when Daddy's around. *No
daughter of mine will wear double-
digit clothes,* he said once, and meant it.

Wonder what he thinks about Mom's
new curves. She's put on
a few pounds. All that
rich food on the
campaign trail,

I guess.

Schmooze
'em with five-star
dinners, high-dollar wine,
and aperitifs; ask 'em for a fistful
of dollars. Calorific politics at its best.

I happen to think Mom wears double-
digit designer clothes pretty
well. She is the portrait
of a beautiful,
highbrow

woman,

curves or no.
What she doesn't look
like is a girl, all narrow hips,
straight waist, and teacup breasts.
And if I have my way, I won't either.

And Tonight Mom's Home

I can eat what I want,
          Daddy or no. After dinner

I help load the dishwasher,
          more to be close to Mom

than anything. Every time
          I brush against her, though,

she stiffens, like a wet sheet
          in January wind. Not fair.

Why can't she love me
          like I love her? Does she

somehow blame me? I ask
          simply, "What's wrong?"

          Mom keeps scrubbing
               the stove, like it isn't already

          spotless. Finally she says,
               Nothing's wrong with me

          that winning this election
               won't cure. It's been a long,

hard campaign, and the polls
        say it's too close to call.

Nothing I didn't know.
        But there's something

more. Something I can't
        quite put my finger on.

I mean, even for Mom, this
        woman is unapproachable.

"Can I ask you something
        without you getting mad?"

        Scrub. Scrub. Scrub. *Of*
                course. Scrub. Scrub. Scrub.

She's gonna get mad for sure.
        "Well, what if you don't win?"

        She stops scrubbing, fires
                at my eyes with her own.

        I can't think like that, and
                I don't want you to either.

Do you think I could just
            tuck my tail between my

legs, come home, and play
            housewife? Never again!

So . . . what? If she wins, she'll
            spend most of her time in DC.

But what if she loses? Either
            way, guess who else loses?

Mom Pours a Glass of Wine

A fine pinot noir, grown here
in the valley. I've come to appreciate
good red wine. Mom allows some
with dinner sometimes. And once
in a while, she allows it after dinner.
"May I have some more too?"

She slides the bottle across the table,
and I fill my glass to the brim.
Mom and I sip in silence for a while,
but eventually the building buzz
in my brain opens my mouth.
"Do you miss us when you're gone?"

Now you might think "yes" would
pop out from between her lips,
quick as a jack-in-the-box wound
tight. No way. She tilts her head
slightly, as if to tip the right answer
into her mouth. The maneuver fails.

Suddenly, she doesn't look like
a politician. She folds up, small,
a woman twice her age, beneath
the burdens she will forever carry.
I don't blame her for not wanting
to be here. Who does?

We Empty Our Glasses

Mom opens another bottle,
pours for us both. I'm getting
drunk with my mother, and

> neither of us can think of
> a thing to say. Finally, she
> says, *I'd better go to bed.*

"Sure, Mom. Me too."
I go around the table,
give her a hug. "Love you."

> She turns, looks me in the eye.
> *Love you too.* She pauses, stutters,
> *A . . . are you . . . all right?*

Anger flares. I want to shout,
"Like you suddenly care?"
Want to cry, "Save me!"

> Something acidy rises in my
> throat. If I break down, say
> those things and more, then what?

But she has already closed
herself again, snapped shut
like a heavy door.

"No," I say simply. Wineglass
in hand, I start to leave, turn
to see her choke back a sob.

In the living room, the TV
is on, but Daddy has drunk
himself into oblivion.

Cool. I'll be there soon
myself. The rest of the house
is dark, and I leave it that way.

I stumble up the hallway,
into my bedroom. Turn on
the little lamp beside my bed.

Think about calling Ian.
But it's late, and it's Friday
night. He's asleep or out.

Out, Where I Should Be

Where any self-respecting
sixteen-year-old should be
on Friday night. Out,

getting drunk

with friends or, better yet,
a really fine guy, instead
of tying one on

at home

with my marble-hearted
mother, no less. At least I
caught a couple of tears, which

leaves

me wondering if she ever
just breaks down or freaks
out. She used to freak out

a lot

before the accident. At least
then we knew she had feelings.
But that was before she came

to be

completely drained of emotion.
I wonder if I would have liked
her when she was young, pretty,

desired.

Did she like herself then?
Before she had children?
Before she met Daddy?

Raeanne
I Called Mick

getting drunk,

at home

leaves

a lot

to be

desired

As soon as the whole house fell
quiet except for whiskey-fueled
snores. Sneaking out,

getting high. What better way
to spend Friday night? Especially
after too many hours stuck

listening to Mom's political
bullshit. Aaagh! Save me.
I, for one, can't wait until she

again. Hell, maybe she'll be
gone by the time I get up in
the morning. I plan to do

in the way of self-medication.
Funny term for getting screwed up
to the point of passing out. I need

that messed up to get to sleep
at all tonight. I'm totally wound.
Besides, I want to feel

for more than what I can bring
to a campaign. A campaign
that only fills our lives with pain.

There's a Party

Up on Figueroa. That's a mountain
not too far from here, but far enough
so parents and cops rarely want
to take the drive, especially at night.
Even if they did, we have our favorite
party place, well off the main road,
and a mile or so back on a dirt track,
not something they'd happen upon.
Great place for hide-and-seek.

Great place for a kegger, too.
And that's our destination.
Mick drives like a maniac,
which would be all right except
I really, really want to get high,
and smoking dope and speeding
don't exactly go hand in hand.

I could be bitchy, and it may come
to that. But I'll try sweet talk first.
"If you slow down a little, I'll roll
a nice big joint. And after we smoke
it, just maybe I'll mess around
with your nice big joint too."
Okay, so it isn't eloquent,
but it works.

He Slows

To right around the speed
limit as I fumble under
the seat, searching for his stash.

> *This slow enough for you?*
> *Damn, I feel like an old woman.*

"Ha. Sound like one too."
Finally, pay dirt. I reach into
the baggie, extract a big bud.

> *Hurry up with that, would ya?*
> *Hey, I saw you on TV tonight.*

I keep crumbling dope.
"Really? You watch the news?"
No frigging way.

> *He snorts a half laugh.*
> *Nah. I was channel surfing.*

Ah, but of course.
"So how'd I look? Like
a movie star or what?"

> *He reaches for my left boob.*
> *More like a rock star, baby.*

God, he's a player. A lousy
player. "Give me your lighter."
Delectable smoke fills the cab.

> Hey, man. You never told
> me your mom was so hot.

My body stiffens and I shove
his hand away. "Shut the fuck
up." I take a giant hit of pot.

> Jeez. Pushed the wrong button,
> huh? Sorry. But she is.

"Mom is not hot! She's fucking
frigid!" Why is this bugging
me so effing much?

> Okay, okay. Really sorry.
> Now give me the damn doob.

Needless to Say

I don't feel much like messing
        around with Mick's "nice big joint,"
not even after killing off the nice
        big joint wrapped in a rolling paper.

Maybe after a beer or ten.
        And hey, lucky me, looks
like the beer's flowing up
        here on Figueroa Mountain.

Twenty or so vehicles are parked
        helter-skelter, like misaligned
zipper teeth. Some I recognize.
        Some I've never seen before.

It's an older crowd. Several
        people graduated with Mick,
and a few last year. Not too
        many my age. Fine by me.

I see enough of those people
        every day at school. Who wants
to socialize with them? What
        I want is to leave them in my dust.

Suddenly a familiar whine
        threatens my jocular mood.

Hey, Mick! I hoped you'd be here,
            even if you had to bring her *along.*

You guessed it. My delightful
            friend, Madison. She rubs up
against Mick like a hungry cat.
            Is she trying to piss me off?

And here I just got unpissed.
            Two choices. Jump into the ring.
Or turn away, move on to
            that really cute guy over there.

I turn to assess Mick's reaction
            to the fur-free feline at his arm.
He looks vaguely intrigued,
            and totally unconcerned about me.

So fine. No use getting into
            a scratchfest. I wander over
to the keg, top off a twenty-ounce
            cup, and go say hi to Prince Charming.

Turns Out

He's not particularly charming,
but at the moment, charm is not
a prerequisite. I'm not looking
for a life partner, just a good time.

"What's up?"

His eyes, the color of creamed coffee,
hold mild interest. *Not much. You
a friend of Mick's?* He tips his head
in the direction of said Mick.

"Not really."

*Hmm. Got the idea you were.
Didn't you come together?* He smiles
at the loaded question. *I mean,
didn't you* arrive *together?*

"Doesn't make us friends.
But yeah, we did actually."
My turn to smile. "And we've
come together a few times too."

He looks me up and down like
he's shopping. *I see. Any plans
to come together tonight?*

"Nope." I part my lips bravely.
"Not with *him*, anyway."

> He nods his head, stands.
> *How's that beer? Need a refill?*

I shrug. "Sure. Don't suppose
you happen to have anything
stronger on you, though?"

> *It's a distinct possibility. Let's
> get those refills and take a walk.*

It's stupid even to consider taking
a walk with this guy. Like I care.
I glance toward Mick, who is now
in the truck with Madison, filling
the cab with smoke. I'm so taking
a walk. With a complete stranger.

We Wander into the Woods

Sit on a big stump, slurping foamy beer.
He's cute, really cute. So what if he's not
much for words? He reaches into his jeans
pocket, digging for treasure. Maybe I'll dig
in there later myself. Meanwhile, I'll content
myself with the giant fatty he lights. The pot
is the same as (or very similar to) Mick's.

"So . . ." I cough out a big hit. "You and Mick
share a connection, huh?"

> *Something like that.* He laughs. *Let's
> just say we move in mutual circles.*
> He draws in a long, deep lungful.

I move a little closer, like I can't quite
reach the joint. "Since we're sharing
a hooter, can we, like, share names?"

> *The name's Ty. I know who you are.
> I saw you on television tonight.*

If he says my mom is hot, I'll kill him.
"Jeez, man. Did everybody just happen
to watch the fucking news tonight?"

> *What? Did I say something wrong?*
> Now he scoots closer. Looks into my
> eyes. *Should I apologize?*

The Guy Knows How

To apologize, for sure. He reaches
across the short distance between us,
pulls me right into him, kisses me
with unexpected hunger. In the

                         time

it takes me to react to that, decide
whether or not to invite more,
he already has my top button
unbuttoned. His hands want

                         to go

under the fabric, insist on it,
in fact. I should say no. Need
to say no. "W-wait," I try,
but no little bit of me wants

                         to stop

and Ty intuits all of that. He
doesn't stop, and I don't try
to make him. And it isn't long

                         before

I throw every ounce of caution
to the nonexistent wind. With only
a fleeting thought of Mick,

                         I give

in to this insane desire to know
this not-quite-stranger in the most
intimate way. And so, I sacrifice
my inner child, give

                         myself away.

Kaeleigh
My Inner Child

Is sobbing, crying for her mother
to please, please come home, stay.
But she is already leaving, well before
dawn, as if to spend any more

time

here might chip her thin veneer.
Her footsteps fall subtly in the hallway,
trailed by Daddy's heavy tread
and garbled entreaty not

to go.

The front door shuts emphatically.
I tense, count his paces. Twenty to his
own bed, twelve to mine. One, two.
Three, four. Wordlessly, I beg him not

to stop.

Five, six. Seven, eight. Please,
go back to bed. Nine, ten. Eleven,
twelve. Pause. The knob turns. Quick,

before

he can open my door, I scrunch my
eyes, will my breathing to slow.
He steps inside, creeps to my bed.

I give

a silent prayer that he'll believe
I'm asleep, take pity, leave me
to my feigned dreams, all
the while preparing to give

myself away.

Daddy Strokes My Cheek

His touch is soft as a dandelion,
ready to release its spores.
I feel his eyes trace my silhouette,

> steel myself against what will come
> next. But the quilt doesn't move.

> > His lips brush my forehead.
> > *You're so much like her,* he whispers.
> > *Why can't I just take it all back?*

He crumbles on the carpet beside
my bed. In the growing light,
I slit open my eyes, watch his face

> fall into his hands. Tears stream
> through the cracks between

> > his fingers. *Why can't I take it back?*
> > *Will you ever be able to forgive me?*
> > Nobody answers. Not her. Not me.

Before long, Daddy's breathing
evens, and when he starts to snore

> I slide out from under the blankets,
> into chill, Turkey-tainted air; tiptoe
> past his sleeping form. Away.

Not a Creature Is Stirring

In the house or out, as I slide open the door,
step out into the crisp Saturday morning,

biting back sudden teeth chatter.

The entire neighborhood seems asleep,
not a single early-morning mower in sight.

But smoke trails zigzagging from chimneys

belie the idea that I'm completely alone.
Someone's awake, despite the fact that the sun

has barely risen. I'll be early to work.

Usually I ride my bike the mile or so to
the Lutheran home. Today I think I'll walk,

inhaling the clean of barely dawn.

Showered, made-up, and blow-dried,
my body is almost as scrubbed as

the daybreak. So why do I feel dirty?

The Old Folks' Home

Has a new arrival, one who has
thrown the place into an uproar.
Seems William O'Connell
is something of a ladies' man.
He's tall, or once was, having
lost a few inches to stoop.
And, despite his years, he's
really quite handsome,
in an aged, Irish way.

Come over here, m'darlin',
he invites, to no one woman
in particular. *I'm thinking
you're in need of a bit of male
companionship.* His offer is met
with a chorus of giggles.

Ah yes, it's a breakfast
to go down in the history
of the Lutheran home, one
to be retold in whispered tales,
passed around by these good
(if lonely) ladies. Only Greta
seems unimpressed.

*Who does the man believe
he is? Sean Connery? Now
there's an Irishman worthy
of consideration,* she jokes.

Unlike some of the home's guests,
William is completely ambulatory.
In fact, he gets around so well,
I have to wonder why he's here,
flitting from woman to woman
like a horny hummingbird.
I watch, amused, until it's time
to clear the dishes. And that's
when he finally catches sight of me.

Ah, such a sweet young rose.
Who might I be addressing,
my lovely little flower?

For no discernible reason,
my arms sprout goose bumps
and my forehead leaks sweat.
I start to say "Kaeleigh," but my
mouth clamps tight around my answer,
squeezes shut around my name.

Memory Strikes Suddenly

Chokes me. Strangles me.
It was dark in my room.
Very dark.
Someone had closed the curtain.
I was small. Maybe nine.
Mommy wasn't home.
But Daddy was.
He lurched through my door.
That scared me. But why?
He'd never hurt me before.
Only touched me lovingly.
Like any Daddy.
So why did I tremble?
Why did I catch my breath,
hold it, as if
I might never breathe again?
Why did my heart feel
like a race-car engine?
Daddy must have heard it.

> *Don't be afraid, little flower.*
> *It's only me.*

And almost instantly, Daddy
made everything seem just fine.
Even when it wasn't.

I Didn't Panic Then

But here in the dining room,
terror inflates inside me

like a flame in a breeze.
Especially when William

>   echoes, *Won't you tell me
>   your name, little flower?*

Blood rushes from my face
to who-knows-where, and I feel

weightless, helpless, a cloud
in a cold, trembling sky.

Just as I think I'll turn and run,
or worse, keel completely over,

dearest Greta takes hold of me,
props me up with the force of her.

>   *Kaeleigh seems to have taken
>   ill, William. You and she can*

>   *chat later.* She guides me away.
>   *Will you come to my room for a while?*

It's a question, not a directive,
and for that I am grateful.

Unlike Everyone Else

In my life, Greta knows when
            to stay silent. She sits me down
in a chair by the window,
            settles into a rocker, opposite me.
Then all she does is rock.

I stare out over the fog-shrouded
            valley. The gray gulps me into
it, infiltrates my brain. Sad.
            Will I ever find a way beyond
this sad? Tears puddle my eyes.

I let them fall, like how they
            feel, then come to my senses.
"S-sorry," I sniffle, not sure
            why, except it's lame to cry,
like it's ever done any good.

            Sorry? What for? Greta asks. *You've*
                        got some powerful demons, girl,
            but I've got a few of my own.
                        Already told you I'm a good listener.
            Talk to me when you're ready.

I Want to Talk

But I'm not   really sure
what I can talk   about. Daddy?
Not ever. Mom? Definitely not now.
The campaign is much too close to call.

Raeanne? How I miss her, miss how
close we once were? Miss
the sisters we used to
be, before . . .

Nope. Can't   crack open
that particular   history book.
Other family members, inexplicably
unable or unwilling to be a part of my

life? Ian? Uh-huh. OMG! Greta is
undeniably right. Some very
intense demons have so
got hold of me.

I Go Over to Her

Wrap my arms around her
neck. "Thank you. But I'm
okay." Of course she knows

                                    it's a lie.

Greta, who patiently
waits for my confession,
can see demons hip-hopping

                                    in my eyes.

She deserves a better answer.
"Maybe someday we can
trade stories, okay? But
I'm on foot today.

                                    Better go."

Be safe, is her reply, and again
I realize I only feel secure here.
Passing William in the hall,
I give his shoulder an easy

                                    poke.

"Name's Kaeleigh. Gotta go.
Be good." He offers the usual
Always, then turns his attention
to a couple of older ladies. Better

                                    them

than me, and their giggles
mean they agree. I step

                                    out

the door, into lengthening
afternoon, carry my demons
home, tucked deep inside.

Raeanne
We All Have Demons

Some inside us, some outside.
(Madison is a fine example
of the exterior variety.)

It's a lie

to say otherwise. Kaeleigh
can successfully stow hers
away in some dark corner, but

in my eyes

it is better to confront them
than let them roil you into
turmoil. And so at the moment
I'm thinking I'd

better go

get in Madison's face. For a day
or two, I wasn't sure Mick was
worth it. And hey, he probably
isn't. But she has to learn not to

poke

sticks at snakes, at least not
venomous ones. Today my
fangs are exposed. All
I have to do is sink

them

into the proper artery, pump
a little poison, watch her bleed

out,

one less demon to contend with.

I Guess I Might

Just leave well enough alone,
                but I've been thinking about Mick.

        One way or another, I have to
                decide whether I want to keep him.

He actually gave me an ultimatum
                when he found me doing the deed with Ty.

        Maybe that's why I got so ballsy, had sex
                with Ty where I knew Mick could

find us. Maybe I had to know if he
                cared or not. He did! He was jealous.

        I'd like to think the reason
                he was flirting with Madison

that night was to make me jealous.
                But I don't think he's that complicated.

        "Complicated" takes more brains.
                Not that Mick is a total dolt,

but he isn't exactly Einstein, either.
                Anyway, most of Mick's brains reside

        in the general area of his groin.
                One thing for sure, sex will never

be about love with Mick. I don't love
                    him, and he definitely doesn't love me.

          Still, he semi-fills a gaping black hole
                          inside me. That place wants love,

maybe even needs love, but love is
                    something I'm pretty sure doesn't exist.

With or Without Love

I'm not ready to let him go, not
without a fight. Besides the easy
sex thing, there's still the pot.

I know they say marijuana isn't
addictive, not like speed or heroin,
which claw into you and won't let go.

Pot is more of a sweet talker, and I'm
all over that sexy voice. I went Saturday
without it, but by yesterday afternoon,

I was getting antsy. I called Mick,
asked him to pick me up after church.
Yes, I sometimes sneak off to Sunday

services, always in need of forgiveness,
if not always exactly sure why. Freshly
forgiven, I was eager for corruption.

> *Okay, I'll come get you,* he said.
> *But not if you're gonna fuck off*
> *on me. What was that about?*

Not like we're exclusive, or have
ever pretended to be. But the dope
was calling. Had to play contrite.

Even if it isn't my best game. "Sorry.
Guess I was jealous of Madison
and wanted to make you jealous too."

> *Yeah, well, I could have screwed*
> *her Friday night too. I didn't,*
> *even though she wanted to.*

Zing! Off went a flare in my head.
My temper [ature] started to rise.
But I kept it in check. "Obviously."

> *Anyway, Madison says you see*
> *other guys all the time. Friday*
> *kind of proved that, didn't it?*

Okay, I was starting to lose it.
"That's just bullshit! If she doesn't
watch her effing mouth, I'll . . ."

> He waited for me to finish it,
> but when all I could do was stammer,
> he asked, *You'll what?*

"Kick her ass."

But Kicking Ass

Could definitely be
a double-edged
sword. Not that
I've ever tried it.

But I can see how getting physical could relieve some tension,
at least in the short run. Hauling off, letting my fists fly, and
feeling them connect with her surprised face just might

make me feel a
whole lot better.
That is, until the
inevitable fallout.
Suspension for
sure. Restitution,
possibly. Maybe
lockup? I could
even find myself
in my dear old
daddy's court.
No, the more
I think about
it, the more I
believe there
has to be a
subtle yet
satisfying
method of
revenge.

I Just Have to Find It

And that might take a while.
        Patience? Not my best thing.

I make it through Contemporary
        Lit, still puzzling over it.

Spanish II. *Si, quiero*
        venganza. I want revenge.

I am on my way to history
        when opportunity falls

smack in my lap, à la
        a quick bathroom break.

As I start toward the girls'
        room, I notice Madison

ahead of me. She reaches
        into her purse, roots inside.

She glances around, but
        doesn't see me watch her

extract a tampon, palm
        it, and step through the door.

I can wait to pee. And now
        I've got my ammunition.

I'll Have to Wait to Use It, Though

First I have to get through history.
I sit in my usual seat in back,
by the window, as Mr. Lawler
passes out last week's essays.
I can't help but notice how
he moves with feline grace.
A big cat. Jaguar, maybe.
Or a tiger. Secure within his stripes.

Pinstripes, actually, on dark
trousers, snug at the waist
and across his hips,
before falling loosely
down over his thighs.
And just as my disgusting
brain gloms onto a sick
image of what those thighs
look like, his voice descends.

Interesting piece of writing.
I'd like to discuss it further.
Can you wait after class,
or come in at lunch?

Interesting, good? Or bad?
My eyes drop, focusing on
a large red A at the top of
my paper. Apparently,
good. "Let's do lunch."

Doing Lunch

With Mr. Lawler will postpone
exacting revenge. Lunch would

have been a great venue for what
I've got in mind. Instead I'll wait

for drama—not my class, but I'll
go to watch Kaeleigh rehearse.

At least, that will be my excuse.
Madison will be there too.

And anyway, lunch with Mr. Lawler
and his pinstripes could prove quite

interesting. Sheesh. Sometimes I turn
into a major vamp. It's a fun game.

I'm all into games, distractions
from the day-to-day crap. All vamp,

I open Mr. Lawler's door. "Ready
for me?" His smile tells me definitely.

> *Come on in. I'm just finishing*
> *up here. Have a seat.* He gestures
>
> to a chair beside his desk, scribbles
> something in his grade book,

and finally looks me in the eye.
I'm fascinated with your take

on the Scopes trial. How did you
arrive at your conclusions?

I outline my research, add a bit
about my father and his take on

this sensational piece of history—
how different attorneys might have

made different arguments, the court
might have allowed the jury to

sentence Scopes, and the Bible
might have been the only source

for schoolchildren for many years
to come. Hard to believe they were

such cretins in 1925, jailing a high
school teacher for offering evolution

as an alternate theory to creationism.
Just who were the monkeys in the "Monkey

Trial"? Anyway, the entire time I talk,
Mr. Lawler's eyes stay fixed on mine.

I'm very impressed. You took
a relatively straightforward

topic and gave it a unique
spin. I appreciate the extra

effort that went into this essay.
And then, in a completely

unexpected move, his hand
settles gently on top of mine.

I should pretend propriety, pull
my hand away. But I like how

it feels beneath the warmth
of his. I give my most vampish

smile. "Extra effort is my middle
name. Thanks, Mr. Lawler."

That Was Fun

Maybe even more fun
than what I've got on my
agenda now. We shall see.
I wander into drama, wearing

"innocent"

like baby powder perfume.
Onstage, waiting for direction,
Madison stands with a couple
of girls and several guys.

Perfect.

God, she's such a cow,
hardly even worth my

jealous

response. I almost change
my mind, but then she catches
sight of me and her expression
puts me on my feet. Totally

guilt

free, I saunter up the stage
steps. Kaeleigh hasn't yet

appeared,

and Ms. Cavendish won't
know the difference unless
I try to sing. I pass Madison's
knot, sniff the air beside her

dramatically,

loudly project, "Ugh! What's that
smell? Madison, are you on the rag?"

Kaeleigh
Everyone's Laughing

At Madison, whose face has turned
the approximate color of pickled beets,
as she struggles for a comeback. I almost
feel sorry for her, not that she's exactly

innocent

of saying mean things to people.
Or about people, behind their backs,
or even worse, where they can overhear.
Most everyone I know thinks she's a

perfect

bitch. Even her friends don't like her
much, that's my guess. Maybe I'm

jealous

somehow. Nah. She's the one
with the problem, not me.
Anyway, the more I remember
how nasty she can be, the less

guilt

I feel about thinking what just
happened is funny. Still, Ian

appeared

just about the time she sputtered
off. He looked at me like I was
at fault. Whatever.

Dramatically,

I tilt my face toward the ceiling,
walk by him without a word.

Ian Retaliates

In his own subtle way, goes
and sits by Shelby, rotates
completely away from me.

I've studied this scene, know
my lines. So why can't I
remember a single one?

Uh, Kaeleigh? You seem
a bit distracted today, says
Ms. Cavendish. *Everything okay?*

Wonder if Ian . . . oh, did she
just ask me a question?
"I'm sorry, what?"

Definitely distracted. Get your
script. You and Ian run lines.
We'll block this scene later.

I slip quietly into the vacant
seat on the other side of Ian.
"She wants us to run lines."

He nods and Shelby retreats.
Ian and I crack our scripts
without exchanging glances.

Eventually

We reach a romantic scene.

>Onstage, Ms. Cavendish
>has the chorus singing a big
>ol' production number.
>It's an unusual backdrop

for Ian's and my scripted passion.

>But even with numerous
>vocal errors, corrections,
>and amended directions,
>so many distractions,

our declarations of love intertwine.

>And even as Madison
>stomps back into the theater,
>to be corralled by Ms. C and
>told to join the others onstage,

Ian finally looks up, into my eyes.

>Just then the bell rings,
>and as everyone deserts
>the stage, locates possessions,
>escapes the building, he says,

Sometimes I just don't know who you are.

Not Exactly

The words I'd hoped to hear.
Then again, what exactly
        were the words I'd hoped for?

Anyway, to be honest,
sometimes I'm not so sure
        just who I am either.

So I admit, "That makes
two of us, I guess." At least
        when I smile, he does too.

He offers me a ride home,
but I opt for the bus. "Maybe
        tomorrow? I need to think."

Ian walks me to the yellow
dinosaur, bends down,
        kisses a sweet good-bye.

As the bus belches and squeals,
pain bubbles up inside, an evil
        spirit, demanding escape.

And by the time I reach home,
I know I've got to uncork
        the bottle, free my evil genie.

It's Been a While

Since I've really binged.
Mostly, I guess, because things
have seemed fairly flatlined
recently. No major upsets.
No major downslides.

But that episode with William
has bothered me since
it happened. I let it fester,
though on the surface
the blister has popped,
scabbed over. William didn't
cause the infection, he was just
its manifestation. God, I'm so
in need of spiritual antibiotics.

Then the Madison thing.
She is a major, total shit
stirrer, vicious clear through,
and obviously out to shred
any living thing that stands
in the way of what she wants.
On one level, what happened
in drama was the funniest
thing ever. I laughed out loud,
along with most everyone
else. So why did I feel bad later?

But When It Comes

To my personal sundae
of interior upheaval,
Daddy is the ice cream.
Raeanne is the hot fudge.
Mom is the whipped cream.
And Ian is now, and maybe
forever, the cherry on top.

Why can't he and I find
a way to accept each other,
lose ourselves in all-
encompassing love,
the kind that can save you?
The kind that can glue
all the fragments of two
broken hearts together.

Sometimes, every once
in a while, it feels like
we're almost there. Close.
So close. But then something
happens, something out
of my control, and mostly
it comes from inside of me—
this terrible black energy,
wrenching us apart. I think
I should be able to control
it, make it go away. But I can't.

And So, Right Now

I will control one of the few
things I can. Gaining curves.

Funny thing is, I still haven't
graduated to double digits,

despite semiregular binges
amounting to amazing quantities

of food. Maybe stress burns
a lot of calories or something.

But hey, I'm gonna try, at least
as long as there's food in the house

and Daddy isn't home. He's not.
The garage is vacant, awaiting

the Lexus's return. I glance at
the grandfather clock in the hall.

Not yet four. I should have an hour
or more, all to myself and my genie.

It's screaming to be fed.
Begging to be satisfied.

It's Probably Weird

To think about an addiction
like it's a sentient being,
but that's how it feels.

Like it's something living
inside you. Something
you can't get rid of because
killing it means killing you.

I can't really understand
addictions to drugs or alcohol.
Things that control you.

But an eating disorder
is an addiction you control.
Wait, is that paradoxical?
I prefer to believe not.

Either way, I kick off my shoes,
slide along the tile and into
the kitchen, calming my genie

with promises. Twinkies. Ice
cream bars. Halloween candy.
Screw the trick-or-treaters.
Little heathens are bums.

Sweet Stuff

Sounds good, but I know from
experience I'll get sick before
I can eat enough sugar to satiate
this kind of need. I should start
with something else. Hey.
I know. I'll binge healthy
and do the five food groups.

Crackers. Chips. Both whole
grain. Salsa. Fruit salad.
Canned, but oh well. Cheese
for the crackers. (And later,
ice cream, dessert dairy.)
Protein? Think there's lunch
meat in the refrigerator.
Hope it's bologna.

That just leaves fat. So I'll
butter my bologna. First,
I spread a quarter roll of paper
towels on the table. Have to
do this crumb free. Next
I arrange silverware in
a perfectly straight line.

About the time I turn toward
the cupboards, I notice
the obnoxious repetitive noise.

The Answering Machine

Is beeping, accompanied
by a red warning light.
Blip-blip-blip. Three messages.

> One: Mom. *Can't talk*
> *long. But thought you'd*
> *want to know, in case*
> *you haven't checked,*
> *the campaign is picking*
> *up. I'm ahead in current*
> *polls. Will be home to watch*
> *the election coverage.* Click.

Awesome. Looks like we'll lose
her completely. Not that I expected
anything else. No, not at all.

> Two: Daddy. *Can't talk*
> *long. But wanted to let*
> *you know I'm going out*
> *to dinner with a colleague.*
> *It could go pretty late,*
> *so don't worry if you don't*
> *see me tonight. Any problems,*
> *call my cell phone and I'll*
> *get back to you ASAP.*

"ASAP," pronounced like a word,
instead of initials. No problem,
Daddy. I'm feeling pretty good now.

My Head Is in the Fridge

When the third message
fires up. The voice is unfamiliar,
but it's someone I sort of know.

> *Hello? I'm trying to reach*
> *Raymond Gardella. Ray?*
> *This is your father. I know*
> *it's been a long time with*
> *no word from me. But*
> *something has come up*
> *that I thought you should*
> *hear about ASAP. . . .*

A-S-A-P. Unlike Daddy,
Grandpa Gardella uses
the initials, not the acronym.

> *I had a visit from your mother,*
> *returned from who-knows-where.*
> *She wanted to know how*
> *to find you. Apparently, she's*
> *actually paid attention to*
> *the news lately. She knows*
> *your wife is running for Congress.*
> *My guess is she's out to make*
> *trouble unless you shove*
> *a few dollars in her direction.*
> *If I were you, I'd expect a call.*

The Impossible News

Steals my breath, chases away
all desire for food. I thought
for sure my grandmother was dead.
And now this not-so-distant
relative crawls from the grave,

                                            a ghost.

I wonder where she's been,
why it's taken so many years
for her to reappear. And now,
three weeks until the election, she

                                            materializes

from the ether, robed in evil
intent? What information
can she possibly have? What
dark recess of Daddy's past

                                            harbors

secrets that could sway voters
away from Mom now? Will
my grandmother really, truly
appear on our doorstep, hugging

                                            malevolence,

money her only motivation?
Has she no desire to reconnect
with her son, meet his family,
become our family too? Do we

                                            want

that, even if she does? One
of those faded filmclips
flickers in distant memory.

Raeanne
Rich!

A ghost

Both the Häagen-Dazs bar
dripping into my mouth
and Grandpa Gardella's
phone message.

from Daddy's past, one
who has remained invisible
(almost so, anyway) for a very
long time,

materializes

from some sordid history
we probably don't want
to know about. Kaeleigh,
the dimwit, is thrilled. She

harbors

some idiotic curiosity
about our genealogy,
as if dissecting the beast
could help us escape its

malevolence.

But I know that this poorly
timed turn of events can only
lead to more pain. Sorry, Kaeleigh,
but Daddy's mommy can only

want

one thing: more than a few bucks.

What a Great Thing

To come home to. Something
new. Sure to cause a major stir.

    Life is rarely dull around here.
    I consider calling Daddy,

        more to mess up his dinner out
        than anything. But then it strikes

            me that I want to see the look on
            his face when he hears the news.

        Maybe I should call Mom instead.
        Someone should break it to her.

    Wonder how long she'll be ahead
    in the polls, should the ghost decide

to spread some unimaginable
rumors about dear old Daddy.

What Could the Gossip Be?

She can't have a clue about Daddy
and Kaeleigh. Unless she's been
spying, completely covertly, for a
very long time. Grandpa Gardella
didn't even know
about us until just
a few years ago.
And our grand-
mother was still,
to everyone's
knowledge, totally out of the
picture then—gone or dead.
So what can she possibly
hold over Daddy's head
now? Could it
have something
to do with why
Grandpa and
Daddy don't
speak to each
other? Did my
father shoot up
heroin? Sacrifice neighborhood
pets? Hit-and-run, DUI, or shoot
someone, by accident or on purpose?
My curiosity is killing me because

n q u i r i n g
minds want to know.

Mom Will Want to Know

Although maybe not from me.
But hey, what's a daughter for?
Not sure what city she's touched
down in tonight, but it will
be pretty late. It's ten here.

> Mom's cell rings five times,
> threatens to go to voice mail,
> but she picks up before it does.
> *Yes?* Okay, she's miffed, but not
> as miffed as she's going to be.

"Uh, Mom? It's me. We got
a phone message today that I
think you should know
about sooner rather than later.
Let me play it for you."

> I hold the receiver up to
> the speaker. When the message
> finishes, I wait out the silence.
> Finally she says, *Thank you.*
> *I'll put some people on it.*

People? Mom has people?
I mean, I knew she had a staff,
connections even. But "people,"
as in people who handle stuff
like a crazy long-lost relative?

Wonder If I Should Be Scared

Or at the very
least, a little nervous.

Wonder what it would
take to make

Mom decide to
put her people on me.

I know a secret or two
myself. What if

I threatened to
go public unless she bought

me a car, paid for my
insurance, took

two hours of her
precious time to help me

get my license? Hey! Great
idea. Or not.

Really, how far
would I go if she said no?

How Far Will I Go

To enjoy this little game?
Daddy will be home soon,
at least I assume he will be.
It might be fun to watch
him pick up the message,
squirm. Freak. Go ballistic.

But just imagine the fun
if I erase the warning, wait
things out. See if my loser
grandmother actually rings
the bell one day. Surprise!
Guess who's coming to dinner,

Daddy o' mine. Wow. Decisions.
Decisions. Kaeleigh would want
to tell, but she's crawled on off
somewhere. To erase or not to
erase, that is the question.
While I think it over, I'll make

an easier decision. Another
Häagen-Dazs bar? Why not?
Ex-Lax awaits. Chocolate melting
into my mouth, I go over to
the counter, watch the red light
flash three times, extinguish it.

In the Dark

Of my room, I try to sleep,
but thoughts whirl through

my skull, cerebral tornadoes.

Life, I'm fairly sure, is about
to change. But for better or worse?

Any guess is as good as mine.

What would happen if all our dirty
laundry was hung out on a line

where the entire world could see it?

Would Daddy still be a judge?
Would Mom still run away?

Would Kaeleigh and I be taken,

forced into foster care? Would our
lives be less filled with misery?

Or would it just be more of the same?

My eyes grow heavy, less with
weariness than with remembrance.

A certain night blurs into focus.

Mom Was Gone Again

Can't exactly remember why,
only that we didn't expect her
to come home until very late.
It was dark in our room.

Velvety black. Someone had closed
the curtain. Kaeleigh was scared.
I tried to tell her not to worry, but just
then, Daddy burst through the door.

I closed my eyes tight, made myself
no more than a shadow. Something
about him was different. I didn't
want that something to find me.

I cracked my eyes just a slit as he sat
on Kaeleigh's bed, pulled her into
his lap. He smelled of Brut and Wild
Turkey. His peculiar potpourri.

> *I love you so much, my little*
> *flower. Daddy needs something*
> *from my girl, my sweet rose.*
> *Will you give it to me?*

I wanted to be his little flower,
would have given my daddy anything.
What did he want from Kaeleigh?
She laid her head on his chest. "What?"

I want you to see something,
something that proves how
much I love you. This is only
for you, Kaeleigh girl.

He lifted her gently, sat her
down on the bed beside him.
Then he opened the snaps on
the fly of his flannel pajamas.

It stood up, stiff as a stalagmite.
See how much Daddy loves you?
Show me you love me, too. Touch
it. He closed her hand around it.

I know it sounds bad, but I wanted
to touch it too. I didn't know
what it meant, only that it made Daddy
happy. I wanted to make him happy too.

That's right. That's right.
His voice rocked in rhythm
with his body. *Oh yes, my Kaeleigh*
loves me. My little flower . . .

Kaeleigh Didn't Know

What any of it meant
either.
But we both knew

somehow it was
important,
because when Daddy

finished, he burrowed
his face
into Kaeleigh's hair

and wept. Confused at
his tears,
and at the sticky stuff icing

her hands, still Kaeleigh
pleaded,
"Don't cry, Daddy.

What's the matter? Didn't
I love
you good enough?"

That Brought Him Out of His Trance

Like he suddenly realized just what
he'd done. He scrambled for cover.

> *Yes, you loved me good enough.*
> *So very good! But it's our secret, okay?*
>
> *Because if anyone knew how much*
> *you love me, they'd be jealous.*

Now Kaeleigh was really confused.
"Can I tell Mama our secret?"

> *No! Especially not Mama. She'd get*
> *mad because she doesn't love me*
>
> *like you. She might even go away.*
> *You don't want that, do you?*

She thought it over. Again and again.
But she finally agreed, "I won't tell."

> *Daddy pulled her against him. Good.*
> *That's very good. It's okay to have*
>
> *secrets between Daddy and his girl.*
> *Just remember. No one likes a tattletale.*
>
> *Especially not Daddy.*

She Never Tattled

Didn't want Daddy to get mad.
Didn't want her mama to go
away, though she'd already
gone in spirit, if not yet

                physically.

Hard to understand.
Harder yet to believe.
Especially when your own
need is so great. The simple

                need

to absorb your mother's love.
Kaeleigh always needed
that more than I. No, I

                crave

more our father's affection.
But can anyone really love him
good enough to fill a well of

                want

so deep it must extend all
the way to his core, the very
"who" of who he is? And one
bigger question remains, begging
an answer: Just

                who (or what?)

drilled that well in the first place?

Kaeleigh
This Morning I Wake

Mired in confusion, an odd
sort of throb in my torso.
Hunger. The specter of my genie,

physically

haunting me. Stalking me.
Beneath my silk
pajama top, my empty
belly lies, flatter than ever. I

need

that binge, and something
more. Something to make me
feel necessary. Alive. This thing I

crave

(no, can't) is new. Forbidden.
(No. Don't.) What's wrong
with me? I can't believe I

want

this. Why me? Why now?
Why at all? My hand floats
across my curvelessness,
moves lower, to the need.

Who (or what?)

can I make believe is loving me?

Am I Sick?

My skin is hot. Fevered. Demanding
to be soothed. Touched. Satisfied.

Have I gone crazy? I have never, ever
done such a thing. Never unlocked

this private room inside of me. Never
ever wanted to take a look inside.

Am I possessed? Entered by a demon,
chained and padlocked, inside of myself?

I feel possessed, taken by some evil,
sick desire. Desire I can't control.

What is wrong with me? I don't want
this. Oh God. It can't feel good.

But it does.
But it does.

It does.
It does.

Does.
Does.

Totally Humiliated

I go into the bathroom.
        I'd like to take a hot bath,
                but no time now. I'll have
                        to settle for a shower.
                                The steamy cascade
streams over my body.
        Sandalwood soap
                lifts in a fragranced
                        fog, cleanses and
                                perfumes skin and air.
Nasty stickers of hair
        defile me, the goddess
                within. I reach for my
                        razor, triple bladed
                                and critically sharp.
I've shaved my legs for
        years, know to be careful,
                yet suddenly I don't
                        give a fuck and push
                                hard. The consequences
are immediate. Blood
        streams from the long,
                wide slice I've opened.
                        It vanishes down the drain,
                                and I can't help but smile.

Yeah, It Stings

But at least I feel something.
Something besides hungry.
Something besides afraid.

Weird. I always thought
cutters were sick. Sicker
than me, even. But with

a single swipe I understand
why they do it. Why they like
it, even though they hate it.

I let the water run over the cut,
ratchet it hotter, watch the blood
slow, stutter, almost halt.

I like the way the exposed flesh
looks, all pinkish white. It looks
new, although I know that isn't right.

It's the same age as my skin,
my bones. Me. It's been there
with me since the beginning.

Been there with me through
thick. Thin. Daddy. Suddenly
I don't like how it looks at all.

Ugly Flesh

Still exposed, I dress in loose
drawstring pants, a soft, baggy
blouse. Definitely not haute couture.

In fact, I look like a pregnant hippie.

To complete the look, I make two long
braids with my grown-out bangs,
pull them together in back. All I need
now is some daisies to weave in.

Several minutes behind my usual
schedule, guess I'd better skip
breakfast. Somehow I've lost
my appetite anyway.

Not gonna go double digits like this,
but I've got plenty of time to work on it.
And the baggy pants make me
look larger than the size seven

I keep trying to outgrow.

Backpack Stuffed

With homework and books, I maneuver
the hallway as quietly as possible.

Right hand on the latch, I'm almost out
into the cold, cold morning when

> the sledgehammer falls:

> *Where do you think you're going,*
> *dressed like some lunatic street person?*

Just the tone of Daddy's voice makes
my entire body quake. I don't dare turn

around, don't dare look into his eyes.
In them, I know I'll see the *real* lunatic.

I find an excuse. "Uh, we . . . we have
a play rehearsal this morning. This will

help me get into my role, that's all."

> He doesn't buy a word of it.

> *Today is Wednesday. You have drama*
> *Tuesday and Thursday afternoons.*

Has he actually memorized my class schedule?
Does he really keep an eye on such things?

I mean, yes, he's a control freak and all. . . .
I finally face him, crazy man in the eyes and all.

He's there, okay, daring me not to admit
the lie. I know better. "Yes, that's right,

but I'm already running late. I don't
have time to change now."

The lunatic levels me.

No daughter of mine goes out in public
like that. Go change. I'll drive you.

I Back Up the Hallway

Eyes firmly planted on Daddy,
who follows. Why does it have
to be just the two of us here?

I want my sister. I want my mom.
Surely he won't trail me into
my room. Won't watch me undress.

Won't stop me from transforming
from hippie to soc. Right? Right?
Please tell me I'm right!

I back into my room, start to close
the door, hoping he won't push
inside. "I'll hurry, okay, Daddy?"

I stare at him, try to measure
him, and the weirdest thought
flashes inside my head: He must

have been incredibly good-looking
once, before life crashed around
him. Took him down. He pauses.

*Should I help you choose
what to wear?* His voice
is soft as baby skin.

This can go a couple of ways.
Say no and face his anger?
Say yes and face . . . what, exactly?

Instinct tells me to accept his offer.
"Uh. Sure." But I start to shake
as he steps through the doorway,

moves swiftly across the floor to my
closet, pokes inside, swaying back
and forth like an Indian cobra charmer.

> *This,* he says, *has always
> been one of my favorites. You
> look like your mother in it.*

He Caresses

A pink angora sweater, pets
it softly, as if it were the bunny
the fur was stripped from.

He hands it to me, along
with a slim pair of burgundy
jeans. Daddy has good taste.

I take his offerings, start toward
the bathroom, but he stops
me with the force of his eyes.

I know what he wants. Sudden
nausea rocks me, but just as I think
for sure I'll vomit right here,

the telephone rings, yanking
Daddy from his trance.
His head turns toward the door.

Oh. Been expecting that call.
Hurry and change. You don't
want to be late for school.

The Jeans Rub My Cut

And painfully so, but the pain
reminds me that I'm still
alive, still in control
of at least one
thing.

Right now I need to feel more
in control, so I stash my
hippie clothes deep
in my book
bag.

Daddy is still on the phone.
I call "good-bye," rush
out the door, down
the street, after
the bus.

I can see the flash of its taillights, breathe its greasy
exhaust, but I
can't catch
up to it.

I watch it swing wide, onto
the highway and up
the hill toward
school. Now
what?

Behind me, I hear a well-
tuned car and know
without turning
it's Daddy's
Lexus.

He Pulls Up

Not quite scraping the curb.
The window lowers, and I wait,

expecting a hot wave of anger.
Instead his eyes sweep over

my body, assessing. He catches
something he doesn't like.

> *Much better, except for your*
> *hair. Take them out.*

Take what out? Oh, the braids.
I do as instructed. Wait again.

> *That will do. Now get in. Why*
> *didn't you wait for me?*

"You were still on the phone.
I thought I could catch the bus."

I settle into the plush warmed
leather, unworthy of its comfort.

> *You know I hate disobedience.*
> *I hope it won't happen again.*

"I'm sorry, Daddy. I was just
trying to save you the trouble. . . ."

His head snaps in my direction,
and his hand flashes toward me.

It takes all my willpower not
to flinch, not to bloat his anger.

His fingers catch my cheeks,
pinch until my mouth opens.

I'll decide what is or isn't trouble.
You just follow orders. Understand?

Drool dripping from my open
mouth, all I can do is nod.

His hand falls away from my face,
and stress falls away from his.

That's my girl. You're the one
person in the world I can count on.

After That

He pulls carefully away
from the curb, turn signal
doing its obligatory thing.
To the casual observer,

                    I know,

we are quite a picture.
Judge Gardella, dashing
in tailored navy blue,
and his teenage daughter,

                    pretty

in pink angora. But what's
underneath that sweater
is the antithesis of normality,
however that word

                    is defined.

And hey, when it comes
to abnormal, I can only
be one-upped

                    by

the man driving the car. What
would the neighbors think if they
could look through our windows,
beyond the closed curtains, and see

                    what's inside?

Raeanne
School Drags Today

Not that it's ever exactly exciting,
with the possible exception
of Lawler's history class.

I know

it's terribly warped of me
to spend an entire block
thinking about what's tucked
behind the man's zipper. Oh yeah,

pretty

damn sick, okay. But at least
I'm not bored. Right now I'm
in English, trying to figure
out how the word "faggot"

is defined,

other than by a homophobe.
We have to do a paper about
how English has been bastardized

by

popular culture. But, much
like Kaeleigh's door, the cover
of a dictionary is not particularly
something I want to open to see

what's inside.

I'm Trying to Avoid

Exactly that when Shelby
taps my shoulder. *Look.*

Outside, clearly framed
by the window glass,

my best and dearest friend
Madison sidles up to Ian.

A deep shade of anger
blossoms beneath my skin.

Screwing around with Mick—
and so me—is one thing.

Messing with Ian is something
else, something unforgivable.

I can't believe I'm standing
up for Kaeleigh, but I so am.

I raise my hand. "Excuse me,
Mrs. Finch, but I feel sick.

May I go to the rest room?"
Clearly unwilling to invite

diarrhea or vomit, she waves
me out the door.

I Have No Real Right

To play stand-in for Kaeleigh, but
she wouldn't have the nerve to do
what needs to be done anyway.
Sorry, twin o' mine, but it's true.

I watch from a short distance
for a minute or two, trying to size
up the situation, head to toe. Or
maybe boob to chest is more apt.

Not a millimeter separates Ian's
T-shirt from Madison's blouse.
In his defense, I will say Ian looks
immensely uncomfortable.

As I start toward them, he sees
me, and his demeanor shifts
from complacency to sheer panic.
Oh darlin', you just wait.

At the terrified look in his eyes,
Madison turns to face me. Smiles.
Oh, girl. That is so not the way
to deal with this. I'm ready to rock.

But since I'm supposed to be
Kaeleigh, I'll notch it back
to something more like passive.
At least for the moment.

As I Move Closer

The tenor of the scene changes
yet again. Madison remains
possessive, of course. It's Ian
whose body language alters.
I had expected contriteness.
Instead he seems unmovable,
despite the certain emotion
betrayed by his eyes: hurt.

Okay, what did that bitch tell
him? All thoughts of Kaeleigh
tossed aside, I move faster toward
the two of them. With
obvious intent. Madison's smile
falls from her face and I know
she has read the message in
my eyes: Get the fuck
away from him! She does, too.

But not far. She's a total player,
and all in all, a worthy opponent.
Oh, hey. Hope you don't mind
my borrowing Ian's ear. I was
just asking him to vote for me
for junior class president.

OMG! She's got to be joking.
"Oh, really? Brave of you to
run . . ." I leave the obvious

message hanging. Think better
about letting her off so easy.
"I'm sure Ian is smart enough
to vote for the best candidate,
though." Then I move between
them, turn to face Ian's sad eyes.
"May I talk to you for a minute?"

His response is unexpected.
He levels me with his dark
gaze. *Not right now. I'm late
for an appointment with my
guidance counselor. Later.*
And off he stalks, leaving

Madison and I standing here
together. We both stare
after him, nothing left to say
to each other. We both know
exactly what the other thinks.

Maybe That Wasn't

Such a good move. Then again,
maybe it was. Hopefully I at least
managed some sort of damage
control. Then again, maybe not.
I wonder what she said to Ian.

Well, it still isn't really my business.
And right now my mind is wrapped
around Mick, who's supposed to pick
me up during third block. Spanish.
Uh-huh, I'm ditching. Oh, well.

I stand on the side of the gym,
where hopefully no teachers will
notice me, waiting to do one
more wrong thing. Okay, several
wrong things, all at once.

I can't help but think about Ian,
and I can't help but wonder
what I can do to shut Madison's
big mouth once and for all.
It's a quandary, needing a fix.

Maybe getting my head will
fix it. I sometimes believe I think
best when I'm the most loaded.
Probably just wishful thinking.
But hey, here comes my ride.

Once Again

            My escape is successful.
Once again
            Mick greets me with an
            uncomplicated *Hey.*
Once again
            he points the Avalanche
            away from town, heads
            into the countryside.
Once again
            he leaves it to me to roll
            and light a fatty. Has it only
            been a few days since I last
            indulged this not-so-bad habit?
Once again
            we engage in easy sex,
            hardly a word exchanged
            between us. We are so not
            about conversation, and only
            body-to-body communication.
Once again
            we clean up the obvious,
            straighten our clothing, pop
            a few breath mints, and start
            back toward school. Only
            this time, Mick's erratic driving
            draws unwanted attention.

He Announces the Problem

With a most eloquent
Holy fucking shit.

It is then I notice the flashing
red and blue lights coming
up fast behind us. Holy
fucking shit is right.

Down go the windows,
nothing obvious about that,
but the damn truck smells like
a den of promiscuous skunks.

Mick doesn't have a choice
except to pull over.

This could go a number of ways,
from a simple ticket to a trip
to county lockup. I hope
it's Option Number One.

But as the cop—
a burly deputy sheriff—
strides purposefully closer,
my heart slides down into my gut.

Poor Mick is white.
Do something!

Do Something?

Is he talking to me?
"Like what, exactly?"

I dunno. Tell him
you'll give him head?

Hmm. Nah. "Just shut
up and don't panic."

Believe it or not, he shuts
up. As the cop reaches

the window, he sniffs.
Uh, license and registration.

Mick digs for his wallet,
reaches too quickly toward

the glove box. The cop's hand
dives in the direction of

his holster. *Easy now,*
he urges. *Open it slowly.*

What? Is he thinking gun?
"No problem, Officer," I say.

He looks across Mick, to
me. Instant recognition.

Hey. Aren't you Kay
Gardella's daughter?

Damn news conference!
What can I say? "Mm-hmm."

This, Too, Could Go

A number of ways, depending
on how the guy feels about Mom.
Maybe even how he feels about Daddy.
Both of my parents carry plenty
of baggage—both good and not so—
with local law enforcement.

See, before Mom ran for Congress,
she was a county supervisor.
Not everyone was always happy
about the decisions the board
made, especially when they
involved money. Still, she has always
been a fan of law enforcement.

As for Daddy, his decisions aren't
always favorable toward the arresting
officer, although Mom is right. He's
a reasonable judge who does the best
he can within the structure of the law.
So, depending on too many variables
to have a clue, the outcome of this
particular encounter is unpredictable.

And beyond all that, it just may come
down to how much of a tight-ass
this particular cop happens to be.

Unfortunately

It's so tight it squeaks
when he walks. He takes
Mick's information back
to his patrol car. We watch
in the rearview mirror as
he radios in. This is not
looking particularly good.

Back he comes, hand
dipping toward his hip
and what's attached to it.
He stands back from
the door. *Please exit
the vehicle.*

Okay, really, really not
good. We exit the vehicle
and Mr. Policeman gestures
for us to move to the front
of the truck. I am an idiot!
Holy shit. My dad is so
going to be pissed!

*I noticed a definite odor
of marijuana in your vehicle.
Have you been smoking
pot this afternoon?*

Can't see how lying is going
to help at this point, but I'm
not real keen about admitting
it either. I shake my head

just about the time Mick
is dumb enough to say, *Yeah.*

Which seems to amuse Deputy
Dawg. *I should probably haul
your ass in just for being so
stupid, Mr. Moron. . . .*

That's Morona, with an a, replies
the moron(a) in question.

The cop pretends to look
at Mick's license. *Oh yes, I see
it now. Well, Mr. Morona, you
wait right there for a minute.
Ms. Gardella, would you
please come with me?*

Not Sure Where

This is headed, but I trail
the deputy to his car, out
of earshot of Mick.

The cop gives me a hard
glare, then softens. *What
exactly do you think*

*you're doing? This is
too stupid for words,
you know that, right?*

I nod and finally glance at
the name pinned to his chest.
Deputy Carson. Familiar.

*Okay, here's what I'm
going to do. You go
get whatever is stashed*

*in that pickup. I'm going
to write Mr. Morona
a ticket, sixty in a forty-five . . .*

Holy crap. He's going
to let us walk. My eyes
must betray my disbelief.

I'd probably do things
differently, but Kay
deserves to win that seat.

Won't happen if the press
gets hold of the news that
her daughter is a stoner.

Kay? Sounds terribly
informal. Exactly how
well does he know her?

The man is good at reading
body language. *Yes, I know*
her. We met eight years ago.

I was a highway patrolman
then. First on the scene
at a certain accident. . . .

I stare hard at his face,
try to erase several years,
and sure enough, it swims

into view, just as it did
in the backseat of Daddy's
wiped-out Mercedes.

I Rejoin Mick

As Deputy Carson writes
the ticket. When I break
the news about his pricey
ounce, he actually gets mad.

What? No way! That cost
three bills. Add the fine
for speeding, I'm out more
than five hundred dollars.

"Shut the hell up, would you?
At least you're not going to jail. . . ."
And I'm not going to juvie, and
my parents won't be involved.

As the deputy hands Mick
Moron his ticket, I'm feeling
all warm and fuzzy, until
his final admonition.

I know the last eight years
cannot have been easy.
But hanging out with losers
won't make your life better.

I've come to believe that people
who survive accidents like that one
are either just plain evil, or saved
for a reason. Which are you?

Most of the Time

I don't feel evil. But saved
for a reason? Like what?
I guess I'm pretty good
at sex, but I don't think

                                    I was saved

because the world needs
more (even better) sex.
Maybe Deputy Carson
is completely full of it.

                                    Was I saved,

or was fate simply too
damn busy killing other
people that day to catch
up to me, too?

                                    I don't

let myself return to that
backseat very often. It's
the place every waking
nightmare began. I

                                    know

(think, anyway) that had
that day gone any other way,
nothing would be as it is
now. Right? Right? I guess

                                    I really don't know.

Kaeleigh
PE Today

Could have been ugly.
My leg is swollen, the cut
raw and inflamed. Jean germs?

I was saved,

believe it or not, by a bomb
threat. They evacuated
the whole school. Turned
out it was just a prank.

Was I saved

or was it only a fabulous
coincidence, one that kept me
fully clothed (hippie style) but
shivering in the pale afternoon?

I don't

think rescue is a big focus of fate,
or whatever (whoever?) may
or may not orchestrate history's
page turns. I'd like to

know

that I have the ability to
mold my own future, that if
I work really hard, I can turn
it all around. But truth is,

I really don't know.

Maybe Life Is Random

No fate. No God. Just time.
The concept of God escapes

me. Some all-powerful being,
who rules sometimes gently,

and often not so, all in the name
of love? Who dreamed that up?

I see people who really believe
in God, in hope, in charity.

Mostly, they look pretty happy
and, on the surface, satisfied.

Christian. Like Christ. So why
are so many Christians unlike him?

We don't go to church, but in
my search for personal answers,

I have explored the Bible some.
(Weird, I know, but when you get

no answers at all, you reach.)
The Old Testament is scary,

filled with misery. That God
was pretty creepy, all in all.

But Christ's testament asks
for patience, harmony. Not war,

nor ostracism. Not hate crimes, lies,
or offering plates filled to the brim.

I wonder if there's really a place
in heaven for hypocrites

who preach love, all the while
kicking the downtrodden.

Still, I might have bought into
the essence of Christ, except,

according to the scriptures, he
also asked for understanding

and forgiveness, even of our
enemies. And if he really expected

that, I could not pass muster.
Some people I'll never forgive.

It Was Greta

Who first turned me on to the Bible.

> *Whenever my life takes a wrong*
> *turn, I look there for direction.*
> *I went there often,* she said, *when*
> *I was no more than your age and*
> *the Nazis overran my country.*

The Bible, she said, offered comfort.

> *But it couldn't save the Jews who*
> *were marked for execution. It took*
> *people to do that, and my people,*
> *Lutherans, were not afraid to*
> *interfere. Every life is precious.*

The Bible, she said, gave no solutions.

> *But it did let us know God*
> *helps those who help themselves.*
> *In our Danish eyes, Lutherans,*
> *Jews, and all in between were no*
> *more nor less than Danes.*

Comforted, validated, they went to work.

Once we got word the Germans
were definitely coming for our
Jewish brothers and sisters,
we smuggled them to safe houses
along the eastern coastline.

And, to make the original "fisher of people" proud,

Mostly at night, but sometimes
day, we put them on fishing boats
and took them safely to Sweden.
We lost four hundred, but saved
thousands from the camps.

They lost more than their Jewish friends.

At first the Nazis took little
except food, but with the Resistance,
they confiscated property, possessions.
The freedom fighters they caught
went to the camps. Or disappeared.

Some were even martyred on the spot.

Many of us were just children.
I saw a friend gunned down in
the street. But we were doing
the Lord's work, and we reaped
his mercy from that time forward.

She Believes That Too

Must be nice to have that kind
of unshakable belief
in a merciful higher power.

I believe in a higher power,
but you can't call
it merciful. No, not at all.

It's the power of my father, all
will and rules and law,
and governed himself by

Deadly Sins, chief among them
avarice and lust.
The only two that don't apply

are sloth and gluttony. That last
one I lay claim to, and
before I go to work, I plan on

giving into it wholeheartedly.
Gluttony interrupted
leads to Gluttony, with a capital G.

No Time for a Major Lovefest

I'll have to make do with
a sugar OD, leave the five
                    food groups for next time.
          Look at me, already plotting
a next time. What's up?

          Stupid question, Kaeleigh.
What isn't up? You can't
                    maintain a relationship
          with the only guy in
the world worth loving.

          Your father's a freak,
your mother is invisible,
                    your friends don't get
          you at all, and you for
real like it that way.

          School used to be an escape.
Now it's just another place
                    with too much pressure,
too much confrontation,
          and so not enough joy.

          Your entire life is joyless.
Go ahead. Eat. Pig out, in fact.
                    Food is real, too much
of it the only thing you feel.
          (Except the razor.) So feel.

Still Feeling It

As I pedal my bike up the hill
toward the Lutheran home.
Several days until the time
change, it shouldn't be too dark
when I leave. But I'm going to
have to figure out a better way
to and from this place once night
falls when it's still afternoon.

I despise the short days of winter.
Don't even like the holidays,
and why would I? The only good
thing about them is the omnipresent
food. But all that phony good cheer?
Spare me. Or jump me straight
from Halloween to Easter.
I definitely do candy, so I'm great
with those noncelebrations.

Halloween is actually stupid,
unless you're under twelve.
I know some adults like to dress
up (or down) in costumes,
drink too much, and ogle
one another. I remember Mom
and Daddy doing that when
Raeanne and I were little.

But I totally think everyone
past middle school really ought
to give it a break. Except maybe
witches and vampires. I don't
believe in werewolves. But moon
worship, bonfires, and—oh yeah,
especially—a little bloodletting
seem like reasonable things to me.

I doubt anyone here at the old
folks' home would want to play
those games. But they are having
a Halloween party. William, dressed
up like a pirate? Greta, maybe
a French maid? Ha! Too funny.
I was invited, and, thinking about
it, I might just have to go.
Sounds like more fun than spending
the evening answering the doorbell
and topping off greedy kids' pillowcases.

I'm Almost to Work

When a car beeps and slows
to a stop nearby. It's a truly
forgettable vehicle—a well-
used Toyota something, silver.

The surprise is who's driving.
Brittany. She and I have known
each other for years. But not
well enough to swap secrets.

Hey, girl! Bet you can't guess
what I did this afternoon.
She pauses, and must decide
I'm really dense. *Like my ride?*

"Hmm. Let me see. Did you
get a haircut? No. Manicure?
Nah. Your nails look awful.
Oh. What did you say?

Something about . . . your ride?"
I smile. "Got your license, huh?
Oh hey, did you leave school early?
You missed all the excitement."

I heard about it on the news.
Top of the hour on the radio.
Not the best radio, but at
least I've got tunes.

My smile grows. "Yeah, except
for top of the hour. Congrats
on the license. I probably
won't get mine until I'm old

enough to drink legally. Anyway,
I gotta run. Drive carefully. We
don't need another statistic,
as my dear old dad would say."

*No worries. I don't plan
on being a statistic, unless
it's a good one. Hey, want
a ride to school tomorrow?*

I hardly ever take rides from
friends, and I start to say no,
but she looks so hopeful,
I just can't. "Why not?"

We agree on a time and away
she goes, and as I pedal up
the driveway, it occurs to me
that Brittany (plus Toyota)

just might come in handy,
especially when winter
hits for real. Long as her car
has a heater, of course.

No Party Tonight

At the old folks' home,
just more of the same ol',

except for one major thing.
Greta has a visitor. Someone

very special, from the past. I can
tell he's special by the sparkle

behind her spectacles. I can
tell he's from her past because

they're speaking in Danish,
something I've never heard

her do before. I'm fascinated,
and even though I can't

understand more than a word
or two, I keep finding excuses

to exit the dining room (where
I'm supposed to be getting

everything set up for dinner)
in favor of the sitting room.

Greta and her visitor have
parked themselves in front

of the fireplace, and their
conversation seems every bit

as cheerful as the song of wood,
crackling behind them.

As dinnertime nears, more and
more people stir around them,

but they are so caught up in
each other, they barely notice.

If I didn't know better, I'd
definitely guess this was love.

Looks Like Love

And dear Greta   so deserves love,
it makes me happy   to see it glowing all
around her, glowing   inside her, filling her
up with this beautiful light. Such brilliant
light must come straight from heaven,
if such a place really exists. She
believes it does, so for her,
it's real, and maybe
that's enough
to make
it so.

Real
or no, this
gentleman caller
dropped in from out
of the blue, so I'll just go
ahead and make believe he was
divinely inspired to bring a healthy
dose of light into Greta's life. Her smile
is ethereal. It makes   me shiver as all up
and down my arms,   a colony of goose
bumps lifts. And   suddenly, a jab

of jealousy
nails me in the gut.

Envy Surges

Scarlet hot through my veins.
I mean, the woman is like
eighty-two years old or some-

thing. Why should she know
love when I don't? When I can't?
She's only got a few years

at best. Why should they be warmed
by love when my own coming
decades are doomed to frigidity?

Greta's beau shares the dinner
table with a half-dozen old
women, but he sees only her.

And she sees only him, despite
the banter and pleasantries exchanged
all around and between them.

I can't help but watch through eyes
tinged green. Then Greta laughs,
from the heart, like she has laughed

with me, only sweeter. And suddenly
I am ashamed. No, horrified, at myself.
How could I think that way?

That Was an Incredibly Bad Scene

Like looking inside myself
and finding a stranger,
someone not only vicious
but downright

                evil.

How odd, to suddenly
glimpse a facet of me
I didn't know existed.
I guess it really

                isn't

all that unusual to surprise
oneself with an ugly bit
of ego. But was this
unsuspected piece of me

                born

at the same instant I was?
Or was it spawned some
time between that moment
and now? I know, I know

                it's

a question with no answer,
undeserving of introspection.
But was this hideous thing
conceived, or was it

                created?

Raeanne
Kaeleigh Takes Herself

Way, way too seriously.
Everyone has a secret side,
one that's not so nice. But

evil?

I prefer to reserve that
designation for presidents,
terrorists, and Madison.
Okay, I guess the bitch

isn't

really evil either. Too stupid
for evil. Oops. That lets presidents
off the hook too. Terrorists are
rarely stupid, but even they aren't

born

evil. But you know, preach it—
whatever "it" is—loud enough,
long enough, someone will buy in.
Witness Jerry Falwell. Ask me,

it's

a sin to pervert faith with religion.
Despite every church, mosque, and
synagogue in it, this is not the world
any God worth his salt would have

created.

But Whatever Created It

It's my world, the only one
I've got. Might as well make
the best of it, right? Might as
well have a little fun while
I'm here. Or a lot of fun.
Might be dead tomorrow.

I'd call Mick, but he's out
of dope, and anyway, he's
an irritating prick. Stupid,
too, all ranting about how
he's going to sue the sheriff's
department for stealing stash.

I told him to shut up and think
about it, and hopefully he's
doing exactly that about now.
I do know a few other people
who might have some bud.
But the one who comes first
and foremost to mind is Ty.

He gave me his number,
                    for the next time you
                    find your mouth watering
                    for a hot red lollipop . . .
Yeah, he's totally disgusting.
Why do I like men that way?

Oh, and Guess What

He answers his phone first ring,
and he isn't busy at the moment.

Lucky, lucky me. It's a school
night, and I might very well hear

about not coming straight home, but
hey, if I go straight home, I won't

be going out tonight. No-brainer.
I wait for him at a little convenience

store, and about the time I grow
impatient, a sheriff's sedan cruises

by, reminding me I do not want to
be caught in the backseat of a car

in a compromising position. Turns
out that's not a problem. Ty whips

into the parking lot, in a blue BMW
Z4 convertible. Top down. No back-

seat. We won't be smoking or making
out in this stunning little car.

> He smiles at the look on my face.
> *Get in. How 'bout we take a little spin?*

Zero to Sixty

In five point six seconds, says
Ty. Seemed faster to me. I love
the way acceleration presses me
back against my seat. But what's

really interesting is that Ty can afford
this car at all. Might as well just ask.

"So what do you do, anyway?
Or are your parents loaded?"

> He smiles and settles the car
> into an easy cruise mode.
> *Actually, my parents are*
> *loaded. More ways than one.*

I really look at him for the first
time. Handsome face, chiseled,
strong. Works-out-in-the-gym
body. Dark, longish hair, tied back.

Simple black T-shirt and Levis,
though clean, totally belie the Beamer.
And what exactly did he mean
by *more ways than one?*

Might as well just ask. "Your
parents get high? Do they deal?"

Nah, they don't deal. They indulge
plenty, though. See, my dad is
Chumash. When the casino was built,
he made—how best to put this?—more

than a tidy little sum on the deal.
He and my mom now own quite an
operation out Foxen Canyon Road.
Cattle. Horses. Young vineyard.

Who would have guessed?
Certainly not me, not even
after our little private party
up there on Figueroa. Still . . .

"So how about you? What do you do?
Do you live with your parents?"

A bunch more questions pop
into my head, bubbling over
like champagne, but the answers
to those two might answer the rest.

Shit, yeah. In a guest house,
actually. Once our vines mature,
I'll play vintner. Right now,
I'm apprenticing at another winery.

Several questions answered indeed.
Finally I notice we have in fact
been driving along Foxen Canyon
Road. Ty slows the BMW and we

turn up a long driveway through
rows and rows of immature grapes.
We make a left before reaching
the rather overbearing main house.

Finally Ty crunches to a stop
in the gravel. *Here we are. Home
sweet home. Hope you're up
for fun and games.*

Fun, Ty-Style

Begins with tall Jack Daniel's
          and Cokes. As he mixes them,
I wander around the "guest house,"

          thinking half the country would
flip if they could live in a home
          like this. Two oversize bedrooms.

Two bathrooms, one with a Jacuzzi
          tub. Beautiful kitchen, open to
the leather-and-brass living room.

          With a flick of a switch, Ty lights
the gas fireplace, which throws
          a gentle gleam across the hardwood

floor. He gestures toward the rich
          burgundy leather sofa and goes
into the bedroom. Blink of an eye,

          back he comes, holding a big wooden
box. He sits close, opens the hand-
          carved oak, reveals the cache inside.

This Is Something New

My uncle has connections you
wouldn't believe, says Ty.

He pulls out a baggie, a quarter
full of some crumbly brown substance.

When he cracks the bag, the perfume
that escapes smells like heaven.

Opiated hash. Ever tried it?

I shake my head no, but Ty
is quick to remedy that, filling

a small pipe bowl with a miniature
ball of opium-laced hashish.

He takes the first toke, and now
heaven's on fire, and smoking.

Still holding his hit, Ty cautions
around it, *Little tokes, now.*

Don't want to cough this stuff out.
Hold it as long as you can.

Slowly I inhale a taste sweeter
than any before. Greedy me

wants more, but I remember
his warning. The smoke expands

in my lungs, and I'm glad I didn't
take more. I hold it until I just have

to let go. When I finally do,
my head is tingling all over.

> Ty looks at me, measuring.
> *Having fun yet? 'Course you are.*

> *And sweetheart, this is just the start.*
> *We've still got games to play.*

Games, Ty-Style

Don't even begin until we're well
into the fun. Drinking. Smoking.
Feeling the creep of the poppy,
all along my spine, skull to tailbone.

I know the high is mostly hash,
not so different from regular
cannabis (though even tastier).
But the opium topper provides

a whole new set of rushes. Body
rushes, like little shivers. Head
rushes, like turning in circles,
round and round, don't fall down.

> *Shall we move the party*
> *into the bedroom?* Ty reaches
> over, kisses me. Hard. Harder.
> My heart screams in my chest.

> His teeth rake my bottom
> lip, move down over my chin,
> down my neck. Not too hard.
> Not really. But hard enough.

Should I have worn garlic
and a silver cross? I laugh
out loud at the thought, and
I realize how fucked up I am.

Ty stands, holds out his hand,
but I am so messed up, all I can
do is laugh. He pulls me to my
feet. *What's so funny?*

"Nothing. Everything. You.
Me. Especially me. My head
feels like it came unattached,
and my body is all tingly."

His grin is pure evil. *Excellent.*
I know just how to fix that.
He picks me up, carries me
into his bedroom, half throws

me onto the bed. When he starts
to undress me, I burst into a new
fit of giggles. My jeans are so tight,
he can't wiggle me out of them.

"Want some help, my macho
vampire?" I shed everything
and he does too, but before we
do another thing, he asks,

How 'bout another bowl?
Something to take you real,
real low. He leers like a scary
circus clown. *Low as a girl can go.*

True to His Word

He drops me real, real low.
I'm floating on a poppy sea.

Naked. Mellow. But a sudden
wind rouses the breaks and low

tide builds to major swells. Ty
kisses me, all fang, pure vampire.

"Hey. Take it easy." But somehow
my body responds to the pain.

And Ty responds to that, clamping
one hand around both my wrists,

pulling them up over my head
and pinning me helpless.

It is then I notice the nylon cord,
one end tied tight to the headboard.

                Ty's voice is almost a snarl. *This*
                is one of my favorite games.

He wraps the rope around my wrists,
knots it tightly. Escape-proof.

I shake my head. "Don't." But he does.
Should I scream? Would anyone hear?

Would anyone care? The obvious
answer softens my plea. "Please?"

> *Haven't you played this game*
> *before? I guess I'll have to teach*
>
> *you the rules. The proper response*
> *would be, "Please, sir." Say it.*

My heart yells, "No fucking
way." But my brain, the part

that understands my daddy, makes
me acquiesce. "Please, sir."

He flips me onto my belly, yanks
my legs apart. I don't have to see

the restraints to know they're there.
The ankle knots do not surprise me.

I am helpless. Exposed. And, strangely,
somehow I feel at home this way.

> *Say it,* he demands, like I should know
> he means, *Please, sir. Punish me.*

Deliberate, controlled, he punishes me.
I whisper into the pillow, "I understand."

I Understand

Why Kaeleigh liked the feel of
slicing her flesh, releasing
bottled-up hurt. Leather snaps
against my skin, and I remain

         still

as stagnant water, afraid I might
not play by his rules. This is
a new game, and the sick
thing is, I see quickly that I

         like

it, might ask to play again.
The pain is fuzzy at the edges,
blurring toward pleasure.
Maybe it's the hash,

         the gentle

arms of opium. And now
new leather—human, Ty—
falls softly over the heated
welts, a soothing

         balm of

sweat-beaded skin. But then
heightened pain, forced inside
me, stuffed inside me. Seared,
branded, likely marked,

         a moan

escapes me and Ty surges.
After, knots loosened, a rub
of cool eucalyptus oil persuades
me I do want to play again. Soon.

Kaeleigh
Long Night

Unable to slip into sleep,
unable to fall into dreams,
unable to lie completely

still,

snared by tangled thoughts.
Sometimes, usually well after
the witching hour, Raeanne
comes to me, shares my bed

like

she did so long ago. She
listens to me, soundlessly,
doesn't argue or judge.
Eventually, I slip into

the gentle

tide of unconsciousness. But
tonight she doesn't appear.
I am left to wrestle memories
alone, comforted only by the

balm of

cool satin sheets. I force
my body to relax, feel it grow
heavy. Heavy enough to sink
into the satin balm.

A moan

bubbles into my mouth,
from I don't know where—
some inconceivable place where
pleasure and joy are one.

Not Sure Exactly When

I managed to fall asleep,
but it must have been eventually
because I'm tugged like cement
into morning by the sound
of the telephone.

> Daddy's feet pound
> toward the ringing.
> *Hello . . . ? Hello . . . ?*
> *Okay, who the fuck is this?*

Funny, I hardly ever hear
Daddy curse. He must be
really pissed. The thought
is confirmed by his footfall,
in angry approach of my door.

> He bursts through and fear
> swallows me down. *Do*
> *you have any idea who's*
> *responsible for these hang-ups?*

One thought immediately
crosses my mind, but I'll be
damned if I want to get caught
in the middle of the brewing
storm. "No. Should I?"

He softens, but only a little.
*I thought maybe it was one
of your friends. Or . . .* white
glare *. . . a boyfriend?*

Like I would ever let a boy
call here! Like I would dare
say that. "None of my friends
would do that, Daddy. And I
don't *have* a boyfriend."

*Well . . . it's just that this has been
happening for several days. I
answer,* click. *Maybe it's one
of your mom's secret admirers.*

"Mom's admirers aren't so
secret, Daddy. It's probably
just a solicitor or something.
Anyway, doesn't the number
show up on caller ID?"

Now why didn't I think of that?
His voice fairly sprays sarcasm.
*It's a private number. Hurry
it up now, or you'll be late.*

The Clock Agrees

I'm supposed to meet Brittany
in twenty minutes. Still, I just
can't seem to "hurry it up."
Mostly because he told me to.

I slide out of bed, shuffle
to the bathroom, do my thing.
Brush my teeth and hair.
By the time I return to my
room in search of clothes,

Daddy is hustling toward
the door. *Come straight
home after work. Hear me?*

Like where else would I go?
But, of course, despite
the serious resentment
that blooms immediately,
I say simply, "Okay."

He is all the way into the garage
before calling over his shoulder,
And don't answer the phone.

Do This, Don't Do That

I seriously despise the man, would do just

about anything not to obey him, at

least if I thought I could get

away with it or even that

the sure consequences

would be sufferable.

But when Daddy

decides to make

you suffer,

it's more

than any-

one can

bear.

But He's Gone Now

So I'm going to do the likely
less than intelligent thing and
dress exactly how I want. Not
hippie today. Frumpy? Slutty?
Hey, maybe no clothes at all?

Probably not a good plan.
Who knows if Brittany's silver
bomber can even make it to
school without breaking down?
Speaking of that, she'll be here
soon. Better shake my tail.

Where did that saying come
from, anyway? I slide into
a glam velour jogging suit. Not
frumpy. Not slutty. Just soft
and definitely not an outfit
Daddy would want me to
wear to school. Too casual.
(Although, really not casual
enough for a decent jog.)

Out the door, into the cold
morning, I'm glad I'm wearing
sweats, if you can really call
glam velour sweats. Up the
sidewalk, to the corner where
I'm supposed to meet Brittany.

(Wasn't sure Daddy would
approve of that, either, should
he have been home to see me
climb into a half-dilapidated
Toyota.) Hey, maybe I defied
him twice in one morning.
Wouldn't that be a coup?

As I wait for Brittany (late,
go figure!), my mind wraps
around that "shake my tail"
thing. Some deep place inside
my brain latches onto it and
doesn't want to let go. Where
did I hear that? The voice I
don't quite remember is low.
Feminine. Not Mom's, though.
Too scratchy. So whose?

Brittany, Finally

And she's not alone. Riding
shotgun is Joel, who I know
from drama. And in the backseat, next to my apparently
appointed place, is Shaun.
Ian's little brother. Great.

Not that he's not a nice kid,
but sitting back there next
to him seems somehow
incestuous. Oh, well. It's
just a ride to school, right?

> *Oh, hey,* coos Brittany. *Sorry
> I'm late, but I had to pick up
> the guys. Joel was right on
> time, but Shaun?* She giggles.

Oh, yech. Maybe Brittany
as transportation won't work
out so well after all. But
one day won't hurt, right?
Anyway, the bus already
went by. My choices are
limited. "No problem."

Not Being Top

Of the hour, the radio blares.
Hip-hop, no less. Definitely

not my cup of tea, but hey,
it's not my freaking radio.

Joel seems to like it. He jerks
his head back and forth till

he looks like a bobblehead
with a really loose spring.

Beside me, Shaun stretches
his legs till his right knee rests

            against my left, totally creeping
            me out. *Awesome song, huh?*

I jerk my knee away from his.
"Uh, sure." If you like songs

without music. More like ebonic
poetry. Before I finish the thought,

Shaun's leg has found its way
back to mine. "Need more room?"

            Warmer like this, don't you
            think? Here comes his arm.

I turn and give him my most
evil glare. "What are you doing?"

                Nothing. His arm withdraws, but
                only a little. *Thought you'd like it.*

Irritation flares, red in my face.
"Oh, really? And why is that?"

                He shrugs. *Heard Ian talking.*
                He said you're into other guys.

Irritation fans into anger. "Is
that so? Well, you can just tell

your brother for me that I am
most certainly not into other—"

A sudden *thwunk-thwunk-thwunk*
interrupts the conversation.

The Toyota yanks itself hard to
the right and Brittany fights

                to stay in control. *Oh, man!*
                I think we've got a flat tire.

Flat Barely Describes It

The entire sidewall is gone, what's
left of the tread part, shredded.
We're not going anywhere, not on
this tire. "Do you have a spare?"

> *I dunno, but even if I do, I have
> no idea how to change it. Do
> you guys?* She looks at the boys,
> who shake their heads in unison.

We're already late for school.
Not much we can do but be
later. "Okay, then. Do you have
like AAA or something?"

> *I dunno. Oh, wait. My mom
> showed me a number to call.
> It goes with our cell service.*
> She leans into the car.

As she roots through the glove
box, I notice cars slowing a bit
as they drive by. Something
about four late-for-school kids,

looking helpless as hell
beside a useless car, barely
pulled onto the shoulder?
Could be it, I guess.

Then again, you might
think one of them would
stop and offer to help.
But no, they cruise on by.

Here it is! says Brittany,
punching at her cell phone.
*Hi. Um. I guess I need help . . .
er . . . roadside assistance?*

If she giggles one more
time, I'm going to push
her out into oncoming
traffic. We stand, stupid

as hell, waiting for a tow
truck. My teeth chatter,
and Shaun dares to move
closer. Really, really close.

Once again, his arm tries
to slide around my shoulder,
and I shrink from the touch
of his calloused skin. "No."

*What is your fucking problem?
I'm just trying to keep you
warm. Oh, that's right.
You prefer being frigid.*

His Term or Ian's?

It's going to bug me all day.
I always thought Ian was on
my side, that he understood,
if not everything, that I am only
lukewarm because I'm damaged.

Frigid? Maybe I am. But why
should it even be a topic
of conversation with Shaun?
Did Ian call me that? And did
he really say I'm into other guys?

Who did he say it to? And why?
Wait . . . a sudden "aha" strikes.
Madison. Would she have told
him such a thing, sunk so low?
And why would he believe her?

A stronger person would go
straight to the source, confront
him, ask if any of the things
his little brother had to say
could possibly be true.

But I could never do that.
What if I just couldn't stand
to hear what he had to say?
What if he walked away?
What if I lost him completely?

The Tow Truck Finally Arrives

And I still don't have any
answers, despite a good forty
minutes, standing here with
nothing else to do but

think.

Shaun finally gave up on me
and moved on to Brittany,
who's obviously into Joel.
Shaun is a total clod.

How

can he be Ian's brother?
They're about the same as
straight sex and gay sex—
some similarities, but

different

in ways that really count.
One thing I do know is that
if Ian deserts me, I'll never
repair the giant rip in my

life.

I don't dare let him go.
But how do I keep him
without losing me?
Who knew love

could be

such an enigma?

Raeanne
Life Is Rarely Dull

think

how

different

life

could be

At the Gardella house.
Kaeleigh was late for school
this morning. Now you might not

that should be a big problem,
especially considering she had
what for most would be a good
excuse. But that's not

things work around here. See,
one of Daddy's friends happened
to drive by the tow truck scene
and notice Kaeleigh. A

person might have shrugged
it off completely. Not Hannah,
a nursing student who lives
down the block. I cannot for the

of me understand why she felt
the need to call Daddy, but she
did. No surprise it made him
mad. But who knew he

so unreasonable over such
an innocent faux pas?

Kaeleigh Came Home from School

Not particularly worried about the tardy.
Neither Daddy nor Mom (on those rare
occasions she's around to peruse progress
reports) pays particular notice to stuff
sent home from school. Besides, it was
Kaeleigh's first tardy. Ever. No big deal.

> Not, that is, until she played Daddy's
> message, left both on her cell phone
> and on the answering machine at home.
> *I heard you missed school today in favor*
> *of taking a little joyride with a few friends.*
> *I'm surprised at you. Surprised, and*
>
> *disappointed. I'd better see you at home*
> *when I get there. You have some explaining to do.*
> *And then you have to decide what your*
> *punishment will be. Make no mistake.*
> *You will be punished. When I ask what*
> *you think is fair, I hope you have an answer.*

By the time he was finished, she was shaking.
I tried to tell her not to worry, that he'd cool
off before he got here. But she went to work
scared. And she came home from work scared.
Daddy still hasn't arrived yet, so she goes
straight to the kitchen in search of consolation.

One of Kaeleigh's Regular Binges

Is gross. Disgusting. I watch her

      and I want to puke. (And often do.)

But this one is unlike the others

      I've had the misfortune of seeing.

She doesn't care what goes into

      her mouth, as long as it resembles food.

"Stop," I beg. "Stuffing yourself can't save

      you from whatever it is you imagine

he's going to do. Please, Kaeleigh."

      But she keeps on shoving stuff into

her mouth. *Can't eat dinner tonight.*

      He won't let me, and you know it.

Maybe she's right. But I can't watch

      this self-destruction a minute longer.

The Worst Part Is

She does have something to worry
about. So I'll just have to help
her out. I slip into Daddy's bathroom,

and this time when I "borrow" his Oxy,
it's not for me. Okay, one is for me.
The other three are for Daddy.

I can't slip all three into a single drink
or he'd taste it for sure. This will be
a seduction. One I know he can't refuse.

He finally roars in, and I've already
mixed him a highball, long on Turkey,
short on Oxy. That will change

> as the evening progresses. He gives
> me a look but takes the drink
> anyway. *Thanks. I need this.*

> Thank God he gulps it down
> before turning on Kaeleigh. *Well?*
> I rush to refill his empty glass,

not 100 percent sure why
I'm trying to save Kaeleigh,
who refuses to save herself.

I hand Daddy the Oxy-tainted
highball glass as Kaeleigh answers,
I didn't mean to be late, Daddy.

She doesn't dare look him in the eye.
*It's just that Brittany's car got a flat,
and we had to wait for the tow. . . .*

> Daddy pounces. *I never gave you
> permission to ride to school with
> anyone named Brittany, did I?*

Her eyes are like lasers, beaming
the floor tiles. *No, Daddy . . .* She rushes
on, *But she just got her license, and . . .*

> No, Kaeleigh! Too late. Damage
> done. Daddy raises his voice.
> *Just got her license? Are you*

> *plain stupid? Do you* want *to die?*
> The rest is implicit: *Don't you
> remember a certain infamous day?*

Kaeleigh crumbles. Her face,
only moments ago binge-florid,
blanches. *Oh Daddy, I'm sorry.*

She threatens to collapse, and I
whisper in her ear. "Stay strong,
or you know what he'll do."

                    Tension begins to melt from
                    Daddy as the painkiller starts
                    to kick in. *Fix me something*

                    to eat and we'll discuss this
                    further. As he speaks, his voice
                    sputters a little, slurs. *O-ok-ay?*

          Sure, Daddy. Kaeleigh
          rushes to the refrigerator.
          What are you in the mood for?

                    Daddy sucks down his drink.
                    L-loaded question. He crosses
                    the floor quickly, much faster

                    than I'd thought him capable
                    of, half falls against Kaeleigh,
                    who's leaning into the fridge.

I smile. Whatever he had in
mind, punishment or "reward,"
it will not come tonight.

They Extricate Themselves

From the refrigerator.
      Kaeleigh microwaves
            some leftover stew.
                  I watch the two of them
                        stuff their faces, fix
Daddy one last drink.
      Between the rich food,
            stiff Turkey, and three
                  OxyContin, he'll be fast
                        asleep in a few minutes.
Most of the evening's drama
      behind us, I slip off to
            the bathroom. Kaeleigh's
                  disgusting food binge
                      made me want to purge.
It's more than a habit.
      It's a need. Experts even
            call it a disease. However
                  you classify it, though,
                      it's not about body image.
At least not for me. For me,
      it's all about maintaining
            a modicum of control,
                  especially when everything
                      goes completely ape-shit.

Most People

Hate to vomit.

Can't stand

the protest

of an upset

stomach,

the heave

of bile and

undigested food,

the carve of

acid in the

esophagus.

Okay, I don't

like that

part much

myself. But

I do like

the cool of

porcelain on

my face,

the solid

of tile beneath

my butt.

Most of all,

I like my belly

emptied, even

temporarily,

of food.   Of fat.   Of pain.

Face Washed, Teeth Brushed

Puke free, I emerge from the bathroom,
into a house silent but for Daddy's
impressive snores. Now that I've
evacuated my stomach, I can swallow
the Oxy I borrowed for myself.

Pop the pill, chase it with whiskey,
crawl into bed. Pray such seduction
brings dreamless sleep. Seems to take
a long time for the sleep aid to kick
in. As I wait, I feel good about aiding

Kaeleigh's salvation tonight. Too
many times in the past, I've stood by,
powerless to interfere. They say
an ounce of prevention is worth a pound
of cure. There is no cure for Daddy.

Let's hear it for prevention! Of course,
it's not like you can always tell what Daddy
has in mind. I suppose there must be
triggers that bring him to Kaeleigh's bedside.
If only they were more recognizable!

My body slides toward sleep, but my
brain, though fogging a bit at the edges,
is working overtime. The gathering
haze does not conceal memories
of another night. Kaeleigh was ten.

Mom Was Off on a Retreat

Like any of that spiritual mumbo
jumbo ever did her (or any of us)
one miniscule sliver of good.

Daddy had been back to Kaeleigh
for "lollipop licking" (my term) a few
times. She had a vague notion that it

was "wrong," but she wasn't sure
why, and didn't know who to ask.
They'd probably just be jealous.

That warm summer night, she slept
in a thin white nightie, nothing more,
nothing at all under. The moon, full,

shimmered against the tan of her
exposed skin, and her hair whispered
over the pillow like a pale waterfall.

As usual, the smell of Wild Turkey
preceded Daddy. In the bright moonlight,
you could see Kaeleigh cringe in shallow

sleep. Daddy crept through the door,
to the side of her bed, stood looking down
for a very long time before stirring

her with a volley of kisses. Cheeks.
Forehead. Lips. *Oh, little girl. Do
you know how beautiful you are?*

*No one was ever as lovely as you,
not even your mother when she was
a child. I can't believe you're mine.*

Kaeleigh roused at his words,
came into the moment, secure
in the aura of Daddy's love.

She tried to sit up, but Daddy
pushed her gently back down
against the mattress. *Stay just*

*like that for Daddy. I want to
teach you something new.*
He lifted her nightgown,

rolled it up over her belly, coaxed
her Thoroughbred legs apart.
She squirmed, a paltry protest.

Don't move! Daddy's scarlet
face underlined his command.
I thought he might smack her.

But as quickly as his anger
flared, it dissipated, smoke.
Don't be afraid. This won't

hurt. You'll like it. I promise.
He kissed the length of her torso,
down to the small, naked V.

It was only his mouth
that night. He didn't even
ask her to touch him, prove

how much she loved him.
Afterward, she worried.
Didn't he want her love

anymore? What had she done
wrong? And yet, he had taught her
something new. Something awful.

Worse,

Something wonderful.
Something every
girl should
know the
joy of,
though,
of course,
she shouldn't
learn it from Daddy.

At ten, it isn't exactly
easy to separate
good touch
from bad
touch,
proper
love from
improper love,
doting daddy from perv.

But Tonight Will Be Perv-Free

Hugged by my ostentatiously
thick mattress, falling fast, faster
toward blessed sleep, or in my
case, more likely the sleep of the

                                 damned,

the space behind my eyes
is covered by a dark collage.
Bodies. Smiles. Leers. Faces.
Some familiar, some not, as

                                 if

they are people I've yet to meet,
or maybe have already met
in another lifetime. One face
truly haunts me. I'm sure

                                 I

knew her once upon a time.
Her hair is a rich mahogany,
her eyes vivid green, like those
of a wildcat. Where do I

                                 know

her from? And why do I feel
such a connection, if I can't
even recognize her face? I so
want to understand

                                 the truth

of her, of "us." Yes, wanting
and getting are two different
things. But intuition tells me
this puzzle needs to be solved.

Kaeleigh
Daddy's Still Asleep

At seven a.m. Wonder if I should
wake him before I leave for school.
I'm guessing it's a case of

damned

if I do, damned if I don't. He's
going to have a major headache,
though he probably won't have
a decent clue why. Then again,

if

I let him oversleep, he'll be
mad at me, too. It's not like
a judge can just call in sick,
unless he's on his deathbed.

I

will probably die before he does.
Dying, for Daddy, would be
the ultimate defeat. But death
doesn't scare me. To

know

exactly when I might
expect it, up close and in
my face, would actually be
a comfort. Because to tell

the truth,

most of the time dying
seems pretty much like
my only means of escape.

Not Right Now, Though

Not with the election looming.
No use ruining that for Mom.

Although maybe if something
bad happened to me, something

bad enough to make me die,
she'd win the sympathy vote.

Never mind. She'd probably
be too distracted with the funeral

and the burial and the incredible
after-the-graveyard party and . . .

Pht-pht-pht. Rewind that old
film to another funeral. Ugh.

Don't want to go there. Don't
want to see that coffin, or go

to the post-service pot luck.
I huddled alone in one corner,

trying desperately to ignore
the gut-churning potpourri

of smells: tuna casserole, over-
cooked broccoli, onion laced

salads. Booze, in assorted flavors.
Flowers. Didn't know all their names.

But their combined perfumes
smelled like death. Mom sat on

an overstuffed sofa, vacant-eyed,
silently sipping vodka on the rocks.

Daddy gulped whiskey, and might
have passed out quietly except . . .

Someone stumbled through the door,
wearing an aura of Scotch and a marble

expression on her face—the one I just
barely remember. She went straight up

> to her son. *You!* She shoved him
> into the wall. *L-look at you, Raymond.*
>
> *All red eyed and drippy nosed. You*
> *don't fool me. Don't f-f-fool them. . . .*
>
> She gave a vague wave. *W-we all know*
> *just what you are—a m-monster!*

I Don't Want to Relive

That scene, which grew as ugly
as any my mind can replay.

Grandma and Daddy sparred. Verbally.
Then physically, until someone

pulled them apart, spitting poison
as they separated, not just for that

evening, but, at least if Daddy
has his way, forever afterward.

That's the last solid memory I have
of her, broken by secrets. Splintered

by pain. Escorted into the night, out
of our lives. Does she really dare

try to reenter now? What if I decide
to let her back in? I'm guessing

I'd be crematorium fuel. No
coffin. No flowers. Just a hot

white fire, melting me into
bone fragments and ashes.

Then Again, the Sad Fact Is

My parents might think cremation
too good for me. As I slide books
into my backpack, it comes to me
they might just weight me down
and throw me into Cachuma.

Down, down, into that cold blue
lake I'd go, no one the wiser.
Who would even miss me?
Maybe Ian, but after the last
couple of days, I'm not so sure.

We've got drama today.
Hopefully our little love
scene will warm him (me?)
up some and we can talk
after. A long conversation,

like we used to have all
the time. That's what we need.
But first I have to get to
school. Which means it's time
to poke the sleeping bear.

As Expected

It's a less than pleasant
experience, starting with
the obnoxious breath
coming out of his open
mouth. "Daddy? Wake
up. You'll be late for work."

He snorts and his eyes
flutter open. *Wha . . . ?*
What happened? Where
am I? What time is it?

"You're in the living
room. You fell asleep
on the sofa. It's a little
after seven and I have to
hurry to catch the bus."

After seven? He jumps
upright, too fast. I can
see the pounding in his
temples. *Why didn't you*
wake me sooner?

"I tried, but you went
back to sleep, I guess."
Total lie. But he'll never
know it. And right now,
all he's thinking about
is how his head feels.

*Shit. I've got a heavy
docket today.* Finally
his eyes focus. *And I
feel like a truck ran
over the top of my head.*

"Sorry you don't feel
well, Daddy. But I've
got to run. See you later,
okay?" I grit my teeth
and take a step toward
the front door.

That's as far as I get.
Daddy's hand clamps
around my wrist. *Wait
just a minute. Do you
remember last night?*

Now my teeth grind
uncomfortably. What
about last night, exactly,
does he want to discuss?
"Uh, sure, Daddy."

*All right, then. No rides
with any Brittanys,
okay? I want you all
in one piece.* He doesn't
say just what for.

So of Course

Who comes chugging up
as I wait for the bus
                    but the very Brittany
                    in question. *Wanna ride?*

She's alone in the car,
an explanation at the ready.
                    The guys got in trouble
                    for being late yesterday.

Well, so did I, but I don't
want to talk about it. "Ah."
                    Get in. My mom bought me
                    all new tires, so you're safe.

Not really, but I don't want
to say that, either. "Um . . ."
                    You're not scared, are you?
                    She almost looks hurt.

I glance around, see no sign
of Daddy. "Oh, why not?"
                    Cool. Let's go. Don't want
                    to be late two days in a row!

No, we most definitely
don't want that.

We Actually Arrive

Ten minutes early. And I have
to admit even Brittany's nonstop
chatter wasn't as bad as listening
to freshmen guys talk about zits.

I can't believe I actually defied
Daddy in such an overt manner.
But it feels good. Even better,
in fact, than missing the zit talk.

At least as long as I don't get
caught. That probably wouldn't
feel too great. So far so good,
though you never know where

his spies might be hiding. No
use worrying about them now.
Brittany parks. A bit crooked,
but what else could I expect?

She giggles. *Even new tires
can't help my peripheral vision.
I'm supposed to wear glasses,
but they make me look ugly.*

Oh, wonderful. I can just see
the news: *Judge's daughter
killed in accident with not-ugly
half-blind friend at the wheel.*

I File That Away

Thank Brittany for the ride,
head toward the human knots
clogging the locker breezeways.

Pre-first-bell yells. Catcalls.
Laughter. A few tears.
Nothing out of the ordinary.

But just as I reach my own
locker, a loud guffaw makes
me turn to search for its source.

It's Shaun, apparently the chief
of a small tribe of geeks. When
I draw my glare even with his eyes,

he turns his back to me, lowers
his voice, and says something
to his not-so-braves that makes

them all laugh out loud.
Something inside me snaps,
almost audibly. I slam

my locker, take dead aim at
the geeklets' chieftain. Straight
up in his face, "Something funny?"

His eyes dart back and forth
among his stick figure friends.
But no one comes to the rescue.

Uh. No. Not really. Then he tries
to draw strength from numbers.
We were just talking about girls

and what they do for attention.
He pulls himself up as tall as he
possibly can. *What do you do?*

If his buddies think about
laughing, the look on my face
must make them think twice.

Ice-cold anger pulses in my veins.
I can feel it in my temples. And
something else, too. Something

brand-new. "Anything I do is no
business of yours, you little shit.
But if you want my attention,

here it is." That something new—
courage—brings my palms flat
against his shoulders. Hard.

Hard Enough

To make him stumble backward,
bump his head against a post.
I'll probably get in real trouble
for this, but at the moment I couldn't
care less. "Enough attention?"

> This time his friends do laugh.
> Shaun's face turns the color
> of strawberry jam. *What the fuck
> is your problem? Not my fault
> you're a trashy little skank.*

> Suddenly a hand is at my elbow
> and a voice falls into my ear.
> *C'mon. This is beneath you.* Ian!
> He turns on his brother. *You shut
> your mouth and keep it that way.*

Ian puts his arm around my
shoulder, guides me away from
the dissolving drama. Dueling
emotions take aim inside me.
Relief. Hurt. Happiness. Fury.

We turn a corner and at the far
end of the building, few eyes
to see, Ian pulls me into his chest.
My eyes sting and my legs go weak
and I let myself gather his strength.

The first bell rings and I start
to pull away, but his arms grip
tighter. *Tell me what happened.*
He looks down into my tear-
blurred eyes, and next thing

I know we're kissing. Really,
truly kissing, like it's from the heart
and we really mean it and there's no
one else, never will be. Finally I have
to come up for air. "I love you."

It Just Slipped

Out of my mouth, and the strange
          thing is, I really mean it. But still,
I feel all jumbled up inside,
          like someone put my brain in
a blender, turned it to "crush."

          Ian's eyes tell me he feels the same
                 way. *I love you, too, you know I do.*
          But you always have me walking
                 on eggshells. Oh, if you would just
          let me love you the way I want to . . .

Fire. Ice. Honey. Salt. Eiderdown.
          Iron. Every fiber of me twitches
confusion. I love him, and he loves
          me. So, then, "Why did you tell
your brother that I sleep around?"

          He draws back, but only a little,
                 only enough to look deep into
          my eyes, show me the sudden
                 anger in his. *I never said any such*
          thing. Did he tell you I told him that?

"He said he heard you say I'm
          into other guys. Why would
you say that? And who did you
          say it to?" Before he can craft
an answer, the second bell rings.

Saved by the Bell

The hallways
flood with bodies,
faces, voices, hustling
here and there. Locked
together, despite the inner
wedge, Ian and I draw a few
stares. Definitely not the right
time to continue such an intense
conversation. *Can we talk about it
later?* asks Ian, knowing I have little
choice but to respond positively. He walks
me to class, right arm protectively around my
waist. Despite smarting at the wound of his careless
words, I decide I like how I feel, joined to him in such
an overt way. Especially when we turn the corner and
come face-to-face
with Madison
and, just over
there, Shaun.

I'm Generally Not Big

On smirking. But noticing
how the smiles drop from both
Shaun's and Madison's faces,
I can't seem to

                                    help

it. Booyah! Major smirk.
It gets better. Madison is no
more than two feet away
when Ian bends down to kiss

                                    me

good-bye. I so totally let him,
even though a very, very big
part of me needs him to give
me a plausible explanation so

                                    I

can get beyond his brother's
knife-edged words. "Talk to
you later," I say as he walks
past Madison. I can't help but

                                    think

she's responsible, and I'm not
sure what to do about it if Ian's
story involves her. Ian. All
thoughts of Madison evaporate.

                                    I'm in love.

And I like how that feels.
And I hate how that feels.
Because love is an invention
of fiction writers.

Raeanne
Glad I've Got History Today

I need a major dose of Lawler
to keep my mind off other
things. I wish I could

help

Kaeleigh work her way past
all the major crap so she could
accept the good things waiting
for her, almost within reach. Ask

me,

she doesn't need someone
like Madison to mess things up
for her. She sabotages herself.
C'est la vie. It is life. Her life.

I

suppose I myself am something
of a self-saboteur, in a constant
search for "more." More drugs.
More men. More sex. Do you

think

there's really such a thing as
"enough"? The rhetoric draws
a heartfelt sigh, and Mr. Lawler
turns. Smiles. Oh yeah, I think

I'm in love.

I Swear His Smile

Means more than "How's it going?"
Not that I'm a smile expert or
anything, but something about
that one sure reads "Damn, you
look fine." Even correctly
interpreted, though, it doesn't
necessarily mean, "Let's sneak
on outta here and do the dirty."

Whatever it means, as he passes
out Monday's graded pop quizzes,
he bends just enough for me to make
out the thick ropes of muscles
beneath his trousers. Abductors.
Hamstrings. Gluteus. Mm-hmm.
Oh yeah, I remember human
anatomy. Especially his.

Committed to memory. He works
his way down the aisle, and now
his cologne settles around me,
a soft, masculine cloud. When
he reaches my desk, he leans
slightly forward, and I notice
the not-too-massive, totally
hot patch of blondish hair
peeking out of the open
buttons just below his collar.

His eyes smile. *Great job,*
Ms. Gardella. If only everyone
in here cared about history
the way you do. He holds
out my quiz, a big red A+
at the top. When I reach for
it, our hands touch. Definite
fireworks, and I'm 90
percent sure it's mutual.

I try to say thanks, but
my voice feels like a wad
of gum in my throat and it
comes out all hoarse and weird,
"Th . . . nksss." That makes me
snort a little laugh. "Sorry.
Not sure what's in there . . ."
I leave the rest hanging.
And he so totally gets it.

Am I Sick or What?

I mean, how many guys do I need on the line?

I haven't seen Mick in several days, but he left

    a voice message on my cell: *Are you mad*

    at me or what? Call me. You'll like what I've got.

I assume he's talking weed. It's been a couple

of days and the truth is, I'm so wanting a buzz.

I could call Ty, ask for a bit steeper high (low?).

Oh yeah, how low can we go? Loaded question.

But even without those two on my "available"

list, why would I even consider Mr. Lawler?

He's not only "mature," but a frigging teacher.

Cute teacher, sure, but that's not the point.

The point is: Why do I think he'd consider me?

It's a Game, That's All

And I'm good at games,
and betting Lawler is good
at them too. I watch him

lecture, trying to reach these
dimwads who couldn't care
less about why yesterday

influences today, thus creates
tomorrow. He's so sincere,
so well-learned (so disgustingly

cute), and I seem to be the only
one who even bothers to notice.
More power to me, I guess.

And power, after all, is what
I'm after. At last, the bell
rings and once everyone leaves,

I decide to up the ante a little.
(Okay, a lot.) I corner Mr. Lawler.
"Excuse me. I've got some

questions about the term paper.
Could we possibly get together
to discuss the direction I'm taking?"

Cat and Mouse

That's the name of this game,

old as the Garden of Eden.

I lead. "I'd appreciate your
advice. Maybe after school?

His eyes flash interest. *After
school? Why not now?*

I shrug. "Have a lunch date."

He smiles. *I see. Well . . .*

"Please? I'll buy you a cup
of coffee." I lock his eyes.

He does not look away. *I can
give you some time, I guess.*

Ka-ching! Damn, he is fine.

Where should we meet up?

"How 'bout the library in town?
I'll be doing some research."

*Sounds like a plan. Maybe
around four o'clock?*

"Perfect." He so totally is.

And he so totally knows it.

I Really Do

Have a lunch date. I haven't
seen Mick since the scene
with the cop. Can't believe
I miss him, but I do. He's not
the brightest guy out there,
for sure. But he knows how
to show a girl a good time.

Truth is, more than missing
Mick, I miss catching a lunch-
time buzz. I wish I could just
buy a personal stash, keep it
around. But no way do I dare
take that kind of a chance. Not
sure who would kill me first
(or worst)—Daddy or Mom.

Not to say I won't taunt fate
just a little. Or maybe a lot.
I refuse to smoke in transit.
That cop probably looks for
the Avalanche. And me. So
after Mick and I rendezvous,
we will take a little spin to
the Gardella residence, which,
hopefully, will be vacant.

While I Might Taunt Fate

I will not taunt Madison, who
seems ever more determined
        to interfere in my life. Not to
        mention Kaeleigh's life, like *she*
needs any more drama! I couldn't
help but notice her with Ian
        this morning. If she could be
        like that with him more often,
they both just might find a big
scoop of happiness with each
        other. But that won't happen
        if Madison has her way. Guess
she thinks fucking with Kaeleigh
is fucking with me. And she's right.
        Anyway, I'm not in the mood
        for her stupidity, so instead of
Mick picking me up at school,
I told him to pick me up at
        El Rancho. The market has
        served the fine folks here in
the valley since before I was
born. Glad to know some things
        have staying power. In my
        admittedly limited realm
of existence, El Rancho has
outlasted every relationship
        I've ever had. Then again, in my
        realm relationships are meaningless.

I Hoof It North

A hundred or so yards, pause
before crossing the highway.
And who should happen to go
screaming past but my unique
(if meaningless) relationship, Ty.

Taillights flash red and brakes
squeal displeasure. Guess he saw
me standing here. Guess he has
something to say because he flips
a dangerous U-turn, pulls over

opposite me. I look both ways
three times, decide it's safe to
cross, and walk real fast (running
would not be cool) in his direction.
I bend into his car. "What's up?"

He looks into my eyes, licks
his lips. *Give me your hand.*
I'll show you what's up. I do,
and he does. And it is. *Haven't*
heard from you. I'm really

surprised. Thought you kind
of liked the play. Was I wrong?
He reaches up, strokes
my cheek gently. *No encore?*

Rough Play, He Means

And I really did like it because
I'm sicker than he is. Giving
is one thing. Taking—and
enjoying—is something else
altogether. "An encore would
be nice." I smile. "Maybe nice
is not the right word, though."

Nice works. So how about it?
When can we get together
again? He winds his fingers
into my hair. Tugs gently,
brings my face right down
against his. Opens his mouth.
We are tongue on tongue

when the beep of a passing
peeping Tom reminds me
I'm standing beside a quite
public thoroughfare. Any-
one could pass by and, oh
yeah, I'm supposed to be
hooking up with Mick.

For once, I'm glad he's late,
although if he doesn't show
pretty soon I might just have
to take off with Ty. Sheesh.
I really am sick, aren't I?

Guess the best thing is to play
coy. "I'll check my schedule
and get back to you, okay?"

                    He looks like I slapped him.
                    Hurt? Pissed? Totally surprised?
                    What? Does every girl he asks
                    jump straight into bed (cuffs)
                    with him? Has he never been
                    on the far side of "coy"? The
                    game moves to level two.

I Triple Promise

I'll give him a call.
Straight up, I will, because
one guy will never be

enough for the likes of me.
Truth is, I can't
believe one anything (guy,

girl, whatever you
happen to be into) could be
enough for anyone.

Too, too many "anyones" in
this ol' world.
Let's see. I'm currently

working on three.
All different. Smart. Not so.
Accomplished. Not

so. Older. Not so. Oh, and
speaking of Not So,
better late than never, Mick

arrives.

Ty's Quite Recent Invitation

Was totally beyond my control.
I didn't solicit. Didn't even agree.

So why, pray fucking tell, do I feel
guilty? Guilt is not a Gardella trait.

Certainly not a Raeanne trait. What
the hell is up with me? Mick parks

with an overt flourish. Not much
subtle about Mick. He reminds me

of a Rottweiler. Eighty percent
brawn. Twenty percent affection,

long as you treat him right. I jump
up into the Avalanche, scoot almost

into his lap, give him an over-the-top
kiss, hoping he doesn't taste guilt.

Whatever he tastes, he likes it, wants
another dose. I stop his tongue (not

to mention his hands) with a single
word. "No." Then I assuage his obvious

disappointment. "Not enough privacy
here for what I've got in mind. Let's go."

He Starts to Turn South

But I stop him, with a hand on a spot
too high on his thigh to qualify as
"thigh." "Let's go to my house.
It's empty." And, of course, it

                                        should

be empty, with Manuela out sick.
It's a gamble, inviting Mick
to my house to party. But Mom's
campaigning, Daddy's judging, and

                                        I

am the only one brave enough to
veer from the "should do" straight
into the "want to do." And that is
so what I'm going to do. Better to

                                        be

a little reckless than like Kaeleigh—
all uptight and frozen all the time.
Okay, so maybe I lean a bit
too far the other way, but

                                        scared

is something I refuse to be. I'd
rather spit in the devil's face.
So Mick and I will smoke up
and make out in my bedroom.

                                        I don't

think we'll get caught, but the very
possibility is half the fun. And, with
a modicum of luck, no one will

                                        know.

Kaeleigh
I Thought Last Block

Would never come. I've had
Ian on my mind all afternoon.
I know right now I

should

concentrate on Ms. Cavendish
and her impassioned stage direction.
But I'm standing here, so close
to Ian. And he smells good and all

I

want to do is kiss him again, like
we kissed earlier. Because for
the very first time, a kiss felt right,
and exactly the way a kiss should

be,

instead of like something dirty.
And what rose up inside of me
was something so intense
and so completely new, it

scared

me, only it scared me in a good
way instead of making me want
to crawl in a hole and die.
I slip my hand inside Ian's and

I don't

want anyone to see because
I'm afraid someone will pull
me away from him if they

know.

Our Fingers Interlock

And it feels like commitment.

    And that begins a tug-of-war

        inside me.

I want Ian to give me all of himself.

    But that means returning

        the priceless gift.

I want to open myself, let him inside.

    But how do I give what has

        always been taken?

I want to know what it means to be in love.

    But in my dictionary, "in love"

        is indefinable.

We Have to Unlock

To rehearse. And I feel regret,
and I know Ian feels it too.
At least our love scenes should
come easy for once. If I can
just remember my lines!

> *Places, everyone,* directs Ms. C.
> *From the top, no music today.*

> Reluctantly, I start stage right.
> Ian stops me with a gentle hand,
> whispers, *We need to talk. Can
> I take you home? Please?*

Yes. No. Oh God, what does he
want to talk about? A wave
of fear crashes over me. Makes
it hard to draw breath. Still I croak,
"Okay," look into his eyes, try
to discern what's hiding there.

I cannot see anything secret.
only love and something
I myself know only too well—fear.

Ian, Afraid?

What can he possibly
be afraid of? He's
the strongest person
I've ever known.

I fret on that all
through drama,
flub my lines every
time the thought
blankets my brain,
disrupts rote memory.

Finally the bell rings.
As we gather our things,
I notice Ian barely looks
at me, or at anyone
else for that matter.
And believe me, we
are the focus of more
than one person's attention.

The one who I notice
most, beaming evil
rays from her charcoal
pencil-smeared eyes,
is the most-likely-to-be-
our-next-class-president,
the ever-amiable Madison.

Ian Walks Past Her

Without so much as a nod,
despite the come-on smile
she gives him, as an obvious
jab at me. What's up?

                    Ian slides an arm around
                    my waist. *Ready?*

His touch sends little electric
jolts through parts of my body
I usually try to ignore. "Ready."
Madison is still staring as we

exit. I can feel her eyes stab
my back, and when I turn, she
mouths a single word. *Slut.*
I really don't get her at all.

But how can I possibly care?
I am hip-to-hip with the most
incredible guy in the universe.
And for once I will let myself

accept our union. At least until
he takes me home and tells me,
as I fear he will, *This is a mistake.*
You don't deserve my love.

This Afternoon

Comes laced with autumn chill.
Ian insists I wear his jacket,
and the sharp scent of leather lifts
up underneath the helmet's face
shield. My arms hug Ian tight,
and as he shifts the Yamaha,
the muscles beneath his Levi
shirt tense and release. Tense
and release. And my body
tenses too. I've ridden behind
him many times before. So
why is it suddenly new?

His contours, taut and sinewy,
are exactly the same. The mink
curl of his hair creeps gently
from beneath his helmet. Same.
He commands the big bike
with skill and respect. Same
as always. But I am different.
And I don't understand
exactly how. And I don't
understand just why.

All I know is I love how it feels.
And I know I'm going to lose it,
just like I've lost everything
important in my life.

Daddy Isn't Home

Not that I expected him to be.
It's early yet. I climb down
from the bike, biting back
anxiety. "Want to come inside?"

> Ian hesitates. Normally he
> wouldn't chance it. But today
> whatever he has to say makes
> the risk worthwhile. *Okay.*

Knowing spies might lurk,
we don't touch until we're
through the front door. Once
it closes, I'm in Ian's arms.

> Our kiss eclipses all others,
> real, imagined, dreamed of.
> It is the beginning of time,
> it is the end of the ages.

I can't breathe, don't want
to breathe. I want to give my
breath to Ian, die in the giving.
I want to give him more. . . .

Desire Strikes Like a Cobra

Sinks its fangs between my legs,
injects its venom. The heady
creep wanders from groin to belly.

I lift Ian's hands, urge them
against the throb beneath
my blouse. "Touch me. Please?"

       He wants to, does, and I love
       his skin on mine. And then
       he moans, *Oh, Kaeleigh . . .*

              And suddenly a different
              snake strikes, with lightning
              ferocity. Not cobra, but python,

              threading itself around me,
              squeezing. Hissing, *Oh, Kaeleigh.*
              Oh yes, that's right, little flower.

I jerk back and Ian's watery eyes
reflect the horror in my own.
Oh God, Kaeleigh, what is it?

Tell me! Then he softens, clay
in hot-water hands. *Please*
tell me. And he starts to cry.

And I cry too. And I want
to confess. And I fall so deep
into his tears that I think I'll drown.

"Oh God, Ian. I love you
so much. If I could tell
anyone, I would tell you. . . ."

Anger swells inside him now,
bloats like August carrion,
and his eyes fairly sizzle.

You are all I've ever wanted,
and I want you now with all
that I am. I don't mean I want

sex with you, although I do
want that, too. I want the part
of you that you refuse to give.

And I Think

He will do as he's always done
in the past—stalk away, out
the door. Rev up his bike,
leave me here, alone in his
exhaust. Small. Very small.

Instead he coaxes me, *Please,
let me hold you.* And I look,
but the python has dissolved
into the jungle, left me numb
with confusion and need.

The need for a friend. The need
for a lover. The need to trust
someone, and who can I trust,
if not Ian? I lean into the warmth
of him, the truth of him. I look

up into his eyes, find so much
love for me there I know I'll
never be okay without him in
my life. My eyes beg him to
kiss me. And when he does,

it's like rain on drought-starved
desert. I want to give him what he
asked for. Just as I think I will,
it full frontal hits me that
it's best to let sleeping pythons lie.

Speaking of Snakes

I think it's best for Ian to leave
before my personal serpent slithers
home. "I'm not ready to tell you
everything yet, but I want you to
know something changed today. . . ."

Something profound, but I don't
say that. "I've always loved you
like a friend, but I want us to be
more. I want to give you all of me,
and I will just as soon as I can. Okay?"

His eyes are red. Bleary.
But smeared in them is something
resembling hope. He smiles.
I've waited this long. Guess
a little longer won't hurt.

But please try to trust me. Love
is meaningless without trust.
I can't change what has happened
in the past, Kaeleigh. I can only
promise to make the future better.

And he kisses me again, and
there is no need for sex, no
need for hands. No demands.
No control. Only connection.

I Walk Ian to His Bike

Feeling completely disconnected
without my fingers twined in his.

But the idea of spies—Daddy's,
Mom's, or some unknown covert

operatives—nags. I look right, left,
over my shoulder, across the street,

but can't discern a single person
who might qualify as a spy.

Before Ian can put on his helmet,
I sneak one last delicious kiss.

"Oh, hey. You wanted to talk to me
about something, remember?"

> Ian looks nowhere but directly
> into my eyes. *Think we covered it.*
>
> *Guess I'll see you tomorrow.*
> He straddles the Yamaha, turns
>
> the key, pauses long enough
> to say, *I love you,* and he's gone.

My Normal MO

After Ian leaves me alone
is to run to the refrigerator,
empty most of it onto a plate
and smother every bad feeling.

Like an automaton, I go into
the kitchen, open the fridge,
peek inside. But for once,
nothing shouts, *Eat me now!*

Thinking back, I didn't have
lunch, didn't have breakfast.
I should be starving, and in
fact, my tummy's rumbling.

I grab a bottle of raspberry
iced tea, one of Mom's Power-
Bars, and a handful of grapes.
Eating healthy? So not me.

But at the moment, nothing
inside needs to be killed with food.
No shame. No pain. No loneliness.
Every demon is fast asleep.

Notice I Didn't Say Gone

I'm not stupid enough to
believe one magical afternoon
can vanquish my monsters
forever. And what is

                    forever,

anyway, but enough time
for monster to beget monster?
No matter, I take a big bite
of the PowerBar, which

                    is

stale, the texture of rubber,
and mostly flavorless, though
the wrapper claims "great
chocolate taste." It takes

                    a long

while and too many teeth-
grinding chews to swallow
a single bite. I toss the rest, gulp
some tea, and just about the

                    time

I consider my homework,
I hear the garage door open.
If I hurry, I can slip out the front
before Daddy knows I'm here.
Too much of me is happy right
now to allow the rest

                    to worry

about his current state of mind.

Raeanne
The Library

Is busy this afternoon.
Lots of little kids running
around. It seems like it takes

forever

to find a quiet place in an
unobtrusive corner. I put my
sweater on the chair across
from mine. Wait. Mr. Lawler

is

late, and it crosses my mind
that he might stand me up.
I pretend to be working,
and after what seems like

a long

long time (though the clock
insists it's only ten minutes),
I sense eyes and smell Lawler's
woody cologne. *Sorry I'm late.*

Time

got away from me this afternoon.
Is this yours? He points to
my sweater and I nod. "Saved
you a seat." He smiles and sits
across the narrow table from
me and seems not

to worry

at all that our legs touch.

Glad I Wore Jeans Today

I haven't shaved in a few days.
Nothing less sexy than stubble,
when you're leg to leg
with an amazing guy.
And, teacher or no teacher,
ten years (or maybe more) my
senior or not, he is def amazing.

I lean forward slightly, notice
his eyes fall to what almost
passes as cleavage, with a good
Victoria's Secret push-up bra
helping out. Glad I wore that, too.

>   He clears his throat. *Of all*
>   *my students this semester,*
>   *you seem to have the best*
>   *grip on history. Not just*
>   *dates and events, but also*
>   *their relevance to today.*
>   *So how can I help you?*

I smile. "Loaded question.
But what I'd like is your take
on conspiracy theories. . . ."
We spend the next twenty minutes
discussing the Kennedys, Martin
Luther King Jr., Castro, Lyndon B.
Johnson, and government goons.

Who knew conspiracy theories
and sixties politics could be
such a major turn-on?
The entire time, my legs rest
gently between his, knees
touching the inside of his,
and despite my "lunch" with
Mick today, I'm starting to
feel incredibly, um . . . aroused.

And what's more, I can tell
Lawler feels the same way.
While we talk, his hair strays
down close to his eyes and
I start to reach up, move it out
of the way for him. Reconsider.
Damn, the man is totally hot.

Just as I think that, my cell
phone rings. Once. Twice.
I glance at who's calling.
Daddy, of course. "Excuse
me one second?" I turn my
back to Lawler, take the call,
explain where I am and when
I'll be home. After I hang
up, Mr. Lawler says,

Sounds like it's time to go.
Any more questions?

Questions? Yeah, I've Got Them

Do you or don't you have a girlfriend? If you do, is she prettier
than me? If you do, do you
sleep around on her?
If you do, would
you sleep with me?
Even if you don't
have a girlfriend,
would you pretty
please sleep with
me? Have you ever
slept with a student?
If you have, was she
prettier than me? Even
if you've never slept
with a student, would
you pretty please sleep
with me? Is this over-
whelming attraction
really mutual, or
is my believing
that just a sign
of impending
insanity? Is my

lunacy on the
horizon, or is
it already here?

I Don't Actually Ask

Any of those questions, although
I'd really, really like the answers.
Instead I say, "No more questions

right now, at least not about
conspiracies. But I'm seriously
thinking about majoring in history.

When I start looking at colleges,
will you help?" I still haven't moved
my legs. Neither has he, and that

encourages my next move. I slide
my arm under the table, rest
my hand on his knee. Okay, now

this can go either way. "I'd like
your views on schools. And maybe
you'll honor me with a good reference?"

Lawler Doesn't Jerk Away

Doesn't run away.
In fact, he barely
even blinks.

All he does
is smile and cover
my hand with his own.

> His palm is smooth,
> and it wears a thin
> patina of sweat.

> *You know you're*
> *my favorite student.*
> *A good reference is no*

> *problem at all. And of*
> *course we can talk*
> *about schools.*

> *You still owe me*
> *that cup of coffee. I'm*
> *not likely to forget. Next time?*

Next Time!

There's going to be a next time,
and darlin', it's gonna be a lot
more private than this time,

I'm guessing. Don't want to
look too anxious, though, so
I simply agree, "Next time."

Neither of us has moved yet,
not a finger, not a knee. I think
maybe before my next history

class I'll shave my legs, buy
some nylons, and make sure
my shortest skirt is clean.

Finally he lifts his hand away
from mine. I sigh and he smiles.
Thanks for an enlightening afternoon.

He lowers his voice slightly.
*You really are an exceptional
young woman, you know.*

*I look forward to coffee and you
very soon. Better take my leave
before the gossip mill starts to spin.*

I Watch Him Go

My heart races and my brain
buzzes, replaying his words:

> *I look forward to coffee and you*
> *coffee and you*
> *and you*
> *you.*

Maybe I'm reading way too much
into it. It's weird, because I so

believed there was something
between us, but now I'm not

so sure there really is, even
though just a second ago, I was.

> *I look forward to coffee and you*
> *coffee and you*
> *and you*
> *you.*

Take out the "coffee" and what
have you got? Words. Decaf words.

Coffee Actually Sounds

Pretty damn good right now
(coffee and . . . him).
All I had for lunch was a big

fat doobie and an overdose
of Mick. My blood
sugar has bottomed out.

I told Daddy I'd be home about
six, and it's only a little
after five now. I'll grab a quick

something before I try to walk
home. It's not too far,
mostly downhill, but a quick

carb injection will not hurt one
bit. I drop into the little
market nearby, grab a Nutri-Grain

Bar and a Diet Coke. Mmm. Well,
at least it will get me
home. As I exit, a silver car zips

into the parking lot, radio blaring.
Hey! calls Brittany.
What's up? Need a ride somewhere?

I Know Daddy Has Issued

A "no rides with Brittany" edict.
   But that was to Kaeleigh, not me,
   and I really don't feel like walking.

Besides, he's probably halfway
   to drunk by now. If I'm lucky,
   he won't notice me come in at all.

"Sure," I agree. "Why not?" Just in case,
   I point Brittany in the opposite direction,
   around the block from how I usually go.

No need to tempt the devil, I always say.
   As she cruises slowly up the street,
   something makes me turn my head.

We're passing Hannah's house.
   She's the not-yet-nurse with the big
   mouth, the one who busted Kaeleigh.

She's standing on her front step,
   talking to the devil himself. In fact,
   she is standing very close to Daddy.

To an outsider, they are the picture
   of propriety. Neighbor to neighbor,
   discussing the weather, perhaps.

But I see something more
        in the way he leans toward her,
        close, as if he's hard of hearing.

Darkness has closed in, but Hannah
        might recognize Brittany's car.
        I think I am too obvious, and duck.

"Don't slow down. Keep going."
        Yeah, sure, she says, and she does,
        apparently used to such deception.

I poke up my face, barely over
        the seat, look out the back window,
        fingers crossed I remain incognito.

Daddy and Hannah are lost in each
        other, and Daddy's body language
        tells me everything I need to know.

I'm an Expert Interpreter

Of body language: slant
of face, arc of hand,
frame of shoulder,
the whisper of knee
against willing knee.
I know that one well.

> I recognize anger in
> a certain arch of Mom's
> spine; obstinacy, double-
> clenched in her jaw;
> the tip of chin signaling
> imminent tears.

Desire? Every man
displays it differently.
Some, like Mick, wear
it puffed up, peacocks
strutting ostentation
in lieu of real substance.

> Men like Ty are harder
> to read—granite-faced,
> molded smiles that can
> mean anything. You find
> their fire in the unfathomable
> pewter of their eyes.

Lawler-types store lust
not in sinew or bone, but
rather just beneath the skin,
a steady pulse at the wrists
and temples. And when need
rises, easy beat becomes throb.

But I know one man
better than the rest.
I know when it's safe
to be near him—when
booze or pills divorce
every muscle from stress.

I know when it's best
to sneak away—when
he comes in the door
stiff and heavy as iron,
eyelids wide and ears
practically steaming.

And I know when his
face flushes and his breath
comes in raspy little pants
and his red-rimmed eyes
fall on all the wrong places,
it's definitely time to run.

Right Now His Eyes

Fall on all the wrong places,
and those places belong
to Hannah. I should yell,
"Run!" It doesn't really

        surprise

me that he's hitting on her,
I suppose. She's only a few
years older than me, and
looks like she's twelve. I

        guess

she's about five feet tall
and size three. (And how will
someone that little handle ER
work, anyway?) She's married,
I'm pretty sure, to some guy

        who

I've never seen. Soldier?
Merchant marine? Jailbird?
No matter. He's not around
much and hey, lucky her,

        Daddy's

just down the street, and
always up for some young-
looking meat. And just
maybe this little detour
means Daddy won't be

        screwing

Kaeleigh, too, at least not
for the foreseeable future.

Kaeleigh
Today Was Incredible

Today was impossible.
Today was perfect and
terrible and filled with

surprise

after surprise. The thing
with Ian scares the living hell
out of me. Love, I know,
isn't something to second-

guess,

but in my world, love is
always defined by ulterior
motive. To say yes, give
my whole heart away,
simply terrifies me. But

who

can I ever trust, if not Ian?
Trust—another indefinable
word. I'm not sure how to
process learning about

Daddy's

possible affair, not that there's
much overt proof of it. Even
if it's the real deal, I doubt
Mom would care. It's not like
the two of them do much

screwing,

at least not with each other.
So why should I care?

My Parents Aren't Real

Parents anyway.
They're cardboard
cutouts. I mean, aren't
parents supposed
to care about their
kids? Care *for* their
kids? Not abuse
them or use them or
lose track of them.
And aren't they
supposed to care for
each other? Not use
each other or lose
the love that was
once central to each
other's existence.
Not toss each other
aside because life
threw a curveball
their way, even if it
was a major curve-
ball. No wonder
I'm a little paranoid
about giving away my
love. What if I go
ahead, give it, and he
decides to re-gift it?

Of Course, Maybe Daddy

Isn't really sleeping with Hannah.
Maybe it's a harmless flirtation.

(Harmless? Daddy?)

Maybe they were just having
an innocent conversation.

(Innocent? Daddy?)

Maybe Daddy was just trying to
be helpful with some legal advice.

(Helpful? Daddy?)

Maybe he was just trying to offer
a selfless act of kindness.

(Selfless? Daddy?)

And just why am I offering
him such an easy out?

(Easy? You?)

Am I overly generous,
or just totally ignorant?

(Ignorant? You?)

Am I being loyal, or am
I, in fact, a little jealous?

(Enough said.)

Whatever Daddy Did

With Hannah wiped him out. Okay,
that and his usual Wild Turkey dinner,
plus OxyContin dessert. He's snoozing
in front of the TV set, and the TV is off.
Kinda creepy, but oh so very Daddy.

Guess I'll make myself something
to eat. Something substantial.
I'm starving. Too bad the pantry
looks like a raiding party came
through. Manuela usually handles

grocery store duty, but she had
an asthma attack and wound up
in the hospital. Wonder if Hannah
took care of her in the ER. Wonder
if Hannah will do the shopping

this week. Wonder if I can make
spaghetti with tomato soup and
ramen noodles. Sounds disgusting,
but beggars cannot be choosers. Oh,
wait. Two boxes of mac and cheese.

At least it's the kind with the cheese
in a can, not the stuff with fluorescent
orange chem cheese powder. I make
both boxes, because two is always
better than one. That's my motto.

Double the Pleasure

I polish off every bite of both
boxes. Enough, according to
the label, to feed a family of
four. Twice. Not a very hungry
family, if you ask me.

Double the pleasure. Now I
feel the need for liquid fun.
Tucked away in a low cabinet
is my parents' liquor stash.
Can't touch the Turkey.
The smell gags me and anyway,
Daddy would notice it missing.

The Chopin vodka, stashed in
the freezer, is a different
song, and I'm so ready
to drink that slushy tune.
I'll never sleep without it.
Too many conflicts, volleying
inside my head, bouncing
off the interior of my skull.

I don't really like the taste
of vodka, but they say you
can't smell it on the breath.
Not sure if that's true, or
if it matters. Even if Daddy
did wake up, he couldn't smell
the vodka for the Turkey.

Double the Fun

I poke my head into the living
room. Daddy hasn't so much
as twitched, at least that's my guess.
The rest of the house is quiet

as death. Think I'm safe.
I fill a juice glass half full
of fermented potato juice, try
not to think about such ingredients

as I down the clear, hot-and-cold
liquid. Cold, as in not-quite frozen.
Hot, as in its burn down the throat.
Frozen smolder, a popular combo.

Phew! Chopin is definitely
not cabernet. Still, while I feel
it on my tongue, I don't feel it
in my brain. Probably the mega

macaroni meal. This time
I fill the four-ounce glass
almost to the brim, think
about adding some water

to the bottle before I put it away,
decide against it. I doubt
anyone will miss it, and I might
want an encore performance.

Clutching the glass like
a baby holds a bottle,
I pad softly down the hall,
to my room. I try sipping

the vodka, but gulping
it is easier, and very quickly,
the glass is empty again.
Shouldn't I feel inebriated?

Ha. Funny word. Inebri . . .
incb . . . whoa. Wouldn't
want to have to spell it!
I-n-i . . . er, inebre . . . okay,

so maybe the Chopin
is singing a little ditty
after all. I'm usually
a really good speller.

I Start to Feel

A little fuzzy at the edges,
          and warm behind my eyes.
Fuzzy and warm. That makes

me think of Ian. I glance
          at the clock. Not quite nine.
I think I can get away with

a quick phone call. One ring,
          two ringies . . . three ringy
dingies . . . C'mon, Ian. Pick up.

          Finally, *Hello? Kaeleigh?*
              What's wrong? He waits
          patiently for me to explain

just why I'm actually calling
          him. This is something rare.
"Nu . . . nothing. I just wanted

t-to say . . . uh . . ." What *did*
          I want to say again? Oh, yeah.
I remember. "Uh . . . um . . . "

          I can't finish it, and his
              patience comes unraveled.
          Have you been drinking?

I could lie, but he'd know
         I was lying. "Uh, maybe
a little . . ." Ball's in his court.

                He rallies. *I don't get it,*
                      Kaeleigh. Why tonight?
                Wasn't today good for you?

I think back. Good. Good.
         Sorta good. Not so good.
Better now. Or is it really?

Don't say any of that! "It
         was wonderful. That's
why I called. To tell you . . ."

Grow a pair, Kaeleigh. Tell
         him. He needs to hear it
right now. "I lu . . . love you."

                Pregnant pause. About nine
                      months pregnant. *I love you, too.*
                But love doesn't make me drink.

What Does Make Him Drink?

I wonder, trying my damnedest
not to giggle. My entire core
knows laughing will make
him turn his back forever.

So why do I really need to laugh?
(Oh girl, too many reasons to
mention!) "S-so-sorry, Prince
P-p-p-perfect. I guess th-that means . . ."

Brother! Why won't my mouth
work? Straighten up and say it.
"Guess that means you never
found out your dad is s-scr . . ."

I swallow any sort of apology.
"Screwing your neighbor."
There. Said it. React, okay?
Pregnant pause becomes three

        weeks overdue. Four weeks.
        Time for a C-section. *What?*
        Oh, Kaeleigh, I'm so sorry.
        Are you sure . . . ?

Spoken like a true guy. Even
if I'm not sure, I say, "Of course
I'm damn well sure. Do you think
I drink for the fun of it?"

I Regret Everything Immediately

The confession. The out-and-out
meanness. That I called at all,
considering the state I'm in.

"I'm s-sh-sorry, Ian. I just didn't
know who I could t-t-talk to,
except for you. I'll go now, 'kay?"

> *Wait. Are you sure you're okay?*
> *Do you want me to pick you*
> *up in the morning?*

I'm not okay at all, but I never
will be. The thought pierces
me. How can he ever love me?

I struggle to talk without slurring.
"I . . . I'm okay. No, don't pick me
up. I'll sh-see you at school."

> *Love is about helping each other*
> *through dark times, Kaeleigh.*
> *Try to remember that, okay?*
>
> *Getting drunk tonight won't make*
> *tomorrow better. But letting me*
> *love you will. It's all up to you.*

I So Do Not Deserve Him

He *is*
Mr. Perfect
and I'm a perfect
ass to have ever, for
even a moment, believed
we could even resemble a
real couple, in real love,
like such a thing exists
beyond media-fed
fantasies.

He says
he loves me
and he'd never lie
to me, not on purpose.
But would he love me if
he knew my secrets? I go
from Chopin giggles to
a Chopin breakdown,
steeped in Chopin
teardrops.

Time For a Chopin Pee

I force Ian out of my mind, do the best I can to do that, anyway. Head spinning, gut churning, I go into the bathroom, try not to look at the girl in the mirror as I pass by. Every time I think I've gained a little control, actually played an active role in determining my future, reality punches me in the face. I have no control at all. All I can do is hang on for the ride, and it's starting to make me completely insane. The toilet beckons and my body responds, evacuating Chopin and undigested mac and cheese every which way imaginable. Finally I lay my sweaty forehead against the cool porcelain. No! I don't deserve such comfort. In fact, right this moment, all I really deserve, really desire, is pain.

Not Mental Pain

Not emotional pain,
things beyond my
ability to control. But
physical pain is most
definitely within my
limited realm of power.

I pull back from the mac-
spattered toilet, feel a
fleeting sense of shame
and commiseration for
Manuela. But then I
remember she's out of
commission. Just who
will scrub this mess?

Can't trust my shaky
legs. I crawl over to the
tub, hoist myself inside,
slide out of my vomit-
crusted clothes. Ugh!
My legs are fat. Fat and
hairy. Time for a major
shave. And not just hair.

New Blade

No razor burn.

                      No razor nicks.

          No more hair.

                          Legs are smooth.

      But still fat.

                    Open my skin.

         Right ankle.

                       Left ankle.

     White flesh.

              Red polka dots.

Ha! That's funny.

                    Ouch. Stings.

      Behind right knee.

                       Left knee. Oops.

        A little deep.

                    Blood pumps.

Check it out.

                 Thump. Thump.

                          Oh my God.

        Can I stop it?

                    Who really cares?

     The drain runs red.

I've Heard Exsanguination

Is a pleasant enough way to go.
Bleeding out, ebbing away, one
heartbeat, ever slower, at a time.
Thump-thump. Thump . . . thump. Thump . . .
. . . thump . . . . . . until you look

death

right in the eye, decide you like
what you see. I've always feared
dying before, psychological
fallout from my childhood

near

death experience. The accident
replays in a series of black-and-
white snapshots. Raeanne laughs.
Daddy swears. Mom screams, *Ray!*
Glass rains. Darkness. Someone

calls,

Wake up, and I open my eyes
to a swarm of disembodied faces.
Halloween masks. Bloated. Distorted.
Hands, gloved red, reach out

to me.

I fall back into blackness, stumble
toward an orange glow, vaguely aware
of spectral movement. Ahead, a figure
leans into a low-banked fire. He lifts
his horned head. Daddy! I leap

from the shadows

into antiseptic white.

Raeanne
OM–Effing–G

The bathroom looks like a battle
field. Tangerine-colored puke
paints toilet and tiles, and the
whole place smells like

death,

not only because of the barfed-
up whatever, but also because
of the blood, thick maroon drips
all over the tub and towels. And

near

the sink is a sticky crimson puddle.
What's up with Kaeleigh, anyway?
I mean, yeah, I get throwing up.
It's not bad at all, except for the
stomach acid part. The barf monster

calls

to me regularly. But hey, you're
supposed to get it inside the bowl,
and if you don't, protocol dictates
you clean it up. I guess maid duty falls

to me from

who-knows-where this morning. Kaeleigh
is gone, and if Daddy sees this, all hell
will break loose. That girl seriously
owes me, and I'd better collect soon,
before she succumbs to

the shadows

overtaking her soul.

Speaking of Souls, Monsters, Etc.

Tonight is Halloween.
Ghouls. Goblins. Witches.
Avoidable candy. And way
avoidable children in costumes.
Kind of fun to jump out and scream
boo at the little brats. Then *they*
avoid *you*. Woo-hoo.

Not only is it All Hallows Eve,
but it's also Friday. The perfect
excuse to party hearty. All I have
to do is decide who to party with.
Tricks? Treats? Ty? Mick?
A little (a lot?) of both?
(I don't think it's the right night
for Lawler, but never say never.)

Daddy won't try to stop me. He
knows who he wants to party
with. Well, maybe. I could have
read the whole Hannah thing wrong,
I guess. But if he was flirting and Hannah
didn't go for it, he's a bomb with
a very short fuse. *Tick. Tick.*

Daddy and Hannah

As I scrub away Kaeleigh's
disgustingness, I can't help
thinking about them. Truth is,
the idea makes me crazy.

(Crazy jealous.)

Am I jealous? I guess I must be,
because right now, all I can see
(besides orange puke) are still
shots of Daddy and Hannah.

(Doing the dirty.)

Shot one: missionary, Daddy on top.
Shot two: doggie-style, Daddy on top.
Shot three: can't even say it, let alone
dwell on the picture, but Daddy's on top.

(Always on top.)

Being

On top means
never saying you're sorry, not
for any damn thing you
ever say or do. Daddy
has got to be the king
of on top, with Mom a
very close runner- up. Hm.
Wonder who was on

T O P

when they did have sex.

Sex, Sex, Sex

        I have really got to stop thinking
about it so damn much, you know?
                Daddy and Hannah; Daddy and Mom;

Daddy and Kaeleigh; Daddy and whoever;
                Mom and Daddy; Mom and whoever;
Lawler and whoever; Mick and whoever; Ty . . .

                Sex, sex, sex. I have really got to stop
wanting to have it, and more and more of it.
                Clumsy sex (Mick); choreographed sex

(Ty); imagined sex (Lawler, assorted others).
                I've even half thought about experimenting
with a girl or two. Variety is the spice of life.

                Sex, sex, sex. And what goes with that?
Drugs, more drugs, and alcohol, of course.
                I'm a living, walking, waking party on

two unsteady legs. (Not to mention a shaky
                brain.) Tonight is Halloween, a night to
walk on the dark side. Can't wait to hit the road.

First, I Have to Get Through the Day

And that starts with getting
out the door. Standing between
me and that goal is a red-eyed Daddy.

> *Apparently you forgot to tell*
> *me something important.*

Quick. Think. "Uh. Something
important? Like what?" I mentally
run down a long list of possibilities:
He saw the bathroom?
He saw me with Brittany?
He saw me see him with Hannah?
He missed a few "borrowed" pills?
One of his spies saw me with Lawler,
or told him about Mick, the pot, and the cop?

> *You know, the phone call? Listen . . .*

He advances, menacing, and now
I'm thinking about phone calls.
Is he talking about the hang-ups,
or—oh, shit—the call from his father?
He never mentioned it, so I assumed
he never found out about it.

> *If you can't pass on a simple*
> *answering machine message,*
> *don't play them back, understand?*

I Decide to Act Ignorant

And, you know, for the most part
I am. I have no clue what he's

talking about. "Uh . . . I'm sorry,
but I'm not sure what you mean."

> *Your mother called yesterday,*
> *and left a rather lengthy message. . . .*

News to me. "Sorry, Daddy.
I didn't check the machine."

> *Really. And here I thought you'd*
> *made it your mission. . . .*

What the hell does that mean?
Maybe he knows more than

he's saying too. I apologize again.
"Sorry. I usually do, but I was

all excited about writing my term
paper." No need to mention why.

> *His eyes say, yeah right, but his*
> *lips say, Ahem. Okay, well, your*
>
> *mother is coming home to watch*
> *the election returns and expects*

to host a large party here. It's
a big deal, as you can imagine,

and you'll have to help me pull it
together. We've only got a few days.

And with Manuela unavailable,
I'm not sure what to do.

A devious thought crosses my
mind. Do I dare? Oh, why not?

"Maybe Hannah from down
the street would help out."

H-Hannah? he sputters, eyes filling
with uncertainty. *Why Hannah?*

How much do I know, Daddy? Not
as much as I've guessed, but enough.

But I don't say that. Instead
I shrug. "She's always seemed

pretty friendly, and she looks
like she knows how to party."

He Has No Idea

What I mean, or what to say.
His jaw drops, spittle pooling
in the corners of his mouth.

His eyes blink like some annoying
spore has found its ocular target.
Tears puddle, reflect something

like rising denial. No worries,
Pop, I won't tell, as long as you
be nice to me. (Pretty please be nice.)

One thing for sure, his reaction,
silent as it might be, makes me
know my instincts were right.

Somehow, some way, that hurts
more than it should. After all,
he's not married to me. Still, why

not twist the knife a little deeper?
Kind of fun to make him squirm.
"Do you want me to talk to Hannah?

I don't mind. Unless you'd rather
do it yourself?" I ask, all innocent
eyed. "I'll help too, of course."

Finally Daddy snaps out of
his trance. *That's okay. I'll talk
to her. Good idea. She'll be great.*

He stands, hands on his hips, looking
a lot like Wyatt Earp, facing down
bad guys at the OK Corral.

Guess what that makes me.
Better holster my six-shooter.
I'll break out the shotgun later.

School Totally Drags

Tricks and treats are put
        on hold in favor of tests
                and ineffectual lectures.
                        Teachers can be so heartless.

At lunch, I'm still deciding
        who to get witchy with. I'm
                wandering, foodless, when
                        I hear someone call my name.

Ms. Gardella? One minute!
        Would you please honor
                me with your presence?
                        Lawler, sounding all teacher.

So why does a little chill
        shimmy all up and down
                my spine? I'll honor him
                      with more than my presence.

I turn toward his classroom,
        extremely happy that I shaved
                my legs and wore a very,
                      very short skirt today.

Lawler Definitely Notices

Not only that, but he doesn't
hide the fact that he's noticing.
His eyes fall to the source of my
swishing stockings, stay there until
he closes the door behind me.

*How's the paper coming?
Hope I was able to help.*

I turn and he's very close
behind me. In fact, we're just
about nose to nose. I smile my
most vampish smile. "You've
helped me more than you know."

His turn to smile, revealing
perfect white teeth. *How so?*

God, he smells good. I so
want to get lost in him. "You
treat me with respect. Not
many teachers do that for their
students. Power trips, I guess."

*You deserve my respect.
Not many students do.*

I must be totally schizoid. As
much as I like having his respect,
I wonder what it would take to
earn his disrespect. My eyes tell
him that. My lips say, "Thank you."

Welcome. So I was wondering
if you have plans for tonight.

Plans? Holy shit! Stay cool,
Raeanne. Leave the drool
where it belongs—inside your
mouth. But wait. Do I have
plans? Answer: "Not really."

I realize it's Halloween
and you might be busy. . . .

"No!" Easy now. Don't want
to look like you're undateable
or something. "I mean I really
haven't got anything definite
planned." Breathe in. Breathe out.

I was hoping you might be able
to come over to my place and . . .

Yes, Yes, and . . . ?

Okay, I know he doesn't dare
say what I want him to, but
what he does say surprises me.

> *. . . answer my door for an hour*
> *or so. I have an appointment*
>
> *and don't want to leave the house*
> *empty with all the little tricksters*
> *running around. I know it's late*
>
> *notice, an imposition, but you were*
> *the first person who came to mind.*

A deep breath brings several
positives to mind. One: I'll
have my foot, quite literally,

in his door. Two: He probably
doesn't have a girlfriend, unless

she happens to be his appointment.
Three: what might happen after
he gets back from his appointment.

Four: I was on his mind.
What can I do but agree?

He Gives Me Directions

        To his house, which isn't far
        from mine. *Need a ride?*

A ride would be nice,
considering it is chilly

outside, but I don't think
I should chance it. Oh yeah,

just think about explaining
that one to dear old Dad.

I shake my head. "Maybe
a ride home. What time

do you want me?" I am
queen of double entendre.

        Lawler shows his dimples.
        My haircut is at six.

        Can you get there around
        quarter to? I should only

        be gone a little over an hour,
        so you won't be tied up all night.

Okay, vamp, ramp it up.
"How about half the night?"

The Rest of the Day

Crawls along even slower
than the first half did. Lawler
got my "tied up" joke and even
gifted me with an easygoing

               laugh.

I'm pretty sure he's got more
than an abbreviated house-sitting
job in mind. Wonder if he wants
what I do—to wrap ourselves up
in each other, make love until we

               cry

with pleasure. Pain. Both. More.
But to go there, I need to catch
a buzz, which presents a problem.

               It's

one thing to ask Mick for bud,
then "reward" him after. But to
get my head, then ask him to drop
me at Lawler's? He would not
appreciate that at

               all.

Eek! Have I backed myself
into a corner? No Mick, no bud.
No Ty, no better buzz, and he's
much more difficult to manipulate.
Dopeless sex? That could not feel

               good.

Could it?

Kaeleigh
The Bus Seems Slower

Than usual today, and that's
okay by me. Sitting here,
listening to everyone joke and

laugh

about being too old for trick-
or-treating but doing it anyway,
because hey, it's free candy.
Okay, it's lame, but not
as lame as going home to

cry

because Ian is going out of town
this weekend, at a family reunion.
No treats for me. Looks like

it's

going to be tricks, starting
with Hannah, who's knee-deep
in conversation with Daddy when
I finally get home. The topic
seems to be caterers, and it's

all

I can do to be courteous as I pass.
I mean, if she sat any closer, she'd
be in Daddy's lap. And it is Mom's
kitchen. Even if Mom's never in it.
One thing I know. Nothing

good

can come of this "friendship."

But Daddy's Attention

Is drawn to the petite blonde,
and so away from me. Yay.

> I do have to go to work, but only
> for a couple of hours, setting

> up the codgers' Halloween bash.
> Did I just think "codgers"? Where

in hell did that word come
from? Some deep, dark, mean

recess of my brain? Some long-
forgotten conversation? Some

> past-life dictionary? Sheesh. Just
> think if I didn't like those people!

> Anyway, it will be easy enough
> to get out the door, not that it isn't

usually, but usually Daddy isn't
even home yet. What's so special

about today? Planning Mom's
party? The simple chance to get

> together with Hannah? Oops.
> Answered my own question.

I Slip Off My Shoes

Slide down the hall in my stocking
feet, evoking a memory of Raeanne
and me when we were little, playing
champion ice-skaters. Wow. I don't
go there often anymore. Most of my
childhood memories bloat with pain.

Laughter trickles from the kitchen,
the exact same way it used to,
except it is not Mom laughing with
Daddy. It's her . . . what? Fill-in?
Replacement? Divorce would
probably be a better choice.

But considering the reputation
factor, divorce will never happen.
Ah. See? Happy memory dashed
against the rocks of reality. I can't
deal with it in my normal way.
Daddy and Hannah have control

of the kitchen. No stuffing myself
until there's no room left inside
for hurt. Aching from just behind
my eyes to the pit of my too-empty
belly, I go into my bedroom, sit
on the floor, pick open a scab or two.

I'm Kind of Liking

This blood
                    thing. Fetish?

        Fixation? Not
                            quite an

obsession
                yet, but I

        can see it
                            growing

into that.

            Drip. Drip.
                            Steady. Slow.

Drip-drip.
                    Quicker yet.

Drip-drip-drip.
                    Drip-drip-drip.
                                        Drip.
                                                Drip.
                                                        Drip.

I'd Probably Just

Let myself drip, but I did promise
to show up at work and help out
with the Halloween decorations.

I'm rummaging through the medicine
cabinet for a couple of Band-Aids
when the telephone rings.

Will you get that, please? calls
Daddy. *If it's for me, tell them
I'll call back in a few minutes.*

The nearest phone is in the hall.
I rush to reach it before the fifth
ring feeds it to the machine. "Hello?"

No response, but a sharp rustle
on the far end, like someone
has dropped a stack of papers.

I wait, but no voice follows,
so I repeat, "Hello? Is anyone
there?" Still no answer.

Bad connection? Prank call?
Either way, I've got to go. "Sorry.
I'm late for work. Try back later."

Why Am I Always So Polite?

I mean, that was just so annoying.
No wonder Daddy
gets mad about these recent
hang-up calls.
Is that what this was? I'm not sure.
I was the one
who did the hanging up, after all.

Who was it? calls Daddy as I start
toward the door.
"Wrong number," I answer. No
use letting Hannah
see his dark underside, is there?
Okay, maybe there
is, but I'll save that card for later.

I pop my head through the kitchen
doorway. "Bye.
I'm going to work." Hannah looks
up and gives a
small wave. Daddy does not
even turn. *Don't
stay out late. I'll wait up for you.*

His Words

Send ice chips pulsing
through my veins. No,
Daddy, don't wait up,
unless you wait at Hannah's.

And suddenly it comes
to me that not only is he
already home, but he has
not yet started drinking.

No Turkey stink; no
indistinct sentences;
no red-rimmed, tear-
choked eyes. Unreal.

I can't remember the
last time I saw him
look so human. But
how long can it last?

My Hand Is Turning

The doorknob when the phone
rings again. I hesitate, know
I should ignore it. But somehow
I have to find out who's on the other
end. Work will wait. "I've got it!"

Caller ID says only *Private Name,
Private Number*. It's weird, but
my hand twitches as I reach
for the receiver. "Hello?"

Who is this?

Odd way to open a dialogue.
"Uh, this is Kaeleigh. Who's
this?" A long stretch of silence
follows and I repeat, "Hello?"

Kaeleigh?

OMG. Is the woman dense?
But her voice, soft and scratchy
as an old vinyl record, tugs
at a place inside of me. "Yes,
it's Kaeleigh. And you are . . . ?"

Your grandmother.

Not Grandma Betty

Calling from Florida,
no, she's busy with her new
(relatively speaking—
I think he's like eighty)
husband. Yech. Ugly
picture. Anyway, I know
her voice, and this isn't it.

Instinctively, I lower my
own voice. "You mean my
father's mother?" The one
who vanished so long ago?
The one who . . . who what?

That's right. I know
it's been a very long time . . .

"Kind of an understatement,
wouldn't you say? Where
have you been?" Where did
you go? Why did you stay
away so long? "And why
are you calling now?"

It's a difficult story, one
I need to tell you, but not
on the telephone. I'm . . .

A Shadow Falls

Through the doorway, darkens
the entire hall. Daddy. *Who is it?*

Can't tell him! Into the phone,
"Hang on." To Daddy, "It's Shelby,
asking about tonight."

Tonight? What about tonight?
Daddy's eyes betray suspicion.

Think of something quick. "Uh, it
is Halloween. A few of the kids
are getting together. . . . "

*You mean like a party? You know
how I feel about underage parties.*

He'll never go for a party, not
even chaperoned. "No, no party.
To take the little kids trick-or-treating."

He thinks a second, then says,
I guess that's okay. But not late.

He stands there, head cocked,
waiting for me to respond. "My
dad says okay. We'll talk later."

I Don't Want to Hang Up

But I have to.

Will she understand?
She seems to. *Okay.*

But she's not

quite ready to hang up

either. *One question.*

Daddy has retreated

to the kitchen, but he'll

notice if I keep talking.

I force my voice real

low. "One quick one."

Are you all right?

What does she know?

How can I answer?

"Yes . . . no . . . gotta go."

I'm Running Really Late

So I do something I never do.
"Daddy, I hate to ask you,
but I'm kind of late for work.
Could you possibly give me a ride?"

Then I top off the lie, "Shelby's
mom will pick me up after
and bring me home later."
I'll get home one way or another.

> Daddy scowls and Hannah
> reacts. *I'll give you a ride.*
> *That way we can talk*
> *about your mom's reception.*

> I don't want to talk to Hannah.
> I don't want her to give me a ride.
> But Daddy seals the deal. *Great*
> *idea. And I'll start making calls.*

Damn, damn, damn. I hate
when I'm left without a choice.
But that's the situation now.
I follow Hannah out the door,

and down the block to her Mitsubishi
Mirage. Red, of course. Black leather
interior. And still a mediocre ride.
Mediocre. Just right for her.

Thank God it's only several blocks.
Hannah yammers on and on about
food and how much champagne
we should order and

Can you help me out with
a guest list? I have no idea
who your mother's friends
are. I assume she'll invite

her business acquaintances.
Oh, and what about the press?
Should I contact them? Oh, no,
your father will probably want to.

And on and on some more.
And I can't concentrate on
one-tenth of what she says
because the only thing I can

think about right now is my
grandmother. A stranger, but
somehow not. Her voice is a
memory, tucked away so deep

inside that trying to extricate
it makes my head pound.
And it feels like once I pry it
up, a crater will be left behind.

I Thank Hannah for the Ride

Go on inside. Preparations
are well underway, and an
excited buzz carries along
the corridors. Sheesh. You'd
think the old folks would leave
Halloween to the little kids,
but no. Any excuse to get out
of their rooms and party, huh?

So, okay, that isn't so strange
after all. I head straight for
the dining room to see how
the decorations are coming
along. I am not surprised
to see William flanked by
five elderly femme fatales,
hanging cardboard skeletons.

What snatches my immediate
attention is Greta, hand in hand
with the same gentleman who
visited a few weeks ago. They
look like a definite thing.

> When she spies me, Greta
> waves me over. *Kaeleigh,*
> *dear, I want you to meet*
> *Lars. We are old friends.*

346

Speak for yourself, woman,
scolds Lars *in a heavy Danish*
accent. *I myself am forever young,*
especially now that I've found you
again. He turns his attention to me.
So happy to meet you. Greta
has told me so much about you.

No wonder she loves him.
He loves her, and that little
bit of wisdom comes from
more than his words. It's
written all over his face.
"Good to meet you, too.
And I think you're both
forever young."

Greta beams but says, *In our*
hearts, perhaps. But my body
reminds me regularly of just
how many years I have worn it.
No matter. My Lars has found me.
I can leave this world satisfied.

Satisfaction

Not sure what that is or how
to find it, and I sincerely doubt
that it will ever apply to me.
I look at them, so in love, and I

              think

about Ian. Where is he right
now? Who is he talking to?
What is he talking about?
Why should I even

              care,

as long as every now and
again he thinks about me,
pulls me from a place
deep in his heart? Does he

              wonder

what I'm doing? Does he care
that I've hung paper pumpkins,
lit jack-o'-lanterns, baked cookies?
I want to call him, tell him I

              love

him. But no, I won't do
that, won't set myself up
for disappointment. If
he's changed his mind, I

              don't

want to know. Anyway,
I've got to go. I say good-bye,
hurry away from the All Hallows
Eve celebration, into the night,

              close the door behind me.

Raeanne
Lawler's House

think

Isn't at all what I expected.
It's not small, not really. And
it's definitely not untidy. I

care,

I watch too much TV. Aren't
all single guys supposed to be
slobs? Not Lawler. No, not
at all. His yard is tended with

wonder

and I doubt he makes enough
money to afford a service.
His Charger, parked on the street,
is washed, polished. Spotless. I

love

if dirt and bug guts just slide
right off it. I wonder if lowdown
slides right off him, or if he
worries about it. I would

don't

to know if he's even a little
worried about inviting me
here, about what the neighbors
might think. Personally, I

close the door
behind me.

give one good damn about
gossip. So I walk right up, ring
the bell, head on inside,

He's Gone for Over an Hour

Between doorbell rings
and candy grabs, I roam
room to room, sitting in chairs,
straightening photos, opening
drawers and touching
their contents, trying to
absorb Lawler by osmosis.

The last room I enter
is his bedroom. Like everything
else, it is tidy. Spare. Few
embellishments but the wandering
star quilt, in sapphire and rose,
and matching throw pillows.

I flop onto the bed, settle
into the hand-sewn luxury.
Who gave him such a personal
gift? Mother? Grandmother?
No, this feels like the remnant
of a lover. Resentment swells
and I bury my head in his pillow,
seek his familiar leather scent,
breathe it in. In. In. Smother myself
in leather perfumed eiderdown.

The Doorbell Interrupts

My Lawler-scented reverie.
I go to answer, expecting a knee-
high Cinderella or Spiderman.

Instead I find a half-dozen
people my age. A couple wear
masks—a blood-scarred monster,

a long-fanged werewolf, a Dumbo-
eared George W. Bush. The rest
assume they don't need costumes

to look horrific, and that includes
my dearest friend Madison. At
the sight of me, her jaw drops.

> *This isn't where you live, is it?*
> No *Hey, how's it going,* just
> demon-eyed inquisition.

Don't suppose there's any use
lying or denying. "No, it's not.
I'm just answering the door."

I have no idea if she knows who
does live here, but I'm not
volunteering the information.

As if reading my mind, Madison
asks, *Well, whose house is it?*
They all wait for the answer.

The answer I really don't plan
to give. But as I try to formulate
a reply, Lawler's Charger pulls

against the curb. The jig, as
they say, is up. And so, I'm pretty
sure, is any notion of hanging

around now that he's home. Anger
erupts like Vesuvius. "So do you
freaks want candy or what?"

The car door shuts and all attention
turns to Lawler, tall and frigging
gorgeous beneath his new haircut.

Madison turns back to me, and
the smile on her face is not exactly
friendly. *You've got to be kidding.*

Mr. Lawler arrives, all charm. *Hey,
guys. A little old for trick-or-treat,
aren't you? Well, help yourselves.*

Wouldn't want you to knock over
any little kids for their candy.
He smiles and puts handfuls

of the sweet stuff into their
pillowcases. *Anyway, I don't*
need junk food lying around

the house. I'll just eat it, you
know? Thanks for stopping
by. See you all on Monday.

Dismissed! Then he turns
to me. *Thanks so much for*
watching the place. I sure

didn't need any kids playing
tricks on me. He takes my arm.
Come back inside and I'll pay you.

Seamless

And I wouldn't expect
anything less. Still, I suspect
Madison, et al. are lurking
nearby somewhere, waiting
to see when and if I leave.
No Lawler tonight.

"The haircut looks great."
What else can I say?

He stands very close to me,
looks down into my eyes.
Thanks. I had hoped you
could stay for a while, but now . . .

"I know. It's okay." Oh
yeah, real okay. I swear
I will strangle Madison
one of these days. "Oh,
and you don't have to pay
me anything. I was happy
to help out." Happy to lie
on your bed, your pillow.

But Now I Have to Go

And we both know it, and we know
it has to be sooner rather than later.

Do you need a ride home?

I'd planned on staying out later.
Much later. But somehow I don't
feel like calling Mick or Ty.

Somehow, going home and fantasizing
about Lawler will be more
than enough action for one night.

"Okay. If you think it's safe
to leave your house empty."

I'll leave the candy on the front porch.

We walk to the car, far apart,
but the street appears deserted,
except for a few kids well down
the block. "Trick-or-treat seems to
end earlier and earlier every year."

I think that started with 9/11.

He opens the passenger door,
every molecule the gentleman.
I'm pretty damn sure no guy
has *ever* done that for me
before. "Thank you."

                                    But of course, milady.

I might as well melt right now.
Even without Lawler in it yet,
the Charger smells like him.
I think I could just curl up and die
right here in the cushy front seat.
I know this relationship can never
work out. But, oh, how I want it to.

Lawler gets in, starts the car, drives
me home. And although there is so
much to say, neither of us dares
attempt it. The silence crushes.
Finally I chance resting my hand
on his thigh. "I find older men
very attractive, you know."

                                He smiles. *Older than what?*

I Know He Has More to Say

I've got plenty more to say too,
but I'm afraid if I do I'll jinx
myself. Still, home isn't so
far and my curiosity is killing
me. "So . . . what do you think?"

About what?

Is he playing coy? He has to
know what I'm talking about.
This game isn't that complicated.
"About us." Okay. Said it.
He sucks in a deep breath.

There isn't an "us."

Now see? Went and jinxed
it. Oh, well. What's jinxed
is jinxed. Might as well push
things right out into the open.
"I thought there might be . . .

could be, anyway. Kind of
seemed like things were
moving that way." Enough
already. Let him talk.

Lawler Pulls Over

A couple of blocks from home.
I don't move to get out of the car,
and he turns to face me.

> You are a stunning temptation, not
> to mention an amazing distraction.
> You're bright, beautiful, adventurous.
>
> I am totally drawn to you, and if you
> were eighteen and not my student,
> I'd go out with you in a hot second. . . .

No! He's brushing me off.
I want to yell, but I get the feeling
a soft question might work better.

"What if we were really careful?"
I can't believe he's about to
withdraw from the game.

> You saw what happened tonight.
> I guess that was an eye-opener
> for me. Ours is a very small school,
>
> in a very small town. Secrets are
> difficult to keep here, especially
> this kind of secret. I'm really

sorry that I led you on. There's just
something about you. Something . . .
fractured . . . injured, despite how

together you always appear to be.
I wanted to help you. To heal whatever's
broken in you. To make you whole.

Whole. No one can do that
for me. God, why did he have
to go and get so serious?

Game over. I lose. What am
I going to do? Throw a tantrum?
"Okay. I understand. But if you

ever change your mind, you know
where to find me, at least during
second block." Side-out.

A Man with Morals

Or maybe just a coward.

Either way, lucky me,

I had to go and fall for

him. History will not be

nearly as much fun from

now on. In fact, I'm not

sure how I'll go to class,

listen to his lectures, ace

his pop quizzes, etc. etc.,

without staring at his pecs

or better yet, his gluteus.

Then again, I can still stare,

still fantasize, still dream,

can't I?

Anyway, Lawler Seems

Like the "fall in love, settle
down, and have three kids
with a picket fence" kinda
guy. Definitely not my type.

Not that I'm sure exactly
what my type is. Other
than cute. Built. I'd like
to say intelligent, but that

hasn't always proved the case
with some of my selections.
Still, if I could build the perfect
guy, he'd be smart. Just not

as smart as me. Funny.
And, oh yeah, a stoner.
Killer combination. Lawler,
with connections. Sounds

pretty good to me. Yet even
all that can't add up to "happy
ever after." Does anyone
really believe in such a thing?

Happy Ever After

Is a concept I'll never believe
in. I would be content to sample
some little taste of happiness
today, tonight, right now, though

          I know

without a doubt that tomorrow
will arrive, saturated with pain.
Life is like that. At least
my life. And honestly,

          I can't

think of anyone whose life
is any different. The price
tag for joy is misery. I don't
want to go inside, but I can't

          stay

out here on the grass all night.
It's crunchy cold. I watch
Lawler drive away, wish with all
my heart I could keep him

          here

beside me, wrapped around
me, blanketing me with security,
fragile as that might also be.
Oh yes, I would like that

          very much.

But he's gone already, out of
sight, a shadow blurred into night,
and I will weave dreams no

          longer.

Kaeleigh
Sunday Morning

Post-Halloween. The house
is silent, fast asleep, but
despite the seeming calm,

I know

in my bones that I'm straddling
more than one powder keg,
lit torch in hand. Everything
wants to blow, although

I can't

say exactly why I think so,
but it definitely has to do with
Mom getting home late last night.
I guess she plans to

stay

through Election Day. Depending
on the outcome of that, she'll
leave for DC right away to find
a place, or she'll settle back

here

indefinitely. Meaning until she
finds a new crusade to embark on.
Why can't her crusade be me?
The polls say the race is still

very

close. Either way, I feel her slip
away. Either way, our lives
won't be the same

much longer.

Either Way

Mom is sleeping in the guest room.
Maybe that's truly what she is—a guest
in her own home. God, how sad.

For me.

I just want my mommy back,
just want to be the little girl she tells
stories to, whose hair she brushes

every night

until it shines like polished brass.
Why does life have to be so messed up?
Why can't it just keep marching in

perfect order?

I Was Supposed

To be asleep last night when Mom blew
                in through the door, an unsubtle wind.

I wanted to run to her, throw my arms
                around her, snow kisses all over her face.

But something told me to crack open
                my door, sit beside it in the dark, silent.

To listen, no more than a hint of the child
                she loved once upon a time, so long ago.

Then, she would never leave me or Raeanne.
                My sister and I would sit in the dark, like

this, only together. We'd sit very close,
                listening in to our parents' discussions.

Then, Daddy would often ask to go away
                with Mom, who refused to leave us

with an au pair. Then, the only person who
                ever watched us was . . . was . . . a face

surfaces in memory. She looked like Daddy,
                and her breath always smelled like Dewar's.

Oh Yeah, Blast from the Past

I sat there last night, shaking, no Raeanne
to make the jolt of remembrance better.
And it was about to get worse.

Mom greeted Daddy about as expected,
with a clipped *Good to see you.* Next came
several minutes of usual campaign banter.

Daddy went on to talk about plans
for Tuesday, skipping the Hannah
part. I just about fell asleep.

Around the time I decided to go
ahead to bed, Mom began,
Oh, I spoke with your father. . . .

My father? Daddy's voice
was startled. *Why in bloody
hell would you do that?*

Mom's turn for surprise:
You don't know?
Daddy: *I couldn't hazard a guess.*

*So you haven't heard from
your mother? No demands?*
Her words sank in slowly.

I could imagine the expression
on his face. *What in the fuck
are you talking about, Kay?*

She spoke slowly, as if to a dull-
witted child. *Your father called
to let you know you might expect*

*to hear from your mother. His take
was she wanted money to keep quiet.
Quiet about what, Raymond?*

I have no idea, answered Daddy,
a little too quickly. *Frankly, I'd be
shocked to hear from her. . . .*

So long, with no word. What, exactly,
happened between them? Surely
something more than just the scene

after the funeral. I shifted my weight
and the floorboards groaned.
Conversation skidded to an abrupt halt.

Finally, Mom said, *We'll finish this
later. I'm exhausted anyway. We'll
both be clearer tomorrow.* Finis.

I Lay Awake

Most of the night, pondering
mysteries. Where did my father

come from? Who made him,
and who made him the way he is?

Who is my grandmother? Where
has she been all these years, and what

does she know that Daddy wouldn't
want us to know? What happened

between her and Grandpa Gardella?
What happened between Daddy

and him? Does Mom know
the answers to these questions?

If she does, why hasn't she ever
talked about them? If she doesn't,

why doesn't she? Why don't I?
Why are there so many mysteries

shrouding our lives? Will I ever
know the answers? If so, when?

If not, why?

Not a Good Time

For those questions. Of course,
I doubt there will ever be a good
time for those questions.

Our family puts the "dys"
in dysfunctional. And every time
I start to think I'm the sanest

in the bunch, I turn around
and do something completely
insane, like letting myself

> fall hard for Ian. He called
> yesterday, caught me on my
> cell. *Hey, you. What's up?*

Just hearing his voice warmed
me, from the inside out. "Same
ol'. What's up with you?"

> *Not much. In fact, I'm bored
> as hell, so I thought I'd call and
> tell you how much I miss you.*
>
> *I'll be home Sunday morning.
> Think you could steal a few
> minutes with me?*

"Maybe after work. We can
always try, although my mom
is supposed to be home."

Oh, that's right. The election
is Tuesday, huh? How's it
looking for your mom?

"Okay, I guess. Barring some
major revelation, she's got
a pretty good shot."

Major revelation, huh?
He laughed. And what
are the odds of that?

At the time, I thought
they were pretty long.
But now I have to wonder.

I Want to Talk to Ian

About Mom and Daddy and Raeanne
and Grandma Gardella, whose face keeps
trying to materialize behind my eyes, and whose
motives for appearing now can't be guessed.

But I don't dare talk to him about any
of that, because then he'll realize how truly
screwed up my family is, and that includes
me, and if he knows all that, he'll dump me.

I want to talk to Mom about Daddy and his
parents and most of all about Ian, who I
think I might really be in love with. I want
to talk to her about love and what that means.

But I'm not sure she knows what it means
or that she cares in the least that I might
have found it. I'm not sure she cares about
me at all, and that's what I'm really afraid of.

Afraid, afraid, afraid. I'm always afraid
and I'm sick of it and I don't know any
other way of dealing with it than to go
find food and stuff myself with it. So I do.

And Still No One's Awake

So I bundle up against the drear
November fog and pedal off to
work. I pass a church, starting
to fill with early risers, almost
think about going inside.

Like what for, Kaeleigh?

Forgiveness?

You'll burn.

Belonging?

No one wants you.

Enlightenment?

Huh? What?

Confession?

Oh yeah, break down.

Daddy would kill me.

If Mom didn't kill you first.

And if I don't stop talking
to myself, I'll only prove
that I really am crazy.
Schizophrenic, maybe.

Yeah, Kaeleigh, shut the hell up.

Schizophrenic Me

Can barely pay attention
             to what I'm doing at work,
with all the conversation
             going back and forth in my
head. Mental tug-of-war.

Finally I get the breakfast
             table set. The residents start
to trickle in, many dressed
             up for their own worship
to come. Among those women

in cheerful flowered dresses
             is Greta, no gentleman beside
her. She sits and I go over.
             "No Lars today? And you
look so pretty, too!"

             Greta sighs. *Lars will not*
                          come to church with me.
             He says there is no God.
                          He used to think differently,
             once long ago. The war . . .

She's known him *that* long?
             "I didn't realize you've known
each other since before the war.
             Is that how you lost each other?"
What wedged them apart?

Greta's Tale

Comes from a place deep,
deep inside. It takes a few
minutes to surface.
Finally it shudders free.

Lars and I met as small children.
We played together in the streets,
and by the time the war started,
we were in love. Really, we

were still only children. I must
have been twelve or thirteen,
and Lars was a year older.
Our love was pure, and born

of friendship. But when my father
found out, he forbade me to see
Lars. We met in secret, shared
kisses and laughter. Nothing more.

One day my father discovered
us together. He nearly beat me
to death. I feared he would kill
Lars, and so it was almost a relief

when Lars put on a uniform
and went to fight the Nazis.
Almost. Her voice softens, slows.
I mean, he was only a boy inside,

although on the outside he looked
every bit the handsome soldier.
My father tried to stop me
from going to say good-bye.

But for once, my mother
intervened. "Let her go,"
she said. "She may never
see him again." And I didn't.

Not until a few weeks ago,
when he showed up here.
More than sixty years have
gone by. Sixty years we can

never get back, six decades
filled with things we will
never speak of. But we accept
that, and have promised

to share the few years we have
left, create new memories,
joyous and loving, that we
can take with us when we go.

Love, Resurrected

After more than sixty years.
Must be that love never died.

And that means it had to have
been alive in the first place.

I want to know living love.
And I don't want to wait for it.

I go through the motions of this
mindless work, mind totally

locked on Ian and possibility.
As soon as I finish, I call him.

He's home. *Hey. I was hoping
I'd hear from you. So . . .*

He doesn't have to ask. "Pick
me up. Mom can wait."

It's an impossibly long fifteen
minutes. Finally I hear his bike,

and the sound of its approach
fills me with happiness. And

something else. Something
very much like desire.

And Now I See His Face

And the warmth of his smile
intensifies the heat wave
flowing inside me. But I have
to play cool because that's what
good girls do and I want to be
good for Ian. "Hey. Missed you."

> *Not as much as I missed you.*
> *Come here.* And he pulls me
> into him and now we're kissing
> and I want to make this amazing
> sense of belonging last forever.
> *Have I told you lately I love you?*

I fold myself up into his arms,
close as one body can get to another,
except for . . . I go stiff at the thought.
No Kaeleigh, no. That's not what
this is. It's okay to be here, plastered
right up against this incredible guy.

> But the magic has dissipated,
> the warmth frozen over. Ian can't
> help but notice. *What's wrong?*
> I shake my head, cling tighter.
> In the past, Ian would have turned
> away. Today he holds fast. *Stay.*

Like a Puppy

I stay, and for once I stay
long enough for the ice dam
to melt, warm into an easy
flow, burgeoning into

a river

of need. My pulse picks up
speed and I lift my eyes to his,
have to look away or I might
go blind at the blaze

raging

there. "Oh God, Ian, I can't
believe how much I love you."
And he kisses me again, and now
I understand how love can come

alive

inside you, beneath your skin,
beneath your flesh and bone,
a separate entity, breathing
in and out its own special air,

expanding

to fill all those hollow places
that you can't fill by yourself.
I want to be good. Don't want
to go stiff. But if I don't, this
sudden rush of want will become

unstoppable.

So maybe I'd better stop it now.

Raeanne
Home Bitter Home

Mom's home, oh yeah, oh
boy. Waiting for her to light
into Daddy is like standing beside

a river

knowing you're going to fall
in, no matter what you do.
The only real question is when.
I didn't used to mind their

raging

at each other. When I was little,
I thought it was better than
a deep freeze of silence.
Rage meant they were still

alive,

still feeling *something*. Now,
since I know they're definitely
dead inside, I don't want to
listen to their ever-

expanding

list of unfinished rants and
just-boiling-to-the-surface raves.
(Not talking about the fun kind!)
'Cause once the bitch bus
starts rolling, it's practically

unstoppable.

Topping Today's Rant List

Is, of course, my dear grandmama.
And guess who's going to get
ranted *at*. Spot on! It's me.

> Daddy: *Why didn't you bother*
> *to tell me about my father's call?*

I suppose I could deny knowing
about it. But why lie? I shrug.
"Guess I forgot. Sorry."

> Mom: *Sorry? That's the best you can*
> *do? Under the circumstances . . .*

Patience was never my forte.
"Under what circumstances?
I don't even know the man."

> Daddy: *Beside the point. You couldn't*
> *tell the message was important?*

"The guy sounded like some sort of
nut job. Anyway, why don't I know
him?" Way to flip the tables!

> Mom: *Your father and I have reasons*
> *for the things we do or don't allow.*

I hate her. She never lets her guard
down and always has a ready answer.
"So . . . *is* he a nut job, then?"

        Daddy, trying not to lose it:
        No, he's not a fucking nut job.

Not doing a good job of not losing
it, Daddy, love. "Totally okay? Cool.
Next time I'll pick up and talk to him."

        Mom, definitely losing it:
        Are you trying *to make us angry?*

The game's getting fun. Keep
playing. Smile pretty. "Why
would I want to do that, Mom?"

        Daddy, closer and closer to losing it:
        Extremely good question, I'd say.

All of a sudden, I don't want
this to be a game anymore.
I want answers. Honest ones.

This Is a Rare Opportunity

With Mom sitting right here,
Daddy cannot so easily dismiss
my questions. Valid questions.
I look him directly in the eye—
something I don't often dare.

"Why don't you talk to your father?
And why won't you let him be a part
of our lives?" Like anyone is a part
of our lives. Including us. Truth is,
there is no "our." No "us."

> Mom stares at Daddy, waiting.
> Doesn't she know? Daddy glances
> back and forth between us, like a
> corralled coyote. *Let's just say he
> made my childhood extremely hard.*

If he thinks that's communication,
he should think again. Whose
childhood isn't hard? I shake
my head. "Like how, Daddy?
Can you be more specific?"

> His eyes glaze over, and I know
> he's fallen into the past, a place
> he most definitely does not want
> to revisit. He exits quickly.
> *I don't want to talk about him.*

Surreal

I swear, I've never
seen Daddy look so shaken.
So . . . wow. Scared.

He looks like a little
boy who has been sent to
the principal's office

or to the woodshed
to wait for a switching.
I almost feel sorry

for him, operative
word being *almost*. Because
the mold of his face

reminds me intensely
of Kaeleigh, when she knows
he's on his way to her.

Like father, like son?
One day I'll get my answers.
One day very soon.

Meanwhile, Think I'll Dive

A little deeper into the shit pit.
What have I got to lose?

"If you won't tell me about
my grandfather, what about
my grandmother? What's all
the hype about, anyway?"

Daddy shifts gears to angry,
jumps to his feet, stalks
to the counter to refill his glass
from the fifth of Turkey, drained

half-dry since this morning.
It's not even dinnertime yet.

I think he just might leave
the room, highball in hand.

Mom stops him with the weight
of her voice. *Don't you dare*
walk away from her, Raymond.
Tell her about your mother.
She has the right to know.

Daddy Takes a Gulp

Of his whiskey, adds a big splash
    to the glass, rotates toward us
        on one heel. His expression
    is a curious mix of fury,
resignation, and anguish.

    Finally he returns to the table.
        So you want to know about
            your grandmother? Fine.
        Let me tell you all about her.
    What I remember, anyway.

    I remember coming home
        from school and finding
            her passed out in front
        of the TV set, sweating
    cheap scotch and cigarettes. . . .

Holy crap! Déjà vu of the
    most unpleasant kind and
        he doesn't seem to get it
    at all. Only difference
is the choice of booze.

    I remember scrounging for
        my own dinner because I
            couldn't shake her out
        of her stupor and my dear
    old dad worked swing shift.

I remember other kids,
               laughing at my disgusting
                       clothes. Mom was too
               fucked up to wash them
and I was too little to try. . . .

All the while he talks,
       he sucks down Turkey,
               and it's easy to imagine
       the scene, except for the dirty
clothes. Daddy demands clean.

       I remember how excited
               my classmates got about
                       bringing their parents
               to school plays. I prayed
       mine wouldn't show up drunk.

       I remember working my ass
               off to bring home straight As
                       and the day I finally did,
               my mother wasn't home. In
       fact, she'd gone for good.

That Was the Most

My daddy has said to me in almost ten
years. I can barely catch my breath,

and *he* did all the talking. Still, I have
questions. "Why did she leave?"

> He shrugs. *She came limping back several*
> *years later, told me it was my father's fault.*

> *Said he slept around. Like that was a good*
> *enough excuse for what her leaving did to me.*

Lots of people's parents split up,
especially over stuff like that. But . . .

"Why didn't she take you with her when
she left?" What made him so cold?

> *She said she thought my father would*
> *take better care of me. That she had no*

> *resources. That part, I'm sure, was true.*
> *But she never once checked on my welfare.*

There's more to the story. A lot more.
But it involves his father. He won't share

that part—the part I most need to know.
The part about what makes Daddy tick.

The Topic of Conversation

Plunges him deeper into the depths
of his bottle, and he disappears into
his bathroom for a while. I know
what he's after in there. Oxy dessert,
to chase his Wild Turkey main course.

By the time Mom has dinner ready,
Daddy has reached a state of oblivion.
He will not share the table tonight.

Which just leaves us girls. Kaeleigh
watches Mom whip up a Hollandaise
to go with the fresh fish entrée.
She wants a daughter-mother talk
about Ian, but I can't figure out why.

It would be a blistering day in Antarctica
before I confessed any of my extracurricular
activities. Think I'll reroute the conversation.

"So, Mom . . ." I drop my voice to just
above a whisper. "Do you know what
happened between Daddy and his father?"
Does she know? If so, will she break
down and tell us the necessary backstory?

Mom pauses her whisking, but not for long.
Sorry. He never told me the whole thing.
Anyway, that will have to come from him.

She Knows More, of Course

But she won't spill
it tonight. Will we

        ever get the keys
        to this locked door?

I want to scream.
Curiosity strangles

        me until I choke out,
        "Was Daddy abused?"

        Mom opens the broiler,
        flips the fish. Finally

                she says, *There are
                all kinds of abuse.*

This is the perfect
opening, Kaeleigh,

        the way into asking
        for help. But no way.

Kaeleigh doesn't
want to go there,

        doesn't want to
        go anywhere near.

        Mom saves her
        the trouble. *Okay.*

                *Dinner's ready. Let's
                open some wine.*

A Lot of Wine Later

We are no closer to learning each
          other's dark secrets, and much
closer to our own states of stupor.

Kaeleigh has already retreated,
          not a single word about Ian.
No doubt a very wise decision.

Tomorrow it's back to the books
          (and, damn, a.m. history with
Lawler) for me, back to party

planning for Mom. The clock
          says ten forty-five. "Guess I'd
better go to bed. It's getting late."

                    She looks at me through chardonnay-
                              lidded eyes. *You look like her,
                    you know. Very much so, in fact.*

What is she babbling about?
          My head feels wobbly, my
tongue thick as pudding. "Who?"

                    *Your grandmother. I thought
                              so when you were little, but
                    it's even more obvious now.*

I Stumble Off to Bed

But find no comfort
in its feathers and patchwork.
Despite the wine and rich
food, breaking down into calories,
I feel cold, way deep inside,
and it's the kind of cold
that can't be fought

with Hollandaise or alcohol
or a pile of quilts. I wish I had
a joint. A big, fat, stinky j to slide
me into sleep. But no, all I
can do is lie here, brain
turning somersaults.
It's nights like

these when memories
stir, whipping themselves
into stiff peaks of pain. Here
comes one now, materializing
like Daddy did that night.
The night he came to
Kaeleigh, crossed

the final line.

Mom Had Been Spending

More and more time away
from home. We were getting
used to it. But that night,
something was different.
Kaeleigh and I lay in bed,

> listening to Daddy scream
> into the phone. *What the fuck
> do you think you're doing, Kay?
> It's not just me you're hurting.
> Come home. I'll forgive you.*

We had no idea where she was,
or what she was doing to make
Daddy so mad. But whatever
she said on the other end did not
pacify him. The receiver slammed.

The ensuing silence was scary,
scarier than his yelling. In
retrospect, I understand he had
gone to visit his bottles. But he
didn't find enough healing there.

> His footsteps that night were
> soft. Hesitant. I think they even
> turned around. But eventually
> they came toward us again.
> The door opened slowly.

Kaeleigh was used to Daddy's
visits, but that night she, too,
felt something different in the air.
Rage. Lust. Sorrow. Perversion.
All mingled in Daddy's sweat.

There was nothing gentle
about how he threw back
the covers. Already naked,
he pushed Kaeleigh roughly
to one side, flopped beside her.

I could tell she was afraid.
This wasn't her Daddy. This
was a demon, his evil hard
and sharp as a steel blade,
ready to slice into her. It did.

His attack was brutal, bloody,
wordless except for a vicious
Shut the fuck up at her pitiful
scream, a plea to please, please
no, Daddy, no. It hurts. Oh!

I cowered, sick at the sight,
but unable to divorce myself
from the horror. I felt Kaeleigh's
pain. And when Daddy was done
and she cried, I cried too.

No Doubt About It

There's a demon inside him.
Demons, they say, are fallen
angels. The real question is,
who pushed Daddy over

the edge,

into the abyss? I'd say there
are several likely candidates.
And, oh awesome. I'm related
to all of them, heiress

of darkness.

Dark or not, though, I want
to know them. Want to know
exactly what created not only
Daddy, but through him, me.

Is

that so much to ask? We're
probably too damaged to ever
be fixable, but if there's even
a tiny chance, I need to know

where

to find it. In Daddy? Ha. In
Mom? Unlikely. In some guy?
Every single one I know is worse
off than me. My only hope
is to ferret out exactly who

I am.

Kaeleigh
I Can Hardly Wait

the edge

To get to school today,
something totally new, and
all because of Ian. He takes

off my pain. In fact, for once
I don't feel like fighting pain
with food. For once, I feel
like I might crawl beyond this place

of darkness,

the place I've called home
for as long as I can remember.
I jump out of bed, start to dress,
and my bubble of optimism

is

burst almost immediately.
Down the hall, Mom and Daddy
are into it already, scratching
at each other like alley cats.

Where

did their own love go? Why
did it have to die and suck me
down into its shallow grave?
Guess I'll go shave my legs,
then scope out the pantry.

I am

famished, after all.

I Am on My Third Bowl of Cereal

When Daddy comes into the kitchen.
His eyes wear "pissed" and when they
fall to my mouth, stuffed with Shredded
Wheat, irritation grows to outrage.

What the hell are you doing?

He can't know how many bowls
I've downed, and I haven't made
a mess of the table. I swallow a major
mouthful. "What do you mean, Daddy?"

You look like a regular pig.

Good. I'm glad he thinks I look
like a pig. Still, his words sting
and my eyes start to water.
"I'm just having some cereal."

Ladies don't stuff their mouths full.

I'm not a lady and don't want to
be, but Daddy's spoiling to fight
with someone weaker than Mom.
"Sorry. I won't do it again."

That's more like it. Now give me a kiss.

He Hasn't Asked

For a kiss since I was small.
If he wants, he takes.
The passive demeanor has me

totally creeped out, but I am
not fooled by it. This
is no request. It's an order.

I wipe my mouth carefully,
go over to Daddy, who
waits, an impatient monarch.

I reach up to kiss the plump
of his cheek, but he
turns his face straight on

to mine, and our lips meet.
His mouth is wet,
hungry, and he kisses me

like no father should and just
as I think I'll retch,
Mom's footsteps *click-click*

on the hall tile, coming toward
us. Daddy withdraws.
There's my beautiful little flower.

We Are Still Very Close

When Mom enters the room,
queen to Daddy's king.

> *The caterers want a deposit.*
> *I have to—* She takes in the scene

> suddenly. Doesn't like what she
> sees. *Uh . . . is everything all right?*

Like she wants to hear the truth—
yeah, Mom, just making out with

my father. "Everything's fine.
I just had something in my eye."

> Her relief at the obvious lie escapes
> her lungs in an audible sigh.

Speaking of escape, I can make
mine now. "I've got to finish

getting ready for school. See
you this afternoon, okay?"

> I can't help but look at Daddy,
> who wears arrogance like aftershave.

> *Don't be late, little girl. I'll*
> *be here, waiting for you.*

I Exit the Kitchen

Dash up the hallway, and barely

make the bathroom before three

mountainous bowls of cereal

come pouring from my belly.

Stomach acid roils into my mouth,

bitter as the spit on Daddy's tongue.

The thought brings a round of dry

heaves. Once my stomach stops

convulsing, I scour my teeth and gums,

rinse with Listerine to kill the germs.

I dare to look in the mirror. "Tell,"

urges the girl on the far side of the glass.

"Tell. Or run." But she knows me better

than that. Knows I won't do either.

All Hope Dissolved

I catch the bus, sit in the very front
seat, where I know no one will join
me. I lay my head against the cool
window glass, stare at the nothing
beyond, try to shut out the noise.

Everyone here has parents. Maybe
not together parents, and maybe
some are substitute parents. But
no one has parents like mine.
I'm a complete freak, and so alone.

I was a total fool to ever believe
that someone could save me,
or thaw the frozen death inside
me. Oh Ian, if only you could,
I would run away with you today!

The brakes squeal and the bus
coughs up diesel, and as the next
group boards, I notice a Chevy
Avalanche drive by. It's Mick.
And glued to him is Madison.

Fine by Me

Although at least one person
I could name will probably
not be happy about this reunion.

But, hey, if it means Madison
will leave me the hell alone,
more power to Mick. Poor guy.

The bus pulls curbside at school,
and I'm the first one off. I go
straight to my locker, half hoping

I won't see Ian. The other half
needs desperately to see him.
But the bell rings, Ian-less.

I zombie walk between classes,
sit through hours of lecture
without hearing a single word.

Finally it's lunch, and there's
Ian, by the library. I start to wave,
think about running into his arms,

lifting my face to his for a kiss.
But then his face morphs into Daddy's,
and I duck into the bathroom.

Safe in the Far Stall

I wait for the bell to ring,
picking at a scab or two.
The one on my ankle is recent.
I open it wide, encourage
the flow. It's like milking
venom from my veins.
Wonder how long it would
take to bleed out completely.

    Other girls come and go.
    Talking. Laughing. Sniping.
    A couple dare light up
    cigarettes, and I almost
    ask for a drag. Filling my
    lungs with nicotine gas
    just might take the edge off.

        But the last thing I need
        is to get busted smoking
        in the bathroom at school.
        Think what my suspension
        would do to my parents'
        spotless reputations. Second-
        hand Marlboros will have to do.

I'm Watching Blood Drip

Onto a wad of TP when my cell
signals a text message coming.

> Ian, of course. *R u ok? Saw*
> *u run in2 the bathroom. I'm*
> *w8ing 4 u to come out.*

Looks like I'll have to oblige.
Can't hide in here forever.

Into the bowl goes the bloody
tissue. One mighty flush. So long.

Would be nice to so easily get rid
of all of life's varied detritus.

My fingers are tinted with blood.
I go to the sink, drawing a horrified

stare from the freshman standing
adjacent. "Bloody nose," I explain.

> She accepts the explanation.
> *Hate when that happens.*

Excuses. Excuses. So many excuses.
Too bad mine always seem to work.

With Everyone, That Is

Except Ian. When I offer
the bloody nose pretext,
he assesses me head to foot.

> *Really . . . ,* he says. *Did you clean
> up your nose with your pants?
> What are you, triple-jointed?*

I glance down, find one leg
of my white jeans striped
a dark shade of crimson.

My face flares a matching
color. "Oh, that. I cut myself
shaving this morning."

> He pulls me into him. *Be more
> careful, okay? Don't want
> you to bleed to death.*

His sincerity, and the warmth
of him dispel every little bit
of doubt. Okay, maybe not

> every single bit. My heart
> says I'm so, so his. But, asks
> my head, is he so, so mine?

So, So Mine or Not

I agree to let him drive me home
after school. It's a long afternoon
until the final bell releases me from
Monday PE and the usual locker-room
drama. Madison wears "smug" like sunblock, greasing her face to an oily gleam.

What she doesn't seem to get is
it doesn't bother me one little bit.
Once a bitch, always a bitch,
with or without a boyfriend who has
drunk a six-pack or eight too many.
Psychic says: Train wreck on the horizon.

Ian is waiting for me, and I push
all thoughts of Daddy away as I lean
forward to kiss him. Oh, yes. This
is what a kiss should be. Not wet.
Not hungry. No ego here. It's all
about me. I intensely love this guy.

He takes a roundabout route home,
stops down near the river. Okay,
it's mostly a dry river, but who cares?
My heart races, exhilarated at the ride
and at the possibility of what might
come next. Now. Tomorrow. Beyond.

Ian Kills the Motor

Drops the kickstand, takes off
his helmet, and I eighty-six mine.
He reaches for my hand, leads me
across the sand. Finally

he stops, turns to me. I expect
a kiss. Instead I get words.
I know you have to get home,
but I really think we need to talk. . . .

So much for tomorrow.
What can I say but, "Okay."
This is not at all going
where I predicted it would.

You know I've loved you for
a long time. To believe you
might love me back is all
I've ever wanted. . . .

Words spew, an eruption
of emotion. "I do, Ian, I do
love you. I know I haven't
always acted like it, but—"

Shush. Let me talk. Now I need
more from you. I need to believe
you trust me enough to not keep
secrets. To share your secrets.

Here it comes. Cold, bitter
panic, rising up like stomach
acid did just this morning.
"What do you mean?"

>He pauses. Kisses me gently.
>*I'm scared for you, Kaeleigh.
>You're losing weight. And, are—
>don't get mad—are you cutting?*

Every instinct cries out to
deny, deny, deny. "No, I . . ."
It might feel good to confess.
"Things are stressful right now."

>The not-quite-confession riles
>the protector in him. *You can't
>cut, Kaeleigh. Please. If you
>need help, I'll find it for you.*

"No!" No damn help, because
they'd want to know the whys
behind what I do. "No. I'll be
all right, as long as I have you."

>*Then you have to promise
>not to cut, and if you think you
>have to, you'll call.* He kisses
>the promise out of me.

Almost Home

Ian cruises slowly up the block.
I want to tell him, "Keep going."
And going. I know it's impossible,
but how amazing it would be to
just keep driving until we found
somewhere safe for the two of us
to settle down, merge into one.

As we pass Hannah's, I happen
to notice the front door swing
open. Just inside is a familiar
form, standing very close to
Hannah. (Just like in the kitchen.)
The thought makes my skin
crawl. And then he bends to kiss
her. (Just like in the kitchen.)

Before I can twist my head away,
dig it into Ian's back, Daddy
turns, preparing to leave. And our
eyes meet in a moment of mutual,
instantaneous recognition. He
knows who it is beneath this
helmet. And I know how he
has spent this frigid afternoon.

The House Is Crazy

With activity. Odd, to see
Mom so animated, here
            at home, so much more
        the way she used to be.
Holding court in the living
                room, she gives directions
        regally. Wonder if she notices
her nose, tilted so far skyward.

        Delivery guys move furniture,
set up chairs, a buffet table.
                Maids-for-a-day vacuum, dust,
        wash windows, scrub floors.
Some rental place sets up
                a wall-sized flat-screen TV.
        If all this energy would focus
on the polls, Mom couldn't lose.

        Daddy isn't far behind me
through the door. Despite
                a house full of witnesses,
        his hands pounce on my
shoulders, spin me to face
                him. *Haven't I told you no
        rides with young drivers?*
And who was that, anyway?

Spit Pools

At the corners of his mouth,
and his eyes betray insanity.
If we were alone, I'd be frantic
with fear. But we're not. And

          I hold

an amazing trump card. I yank
myself from Daddy's grasp.
"That was Ian. I'm sure it
means nothing to you, but
he and I have been friends

          forever.

That's right, Daddy. I do have
a friend or two, despite you."
His pupils go black with rage.
But suddenly I feel brave,

          in

control. It probably won't last
long, but for once, I've got
as much power as he does.
The house quiets as I continue

          my

taunting monologue. "Of course,
we're not nearly as good friends
as you and Hannah seem to be."
Think I went too far. He's flat

          trembling

with fury. And I know if he
could get away with it, he'd
reward me with the back of his

          hand.

Raeanne
Holy Effing Moly

What got into Kaeleigh?
Has she totally lost her mind?
Still, the (not real high) estimation

I hold

for her just rose a notch or two.
Kaeleigh retreats as Mom snaps
out of her state of shock, hustles
Daddy back into their bedroom.
The shouting match seems to take

forever

to fire up, but when it does,
it's a doozer. Even from here,
my ears are ringing. The cleaning crew
ignores the hoopla, returns to work

in

a matter of seconds. But the delivery
dudes seem completely unable
to move stuff without direction.
I decide to take matters into

my

own hands. "Ahem. Can you
please put that table over there,
under the window?" Beyond
the glass, autumn leaves are

trembling

in the November wind. It's all
going to tumble down soon.
And I'm ready to give it a

hand.

The Afternoon's Drama

Sent us all to our separate corners.

Daddy's holed up
in his bedroom,
shacking up with
his deadly
duo, but no Hannah.

Mom crawled off
to the guest room,
telephone in one
hand, wine bottle
(two) in the other.

Kaeleigh waited
for them to fall
silent, sneaked to
the kitchen, yacked
down five hot dogs.

Watching her made
me go puke up my
Lean Cuisine. Then
I put in a phone call
to Mick. I need bud.

He Picked Up

With some trepidation.
Caller ID totally busted me.

> *Uh, hi. Uh . . . I should tell you, me*
> *and Madison are a thing again.*

"I know. I don't want to hurt
your relationship. . . . " Oh no,
not at all! "It's just I really need
to get my head. Please? I'll make
it worth your while."

> *The greed factor works every time.*
> *Oh. Okay, just so you know. You know?*

Was I ever *really* with this guy?
"Hey, no problem. I promise
to be the perfect lady." Just stoned.

> *Give me fifteen minutes. But hey.*
> *Promise not to tell Mad, okay?*

Fuck. Whatever. I made my voice
real sweet. "Oh, I'd never do that.
But I do miss . . . oh, you know.
It was always so good with you."

He's on his way. And I'm . . .

Out the Window

Cutting through the sea of fog
like an orca on the hunt.

I don't have to wait long before
headlights find me in the mist.

I climb up into the Avalanche,
dive immediately under the seat

without even saying hi. Not nice.
I find the tray, start to roll. "Hi."

> Mick looks at me, laughs.
> *Okay, then. So where to?*

Translation: Exactly how will
you make it worth my while?

Not like that, m' dear. For all
I know, you've got Madison on you.

"Don't care. Just drive. Not through
town. And please don't speed."

OMG. How long has it been since
I've filled my lungs, held it in,

dropped way down low behind
a hedge of "who gives a fuck"?

A Half Hour Later

Mick and I are somewhere
out Foxen Canyon, totally
wasted. When we drove by
Ty's place, I half considered
taunting Mick with a confession.

> Mick pulls over in a deserted spot.
> He probably has to pee. But no,
> he reaches across the seat. *Come
> over here. Make it worth my while.*

"I don't think so, Mick. You're
back with Madison now. Wouldn't
want to mess that up for you."
You so deserve each other.

> He slides over, gagging me with
> the smell of his sweat. No shower
> today? *She doesn't have to know.
> Better not know. Come on.*

Okay. Calling Mick was maybe
not the best idea. I dig for a twenty.
"This should cover what I smoked.
Please take me home now."

> *Don't want your money.* His zipper
> opens, and what escapes is eager.
> Then he pushes my head down.
> *Haven't you missed me?*

I Could Just Do It

Get it over with. Pretend it never
happened. But I don't think so.
It has to be my idea or not at all.

"No, Mick. Goddammit, I said no!"

But he's all over me and I may not
have a choice. He outweighs me
by a hundred pounds and he's got

me pinned against the door. His
fingers, clumsy, work at my own
zipper. I try to push him off.

What's wrong? You know you want to.

"No, I really don't." But I can't stop
his mouth from covering mine, leaving
a wet trail of slobber all over my face.

One hand tugs my shirt over my head,
the other is inside my bra, twisting,
pinching. I could just get it over with.

See? Your nipples don't lie. You like it.

He's too worked up to manage tight
jeans, so he leans up over me, demanding
I do him with my mouth. I could bite.

But he'd probably kick my ass
and finish his business anyway.
I've never seen this side of Mick.

Or maybe I have and ignored it.
I can barely breathe, and the teeth
of his zipper are biting into my chin.

                    Atta girl. You can't say no to . . .

Daddy. Daddy? Kaeleigh would just
give in. The thought of her wide-eyed
surrender gives me a sudden idea.

But I have to play things right.
First I go limp, pretend to acquiesce.
I even give him a taste of what he wants.

"Stop for a minute. You're hurting me."

He hesitates, looks down into my
eyes, which have teared up quite
nicely. He draws back ever so slightly.

I dig down, beyond fear, find Raeanne
again. "If we're going to do this, you
don't get to have all the fun. And can

we pretty please take another hit first?"

The Greed Factor, Again

That, and asking instead of demanding.
I could be a politician one day. Ugh!
Why did I have to go and think that?

        Mick slides to one side of me. *Okay.*

I reach down, grab his tray, complete
with maybe a half ounce of great bud.
Pricey bud. I'm betting on greed.

"Hang on. I need some light." I open
the door wide, send the tray sailing
like a pot-covered Frisbee.

        What the fuck did you do that for?

Mick jumps across me, out the open
door. I slam it behind him, hit the lock
button, move under the steering wheel.

I'm not about to walk all the way home.
Mick can do that. He's on his hands
and knees scouring the dirt for bud,

roaches, rolling papers. I can't help
but notice the crack of his exposed ass.
He was in too big of a hurry to zip his pants.

I think before I do it. I've never actually
driven before. But how hard could it be?
Think again. I might just kill someone.

Hopefully Mick, not me. I laugh, start
the engine. Mick looks up, and I know
I can't let him back in the truck.

What the hell are you doing, bitch?

I have no clue what I'm doing. Fuck it.
I've seen this done a thousand times before.
Drop the gear shift to D. Hit the gas . . .

The Avalanche Lurches Forward

Wheels spinning in the gravel.
        Mick rolls out of the way.
                Good thing. With more force
                        of will than talent, I manage
                                to get tires onto asphalt,
weaving back and forth
        until I sort of get the hang
                of driving a straight line.
                        Almost makes me wish
                                I wasn't so high. Almost.

This isn't so hard. I play
        a little, testing brakes,
                acceleration, and steering
                        capabilities. Not exactly
                                rocket science. Uh-oh.
Here come some curves.
        I ease off the gas, maneuver
                through them, half thinking
                        about what I'm doing.
                                The rest thinks about Mick.
He's pissed, for certain.
        But what's he going to
                do? Call the cops? His
                        word against mine. Still,
                                if the cops come knocking . . .

How Would That Look on Headline News?

CONGRESSWOMAN'S DAUGHTER ARRESTED
for theft of would-be rapist's truck. Says
they were smoking pot after curfew
when things got out of hand.

I could go back, pick him up.
If I could manage to turn
around, anyway. But

you know, I really don't think
I will. He started this game.
I'll play it to the end.

It's one thing to say okay, do me,
do me any way you want
and it's no problem,

because I gave you permission.
But to say no, and have him
insist he will anyway?

No damn way. And as I work it
through, it comes to me that
for once, I did say no.

What's up with me, anyway?

The Road into Town

Is pretty much deserted this time
of night. I drop over the last dark
hill, pull well off the pavement,
onto the shoulder. Wouldn't want
some loadie to come along and
smash into the Avalanche.

Guess I'll leave the keys under
the seat. I think enough to wipe
them off, along with the steering
wheel. Any other fingerprints of mine
would probably be smeared together
with Madison's. Wonder if she says no.

I know it's stupid as hell, but now
I'm worried about Mick. It's a damn
long walk from where I left him.
Oh, well. He deserves it. If he gets
lucky, maybe someone will happen
by. Yeah right. Well after two on
Tuesday morning. Election day.

Better worry about myself. It's
a long enough walk for me, and
I most definitely better be home
well before the sun comes up.

An Hour's Walk Home

Back in through the window.
I listen intently, but all's quiet.

My clothes smell like Mick
so I yank them off, crawl into

bed naked. I don't usually sleep
in the raw. But I'm high and tired,

and the cool cotton sheets feel
like water. I'm skinny-dipping.

Swimming toward deep, deep
sleep, and I'm afraid to go there.

Because when I wake up again,
it will be tomorrow. The day

everything changes. Better?
Worse? Whichever. Looking

back at this afternoon, not
to mention tonight, I understand

the transformation is already
well underway. And I'm scared.

I Wake to a Hailstorm

Of sound:

Footsteps.

Some
news
channel.

Slams.

Daddy.

Mom.

Furniture
scraping.

Orders
barked.

The
telephone.

The
telephone.

Dishes
crashing.

The
telephone.

The
telephone.

Light Through the Window

Informs me I've overslept.
The clock confirms nine twenty-two.
Oh, yeah. Way over. On a normal day,
Daddy would have been in here,
yanking my butt out of bed.

      Oh, but this is not a normal day.

I slink out of bed, naked. Naked?
Last night's clothes are heaped
on the floor. Last night!
Wonder if Mick made it home
yet. Wonder if I'll hear from him.

      Like he could keep his mouth shut.

Oh, well. Not to worry. If he wants
to play rough, I'm up for the game.
Meanwhile, I'll bask in the memory
of him, moonlight falling on his moon.
Shower. Dress. Wade into the madness.

      See if anyone even knows I'm here.

No One Has a Clue

I emerge from my room,
a butterfly from her cocoon,
and no one seems a bit
concerned about the

                    metamorphosis.

I could spread my wings,
let them dry, then fly
far, far away, and no one
would notice my departure.

                    I'm a shadow.

Daddy and Mom have
retreated to their separate
rooms to dress for a joint
trip to the polling place,

                    no longer

at each other's throats, not
until this day settles into dust.
Wonder if I should just go to
school late, pay my pound of

                    flesh,

accept detention without
complaint. But how would
I get there? Can't exactly
call Mick for a ride,

                    and

I can't ask my clueless parents.
I look out the window. Hannah's
home. Delicious. If she'll take
me, I can draw a little figurative

                    blood.

Kaeleigh
The Dreaded Day

Has arrived, and with it total
trepidation. Where will my family
be, once it's all over? What sort of

metamorphosis

will we experience? I'm torn
in two. I mean, most of me hates
everything about my life (except
for Ian, of course). I feel like

I'm a shadow

behind my mother, always
there, but rarely acknowledged.
I love her the way I always
have. How can it be that she

no longer

wants to be my mom? What
have I done? Is it because of
Daddy? Does she know about—
and ignore—his taste for young

flesh,

and not only young flesh, but . . .
No, that can't be. When she
heard about Hannah, she flipped,
issued an ultimatum,

and

I'm pretty sure Daddy will
at the very least be much more
careful about his extramarital
fun. Mom is totally out for

blood.

Most of Me

Does hate my life.
But this tiny sliver
is more afraid of what
life might become
than it is of pain,
ever-present now.

At least I recognize
the boundaries imposed
on me. I know how
far to push. I know
when to step back.
I know when to tuck
tail and run. I know
when not to twitch.

I love my mom, hate
when she disappears.
I love when she comes
home, hate when she
hides inside herself.

I hate my father, love
when he puts distance
between us. I hate
how he treats me.
Love when he makes
me feel loved.

School Is My Refuge

At least for today. At least,
most of it. Mr. Lawler chooses
elections as the topic of the day.
Guess who's front and center.

What can you tell us about your
mother's political ambitions?
he asks, rather pointedly. *Has she*
thought beyond this election?

Is he talking like Mom as president
or something? I shrug. "They're
her ambitions. You should
probably ask her about them."

He smiles. *Fair enough. So*
what about you? How do you
feel about your mother running
for Congress? Are you proud of her?

I really wish he would quit
shining the spotlight on me.
How am I supposed to answer?
"How else would I feel, Mr. Lawler?"

My tone tells him to change
the subject, and he moves on
to infamous elections in the
distant and not-so-distant past.

I Couldn't Care Less

About any election, including
the one going on right now.

All I can think about is seeing
Ian. We have drama today, so

we'll get to rehearse together.
Not that I've had a lot of time

to practice lately. I'll probably
blow every line. But at least

the romantic scenes should take
on an air of definite credibility.

I'm stuck in thoughts of dramatic
interpretation when the door opens.

It's some office intern, with a hall pass.
For me. *Your mom's here to pick you up.*

Everyone stares as I gather my stuff.
Mr. Lawler waves me out the door

and resentment builds inside me.
I know I'm off to be presented

as familial bling, when all I want
is to be left way alone. With Ian.

Bling for a Day

That's me. Photo this. Interview
that. And every damn word is a lie.

"Of course I'm very excited about
my mother's prospects today. . . ."

      The whole thing fills me with dread.

"Oh yes, I think she deserves to win.
She'll work for positive change. . . ."

      For the country, if not for me.

"Well, if she doesn't win, she'll try
again, I'm sure. This is her dream. . . ."

      Does she still dream? I'm not sure.

"The best part of the experience? I guess
seeing politics in action. I've learned a lot. . . ."

      There is no best part of this experience.

"The worst part? Having her away so
much, I suppose. . . ."

      The worst part? That she *so* wants to go.

The Afternoon Ticks By

By eight, when the polls close,
the house has filled with people,
good Republicans all. I swear,
I'm registering Dem. That will
make it just that much easier
to never vote for my parents.

Daddy is up for reelection in two
years, and he's sure working
Mom's crowd now. He's not
about to play bling when there's
so much Money floating around
the living room, drinking Dom
Pérignon and nibbling canapés.

Ranchers. Winemakers. Small
business owners. Developers.
All might one day call in favors
for the votes they no doubt cast
today. Then there are cops.
Prison guards. Other judges.

And, oh yes, there's the mayor,
a stout, youngish conservative
who rubber-stamps growth—
like if he builds enough new
neighborhoods, he might actually
find a life partner in one of them.

Conspicuously absent is Hannah,
who helped pull this shindig
together. Guess my big mouth
made her fade into the background,
at least until Mom takes off again.
In hindsight, it was amazingly
stupid to delete her from this
complicated equation. Idiotic.

Oh. Wait. Here she comes.
Glass in hand, Daddy
glances at the new arrival.
His first reaction is to smile
widely. Then he notices Mom,
weaving through guests on the far
side of the room, and his smile
slips ever so slightly. Hannah waves,
and Daddy moves toward her.

Mom misses nothing, though she
doesn't miss a beat of conversation.
But when Daddy reaches Hannah's
side, takes her arm, Mom starts
in their direction. This evening
might get interesting after all.

I Angle Closer

The last catfight I witnessed
        was my own, with Madison.
This one should prove more fun.

      But, no, Mom remains the steadfast
           politician. She extends a hand.
      So lovely to see you again. Ray?

      Please get Hannah something to drink.
           Too subtly for the untrained eye
    to notice, she extricates Hannah

    from Daddy, who ambles toward
           the bar like a half-trained puppy,
    glancing back for trainer approval.

I move even closer, knowing
      Mom is not about to leave
things up in the air. I am so right.

      *I hear you helped organize this
           evening,* she says. *Thank you
    so much.* Then, smile slipping not

    one inch, she lowers her voice.
           *I also hear the two of you have
    become rather close. I do hope*

you understand the nature of
politics. Scandal will not
be tolerated. My people will

see to that. Perhaps a mutual
decision to move on with
your separate lives is wise.

Mom pauses, but Hannah gives no
immediate response. I wait for
a threat. Instead Mom offers a bribe.

I've told my personal assistant
to see what he can do about
your outstanding student loans.

Hannah remains quiet for several
seconds, as the weight of Mom's
words sinks in. She glances over

at Daddy, who has found her
a glass of champagne. He smiles,
but she doesn't dare smile back.

Before he can rejoin her, she
meets Mom's steady gaze.
And all she says is, *I understand.*

She's In Over Her Head

And she 100 percent knows it. Mom will kick her
figurative butt if she chooses to disregard the overt

       warning. Instead, play it smart, come out way, way
       ahead. Mom, of course, is truly the smart one.

Give Hannah a way out, but make it clear
she'd better latch onto it. Run with it. Run.

          Funny, because, wrapped up in my
          own little corner of the universe,

   I always thought it was Daddy
   who carried the power here.

            Now I see how wrong
            I was. Now I see why

      he wields such a big
      stick when Mom

              isn't around. It's
              the only way he

      can feel like
      even half a

             man.

Daddy Returns

Offers her the glass of bubbly.
I keep my back half to them, at
a respectful distance, but close
enough to successfully eavesdrop.

Daddy doesn't notice me
at all. *So what did she have
to say?* he asks. *I assume
she issued some sort of threat?*

A glance over my shoulder
reveals Hannah, sipping Dom
and scanning the room. *She
said to take a hike. What else?*

I see. Daddy clears his throat.
*And do you plan to take orders
from my wife? Depending on
what happens tonight, she'll—*

*You said the magic word, Ray—
wife. I've always known this would
be a temporary fling. This is
probably a good time to end it.*

She hands her glass to Daddy,
kisses him softly on the cheek,
starts out the door. He looks like
he's going to follow her, but . . .

Just Then Someone Turns Up

The volume on the television,
where regular programming
has been interrupted for an
election update. The polls

                              closed

hours ago and returns trickle
in. In the Twenty-fourth U.S. Congressional
District, Kay Gardella currently
leads with 52 percent of the vote.
That comes as little surprise

                              to me,

of course. A cheer goes up
in the room. Unless there's
a major turnaround, Mom's
got it in the bag. Looks very
much like we've lost her

                              for good.

I look at Daddy, who is torn
between running after Hannah
and strutting beside his wife,
the likely congresswoman.
Guess who wins out. Hannah's

                              gone,

he's still here, where the votes
are. I so despise politics. Pit
them against family. Pit them
against love. The Game conquers,

                              always.

Raeanne
By Midnight

Mom is declared the official
winner. Everyone toasts, a final
round of good cheer before the bar is

closed

for the night. Oops. Make that
morning. I decide to join them.
One more before beddy-bye.
Despite several champagnes,
sleep will not come easily

to me,

not tonight. I might have to
tap into my pill stash. I ignore
the well-wishers and reporters,
go to the window. Hannah's lights
are out. Wonder if that's over

for good,

or if Daddy will coax her back.
If I were the type to wager,
I'd place my bet on Mom.
Especially now, despite the fact
that before we know it, she'll be

gone,

off to DC for the foreseeable
(and perhaps unforeseeable) future.
Who cares? She's not here, even
when she is here, now and

always.

Kaeleigh Has Withdrawn

From the party, crawled away
somewhere to sulk and cry.

                    Not me. Fuck it. The more
                    Mom's gone, the less the stress.

Always plenty of that, nibbling
away at us. Who needs more?

                    And hey, now that this election
                    is over, no more good behavior.

Ha! Like I've behaved so well
over the past eleven months.

                    And, really, with elections every two
                    years, I've only got a year to be bad.

But incumbents generally have
the upper hand, so no worries.

                    Shit, if I don't quit conversing with
                    myself, they'll institutionalize me.

I'm not conversing with myself out loud,
am I? Okay, where's the champagne?

I Finally Limp

Off to bed
around two.
No school
tomorrow,
I figure.
We'll still
be celebrating.
At least Mom
definitely will.

I'm celebrating
pretty good
right now, on
two Oxy and
enough bubbly
to give me
hiccups for days.

Oh yeah, I'm
floating, okay.
But I don't like
how it feels. I
desperately want
solid ground.

Like I've ever
even once in
my life stood
on solid ground.

The Telephone Wakes Me

It has rung incessantly, but not
enough, it seems, to wake Mom
and Daddy, who partied well

into the wee hours of morning.
Their phones are likely unplugged.

I drag myself from beneath
the covers, head pounding.

"Coming, damn it," I call.
Fighting an amazing hangover,
I reach the idiotic phone. "Hello?"

> A very long pause precedes,
> *Hello. This is your grandmother.*

Another very long pause.
Long enough for anger to
blossom inside my traitor head.

"Oh, really? Well, it's a little
late now, don't you think?"
Come on, you old bitch . . .

> *Excuse me? A little late for*
> *what, exactly? Who is this?*

I can't believe I'm rising like this.
Who cares, anyway? Loyalty

to my parents? Definitely not me.
Still, I continue, "A little late to ask
for money. The election's over."

> *Yes, I realize that. But why on*
> *earth would I ask for money?*
> *Who told you that, anyway?*

"Your ex-husband. He told us
you wanted hush money."

> *My ex-husband? Ted? But*
> *why . . . ? W-well, young lady . . .*

> A voice, heavy and masculine,
> falls over my shoulder. *Who*
> *is that?* Daddy. Of course.

I turn to face him, and what I see
in his eyes chills me to my core.
Don't dare lie. "It's your mother."

Daddy Grabs the Phone

Out of my hand, and his intensity
makes me back quickly away.
If he lashes out, I don't want
to be standing in his path.

But no, he's relatively collected.
This is Raymond. May I ask
exactly why you've been
bothering my family with calls?

I can't hear her response, but
Daddy's posture goes from
wood to pulp. It's like he
shrunk sizes. Shrunk years.

He's a small boy, and he's found
his mommy again, only he doesn't
like the idea. *Everyone is just fine.*
Thanks for your misplaced concern.

Whatever she's saying now hits
like hammer blows. His breath
comes in short, stuttered bursts,
and his teeth crunch together.

I couldn't care less about your
"programs." I will never forgive
you, and you will never be welcome
in this house. Good-bye, Mother.

Unable to Guess

What he'll do next, I start to
retreat toward the kitchen.

>Daddy pounces, fists clenched.
>*Why did you answer that?*

If he weren't so angry, I'd have
a smart-ass comeback. But as it

is, I play humble. "It kept ringing,
so I thought it might be important."

>He draws right up against me.
>*What did she say to you?*

"Nothing. Only that she wasn't
calling to ask for money."

>His muscles relax, but only
>a little. *Are you sure that's all?*

"Yes, Daddy, that's all." I finally
chance looking into his eyes,

and this time what I find isn't
anger. It's—can this be right?

Yes, I'm right. It's fear.

The Bad Thing About Fear

Is it requires a reaction. Some hide.
Some cry. But, like a dog condemned
to a walled yard with no hope
of escape or affection, some learn
to bite. Daddy is a fear biter.

> Lucky for me, Mom seems to sense
> the approaching maul and comes to
> my rescue. *Good morning.* Much too
> cheerful. Her head rocks back and
> forth between us. *What's going on?*

> > Daddy snaps out of his fugue,
> > into the moment. *Seems my
> > prodigal mother managed to get
> > one of her calls answered this
> > morning. I took care of it, though.*

> The congresswoman-elect
> searches my face for some
> kind of sign. *Are you okay?*
> At my nod, she detours Daddy.
> *May I speak with you for a moment?*

They withdraw to the bedroom
and I hustle into the bathroom,
determined to reach there before
last night's champagne and this
morning's turmoil escape my belly.

The Bad Thing About Puking Regularly

Is how you come to rely on it.

Hungover?   Go puke.

Feel a bit fat?   Go puke.

Confused?   Go puke.

Frightened?   Go puke.

Entire world falling apart?

Hurry up and go puke.

All of the above?

Puke.

Puke.

Puke.

Puke.

And puke some more.

Totally Puked Out

Esophagus acid-etched,
I'm ready to face the day.

Not.

Despite the insulation
of two closed doors and

a hallway,

I can hear Mom and Daddy
screaming insults at each

other.

I want her to leave now,
leave us within the solace

of silence.

I so need to get high. But Mick,
I'm guessing, is no longer

an option.

And that basically leaves one
person I can ask for a buzz.

Ty.

I Dial His Number

Get only his voice mail.
Leave a subtle message.
"Please call back as soon
as you get this. I so need
to hook up with you."

Sounded a bit desperate
there. And guess what?
I am. Downers are okay,
I guess, but it's not like
you really enjoy the buzz.
Mostly, you sleep through
it. What fun is that?

Besides, I need to feel
desirable, not like a piece
of furniture, something
you can sit on. Something
that belongs to my mom
or my daddy. I need to feel
like somebody wants me,
even if he wants me for
all the wrong reasons.

Mostly, I just need to feel.

But If Ty Wants Me

He's playing hard to get.
Hours pass without a word. I
almost wish I would have
gone to school. I wish Mom
or Daddy would have asked

why

I didn't go, but apparently
they're both so wrapped up
in themselves (and wrapped
around each other's throats),
it was too much effort to even

notice.

All I can think about are two
things. One: Ty calling to say
he's on his way to pick me up,
take me home, and spend
hours doing crazy things with

me,

insane things that will carry
us all the way down into hell,
and maybe, just maybe, back up
again. And two: this morning's
phone call. If not for money, why
did my grandmother bother to call

at all?

Kaeleigh
Three Days

Since the election and things
have finally settled down.
Mom left for DC this morning.
She and I still have no clue

why

Grandma Gardella called the other
day. We talked about it for a few
minutes, which is about all the time
she could spare for me. I swear
I could run away and she wouldn't

notice

me gone. Daddy is a different tale.
Sometimes I turn around suddenly,
sure he's behind me. But he's not.
Sometimes, even though I know
he's miles away, I fccl him watching

me,

monitoring every move I make,
every twitch, every pee, every
thought, even. Sometimes, rarely,
that makes me feel safe, and that
scares me through and through.
Will I ever be able to leave Daddy

at all?

School Was Crazy

For a day or two, like Mom's
celebrity had somehow worn
off on me. Today is better.

No questions. No jokes.
Everything back to normal,
at least as normal as things get.

Thank God for Ian, always
my reality check. And often,
my voice of reason. I guess

it's good to have a conscience
hanging around somewhere.
The fact that he happens to be

a great kisser is a definite bonus.
At least as long as those strange
feelings about my father,

and how he can see beyond
the miles, don't happen to prove
true. Then, considering how much

kissing has gone on between Ian
and me today, I'm toast. If so,
the kissing was worth every crumb.

One Thing Kind of Weird, Though

As hot as our kissing gets (and it
gets pretty intense), Ian has not
tried to take things further. Once
or twice, his hands have strayed
to certain places, places that made
me want a lot more than kissing.

But he always pulls back, intuiting
that, much as I might want more,
I'm really not ready to give myself
to him in that way. All the way.
Not yet. Everything has to be right.
In place. Hopeful. Fearless. Perfect.

He drives me home now and my
heart beats against his back, promising,
"I do love you. I do love you. I do . . ."
He stops around the corner from home,
out of sight of our windows,
of Hannah's windows (just in case).

We are well ahead of the school bus.
We'll let it go by before I walk on
home. Daddy took the week off.
Who knows where he's at, or what
he's doing? Even this is risky,
and we both know it. Don't care.

At Last the Bus Goes By

I haven't much time, at least
not if Daddy is home, aware.

I press myself into Ian, try to
absorb enough of him to get

me through the long night
without him. He doesn't need

the words, but I offer them
anyway. "I love you so much.

More than life itself. I'd be
a total wreck without you."

> He looks into my eyes, smiles.
> *I know. I feel the same way.*

My head shakes automatically.
"You're so together. You don't

need me to keep you that way.
But you are my glue. Without

you, I'd be nothing but broken
pieces. Completely useless."

> *Never useless, Kaeleigh. And*
> *you're stronger than you know.*

I Try to Keep That in Mind

As I arrive home. With Mom gone,
the house wears its usual aura
of hushed nonwelcome. I focus
on Ian as I tread quietly to my room.

Daddy is home, his bedroom
door open a crack, and through
it leaks his voice, thick already
with his usual escapes.

C-c'mon, Hannah. Y-you don't
mean it. She's gone and might
not ever come back to me.
I n-need to see you. N-need you.

Wow. Things went deeper
than I thought. I almost
feel sorry for Daddy. Almost.
Not like he deserves anyone.

P-please, Hannah. D-don't
leave me, just like everyone
else. Please! Several silent
seconds pass before a solid

clunk tells me the phone has
fallen against the floor. And,
sequestered in his dark, lonely
cell, Daddy is sobbing.

I Close My Door

Turn on my music, slip
headphones over my ears. I don't
want to hear him cry.

He's a sad, sick man, who
deserves every tear, at least that's
what I want to think.

I'm shredded, wrecked.
Completely confused because as
much as I hate him most

of the time, every now
and then, a sliver of love for Daddy
embeds itself in my heart.

Hard to tell who's more
messed up. Daddy? Or me? And,
much as it's the end result

that affects me every day,
I really have to wonder who or what
made Daddy become this way.

Babies aren't born cruel
or filled with sick desire. Evil is not
intrinsic. It's fashioned.

Soundless as a Shadow

I stay in my room all evening
Drawing any sort of attention
to myself would be an enormous
mistake. Shh! Turn off the music.

> Every now and again, Daddy
> leaves his own room, on a Turkey
> hunt. Staccato footsteps accompany
> his muttered threats and pleas.

>> *You can't leave me. I won't*
>> *let you. I'm not a little boy*
>> *anymore. I'll go after you.*
>> *Please. Don't leave me!*

I keep the bedside lamp
very low. It sheds a pale,
wheat-colored light, barely
enough to read by. Not

that I can concentrate on
the words. Mostly what I'm
doing is praying Daddy slips
into substance-fed slumber.

Back and Forth

He goes, bedroom to bar. Why
doesn't he just take the bottle

with him? It comes to me with
sudden clarity that his pacing

carries him by my room twice
every round-trip. I extinguish

my light, hunker down in my
bed, as if hiding there might

somehow influence him to keep
on going. Going. Please go on by.

This trip is to the Turkey, and
it seems to take a very long time.

Maybe he fell asleep in the living
room. I start to relax, just a little.

And then I hear him, unsteady in
the hall. One, two. Three, four . . .

He pauses outside my door.
This time, the knob turns.

And I know why he's here. I'm
the only one who doesn't dare run.

I Want to Shout

Leave me alone!
        What's wrong with you?
           Don't you remember
               who I am? Who you are?
                  This is not a father's love!

I want to scream,
        Can't you see what
           you are doing to me?
               What you've done to me?
                  What you've made of me?

I want to cry out,
        I am your little girl.
           I am not your girlfriend.
               I am not your whore.
                  I am not my fucking mother!

But he is on top of me
        and my shout is silenced.
           He is inside of me
               and my scream stays
                  there too. He is finished.

And I don't cry out,
        but I do cry a bucket
           of silent tears. He slithers
               away and at last, I quietly sob
no
      no
           no
               no
                  no.

He Says Not a Word

Except a whispered *I love you.*
And as he exits, an almost-silent something
half-sounding like *I'm sorry.*

Is he? How can he do this despicable
thing to me, expect
me to believe he's the slightest bit sorry?

Once, after an extended "visit,"
he pushed himself up above me, dared to
slur, *Forgive me. Not my fault.*

Whose fault, then? Mine? All I ever did
was try and make
him feel forgiven. Healed. Accepted. Loved.

Mom's fault? Maybe. But why,
then, does he still want her? Still want to
love her, with or without sex?

Hannah's fault? Someone else's? What
unidentified ghost,
wearing Daddy's face, might come to me?

Most of me doesn't care, just
wants him to leave me the hell alone. A tiny
part of me demands to know.

Both Parts

Are exhausted. Too little sleep.
Much too much unsolicited attention.
It *is* unsolicited, isn't it? I don't ask
for it (maybe subconsciously), do I?
Stop it! Can't think like that, even
for a instant, or go completely insane.

My body aches. My brain aches more.
But I have to get up and go to work.
At least I won't have to share a table,
share a couch, a room, a house,
pretending last night didn't happen.
I've done a lot of pretending.

I pry myself from between
the covers, limp off to the shower,
hoping fifteen minutes of hot steam
and fragranced vapors can wash away
the scum. Scrub away the disgust.

Cleansed but not refreshed, I dress
in simple jeans and an unadorned T-shirt,
apply no hint of makeup. I want no
attention, no compliments, no come-
on nor get-off smiles. I want to be
Mother Teresa, helping the elderly.
Okay, it's a ridiculous fantasy,
but one I desperately need right now.

Enveloped by November Fog

I walk to work. Slowly.
        I see now, more than ever,

that I belong to Daddy.
        My father is my keeper.

I can never escape to Ian.
        Ian was only a fantasy.

        Beautiful make-believe.
                A movie poster to focus

on when I have to hide
        out inside my own head.

By the time I reach
        the old folks' home,

        I realize I have to break
                things off with Ian.

        Not fair to let him keep
                thinking we have a future.

        Not fair to me to play
                this game any longer.

        I go inside, drowning.
                Crying, inside and out.

The First Face I See

Belongs to William. He can't
help but notice the state I'm in.

> Straightaway, he puts an arm
> around my shoulder. *You okay?*

I yank away from his touch,
like he's fresh from the oven.

> My muscles twitch, quiver,
> begin to shake uncontrollably.

Greta, nearby, rushes to my
side, latches onto my elbow.

> *Come with me. No ifs, ands,*
> *or buts about it, young lady.*

Next thing I know, I'm in Greta's
room, on her bed, tissue in hand.

> *I think it's time you told me*
> *this deep, dark secret of yours.*

Oh, how wonderful it would be
to break down. Confess. "I can't."

> *This has to do with your family,*
> *yes? Perhaps with your father?*

Any hint of composure vanishes
in a tremendous hailstorm of tears.

> Greta sits beside me. *I should*
> *have told you my story before . . .*

Her Voice Softens

Remember once, I told you I met evil
when I was very small? My Satan
was a butcher, tall, heavyset, and
the face he wore looked exactly
like mine. He was my father, and
he believed he owned me.

A gasp escapes my best effort
to hold it inside me.

Greta continues. *He would come*
home from his butcher shop,
rank with blood and fat. Often
he stripped without washing,
and he would call me into his
bedroom, a calf to slaughter.

I was expected to bring a wash
basin and soap. "Cleanse me,"
he would say. "Take the stench
away." Hands. Arms. Feet. Legs.
And by the time I reached the place

between them, he would be stiff.
And then he would tell me how
to touch him, before he laid
me on the bed and did the thing
no father should do to his child. . . .

I cannot believe she's telling
me this. Cannot believe this
beautiful, strong woman
ever suffered this thing.

> When I met my Lars, I loved
> his gentle way, loved how
> he never demanded. I told you
> my father found us together,
> beat me because of it, and I was
> afraid he would beat Lars, too.
>
> But Lars didn't care. He asked
> me to marry him, and I so wanted
> to, but could not imagine sharing
> a bed with any man. Pleasure
> from scx? Never! When I said no,
> Lars went off to soldier.
>
> How I regretted that decision.
> Later, my father arranged
> a marriage to a man no better
> than he. But that is another story.
> And now, if you will, I think you
> should share your story with me.

Oh, How I Want To

But Daddy would kill me,
and get away with it. I can't
ever tell, not even to someone
else who has had

          sex

forced on her by her father.
What if I ask for it somehow,
maybe subconsciously? Being
brutally honest with myself, it

          feels good.

How can that be? Not that
there's any joy in it. Unlike Greta,
I want to know joyous sex.
It does exist outside of books,

          doesn't

it? I want sex laced with love,
and not warped parental
love, but the honest kind.
I want sex that makes me

          feel right,

not like some freak, some inbred
monstrosity. I'm not, am I?
Damn it, I really don't know.

          Will it

one day be revealed that Mom
is actually my grandmother? OMG,
could there be even deeper secrets
that can't be unearthed, never

          ever?

Raeanne
IMH (not) O

In my not-so-humble opinion,
Kaeleigh definitely asks for it.
Feigned innocence invites

sex

more than a frank come-on does.
Anyway, she tries to pretend
she doesn't like it, but it

feels good

and she knows it. Feels good
with Mick, although that particular
chapter of my life is definitely over.
Even if he has forgiven the whole
truck episode, I prefer a guy who

doesn't

have another girlfriend spoiling
for trouble. Someone like Ty, maybe.
Sex feels great with him, too.
I guess it might be nice for sex to

feel right,

like the person you're with
might even love you. But hey,
I'm not exactly sold on the idea
that love is, in fact, real.

Will it

find me one day, overtake
me, infiltrate my life like sunlight
snakes through the cold of morning?
Can love thaw me? Will it

ever?

I'm Not Even Sure

What love is, or just   what it's supposed to
be. They say you learn by   example. But no one has
set one for me. I only love   one person on this entire
planet. And he only loves Kaeleigh. My daddy loves
Kaeleigh. Ian loves Kaeleigh. And she's incapable
of loving either of them back. What a waste.
She only loves Mom. What in
the hell is wrong with
her, anyway?

Then again, I know   something about
our mother that Kaeleigh   can't quite recall, and
if she did, she'd probably dive off a very tall bridge,
into shallow water. Stop! Can't think about that
now, or I'll have to join Kaeleigh, jump into
ultimate freedom. I must admit I have
considered that leap from time
to time. But I'm afraid
to die loveless.

Afraid to Die Loveless

Because
I think if
you die
without
knowing

love in
this life,
that's how
you'll
spend
eternity.

Alone.
Frozen.

Do you
think hell
is fiery?

I don't.
I think
hell is
frozen.

Before the Other Night

It was a while since Daddy went
to Kaeleigh, saturated with misguided
love and the overwhelming need to
own her completely. To prove
he owns her completely. Prove
it to her. Prove it to himself.

He can never own me. Maybe
that's why he doesn't bother me.
I can give myself to whomever
I please, in any way I damn
well choose. Key word: choose.
If I say okay, well then it is.

I wonder what will happen
to Daddy when we turn eighteen
and Kaeleigh can move away.
I wonder, codependent as she
seems to be on their sick
relationship, if she ever will.

No one will even notice when
I go. I'd leave now, but if I did,
Kaeleigh would have no one
but Ian. And sorry, but the odds
are long that he'll hang around.
Too many easier scores.

Being Easier

Isn't really such a bad thing.
>> It can get you what you want.

Yeah, yeah, I know what
>> they call someone who barters

her body in exchange for
>> something she wants. A wife!

Get it? Okay, never mind.
>> But it doesn't bother me to use

the one thing I've got that's
>> mine, all mine, to get what

I want. Drugs. Liquor. Fun.
>> Not like there's a whole lot

of that where I live. More
>> drugs. Better drugs. Maybe

it's time to graduate from
>> pot, hash, and pills to something

stronger. That opiated stuff
>> was great. Wonder what heroin

is like. I hear it drops you way
>> down, where pain can't find you.

Any Drugs

Would be good right this moment.
Heroin. Cocaine. Maybe ecstasy.
Not too sure about psychedelics.

They say acid and 'shrooms
make you look inside your own head,
help you learn about yourself.

Sorry, not interested. I'm afraid
if I looked inside my head, I'd
find something really scary.

Maybe if I walk into town I'll run
into some way to score. Ty never
called back. He's probably pissed

'cause I took so long to call him.
Or maybe he found someone else,
although I doubt he fell in love and

changed his bachelor ways. Way too
into himself, not the type to move
in a habitual keeper, love or no love.

No love to us, I'd still like to see
Ty. It's been a long week with
nothing to smoke. I'll call him again.

The Biggest Surprise

Of the week was not hearing
a word from or about Mick.

            I expected a call, at the very least,
            telling me what a bitch I am.

What I really expected was a knock
on the door from a tan uniform,

            a trip to juvie, and major dishonor
            to Judge Raymond Gardella, not to

mention his wife, the incoming
freshman congresswoman. Phew!

            But no. Nada. Nothing. Not a hint
            of a problem. Maybe I should call

Mick, apologize. Would he forgive
me? Pick me up? Share a doob?

            I mean, really, it *was* his fault. Maybe
            that's why he didn't make trouble.

Okay, I'm treading a fantasy—Mick,
in my control. A shitload of bud. And me.

But It Isn't Mick

Who comes idling up beside me
at the midtown park where
I spent the afternoon spying on
tourists for sheer amusement value.

No, it isn't a big 4x4 that stops.
In fact, it only has two wheels.
Tuned and well-fed, Ian's Yamaha
hums contentedly. *Ride?*

I know he can't have confused me
with Kaeleigh, who would not
be happy to know Ian gave *me* a ride
home. Like I care. "Sure."

He hands me his spare helmet,
slides forward to make room, and as
I slide my arms around him, I wonder
if he might think I'm Kaeleigh after all.

Nah. He knows her too well.
Doesn't he? One way to find out.
I make my voice all sweet.
"Take me for a cruise?"

He pauses, tenses. Definitely
confused. Then he shakes
his head. Relaxes a level, but
not completely. *Where to?*

Highway 154

Takes you all the way
to Santa Barbara. It winds
past cattle ranches and Lake
Cachuma before cresting
The San Marcos Pass and
snaking down over the
mountain. Just as you
drop, you can turn off on
the potholed road to Cold
Spring Tavern. That's where
I asked to go. I love it there,
where history looms large
in the oak-decked beauty
of old California. It's late
afternoon, and I find myself
wishing I had a heavier jacket.
I bury my face into Ian, inhale
warmth and perfume of leather.
Something very much like
contentment threatens my
equilibrium. Does Kaeleigh
have a clue what she has here?

Longing Lunges

With sudden ferocity.
What is wrong with me?
I can't. Can't. Won't. Will I?

Ian pulls into a narrow
parking space beside the road.
Walk with me? He reaches

for my hand and it dawns
on me. He *does* think I'm
Kaeleigh. How I want to be.

I should tell him. Have to tell
him, but my hand, tucked
neatly into his, is so warm.

I let it stay there as we work
our way along a narrow trail.
So much love, in the palm

of his hand, folded around mine.
Oh, Kaeleigh. Don't you get it?
Oh, Kaeleigh. To be his!

I'm not even drunk, not stoned,
not buzzed on pills. Perfectly
straight, still I'm reeling.

I should tell him. Have to tell
him. But, hidden by forest,
far from prying eyes,

he pulls me against him. My
head falls into his chest and I
listen to the rhythm of his heart.

I look up into his eyes,
find the kind of love there
I hunger for. Love, not meant

for me. I vow to absorb it
anyway, hold on to it as long
as I can, even if for only a few

seconds. I want to kiss him.
Am going to kiss him, though
I know if I do, he'll realize

he's not kissing Kaeleigh.
Hey, maybe he'll fall out
of love with her, and into

love with me. So I stand
on my tiptoes, reach up
for his lips with my own.

Yes, Every Kiss *Is* Different

And this is a kiss
like none before, a kiss
that could overcome the dark
of deep space night. It's a falling
star, flame, ice. It's pure as water from a snow-fed mountain
spring. This is what you dream a kiss to be. To have a kiss just
like this each and every day! How satisfying life would be.
Oh, Kaeleigh. Never let   this man   get away.
Ian is   the key   to your   salvation.

Ian Moans

And that ignites a flame just
below my belly button. This
is so wrong, but I don't care.

Ian is also on fire. But when
I reach down to touch him
the way every guy wants,

he draws back. *Wait.*

"Please, Ian? I want you."

He shakes his head.
What's wrong with you?

Wrong? Everything's right.
I try to kiss him again.

He pulls away, eyes betraying
confusion. *You're not Kaeleigh.*

He knows, of course he does.
I'll make him want me. I fall to
my knees in front of him. "Just let me . . ."

No! I can't. This isn't right.
He turns, stalks off, down the trail.

All I can do is follow.

Ian's Sense

Of right and wrong
overwhelms me. Not
a single other person

                I know

possesses such an unshakable
sense of morality. It's more
than unbelievable.

                It's frightening.

To offer without strings
something all men crave,
and be rejected by him is

                incomprehensible.

Think I'll have to kick
Kaeleigh's ass. Does she have
any idea what it means

                to be

so treasured? He has built
a pedestal for her so tall
that she is afraid to be

                lifted

atop it, because to fall
would mean certain death.
But oh, she would rise far, far

                beyond fear

and be held by arms so strong,
and love so pure, that falling
would not be an option.

Kaeleigh
Falling

Is such an unpleasant sensation.
I'm falling now, down through
a dark blue opiate sea, and

I know

it's all up to me. Sink or swim?
I know how to swim, have practiced
the dead man's float for years, but

it's frightening

how much I just want to drown
in this undertow of booze and pills.
I drank a lot tonight, ingested an

incomprehensible

amount of painkillers, some
borrowed from Daddy, the rest
pilfered from old Sam, who seems

to be

suffering a lot from his arthritis.
His nightstand is a pharmacy.
I doubt he even noticed I

lifted

a handful of Percodans. Lucky me,
Daddy had to work this weekend.
By the time he gets home, I'll be

beyond fear

and well past saving.
I'm falling now, down,
down through indigo. . . .

Tick-Tock

Through the thickening
vespers
the clock on my wall
whispers.

Tick-tick. Tock-tock.
Intones
the passage of time.
Drones.

Inhale. Everything
slows.
Exhale. The exchange
shallows.

Heartbeats mimic,
tick-tick.
Become erratic, stutter,
t-t-tock.

Through the indigo.
Down.
Gradual motion.
I drown.

A Voice

Echoes inside my brain.
A little girl's voice.

> *Get up. When you fall*
> *down, you gotta get up.*

It's Raeanne, and I am with
her on the playground.

> *Get up, Kaeleigh, or I'm*
> *gonna be mad at you.*

I am lying beside the merry-
go-round, head spinning.

> *I hate when you be a baby.*
> *Oooh. Lookie. You're bleeding.*

Scarlet oozes from a slice
on one skinned knee.

> *Stop crying! I hate when*
> *you cry. Mommy! Mom . . .*

Now her voice changes,
hardens, sedimentary stone.

> *Stop whining, Kaeleigh, or I'll*
> *have to kick your ass.*

She sounds like me. Looks
like me. Identical.

> *Goddammit. I'm going for help.*
> *I'll kick your ass later.*

Another Voice

Trails the slam of a door. Door?
Down here? How can a door slam
in so much water? So much deep,

      dark ocean? *Hello? Anyone home?*
      Obnoxious. Intrusive. A lifeline.

Footsteps. Twenty to his bed. Twelve
to mine. I don't want to count them.
Can't help it. One, two. Doesn't matter.

      Three, four. Can't get me here.
      Five, six. Quick! Hide! Seven, eight.

To hide I have to swim. Nine, ten. No
way to swim but up. Eleven, twelve.
The feet stop moving, and even this far

      underwater, I hear a door snitch open.
      Kaeleigh? Kaeleigh! What have you done?

      Up through the indigo, I am lifted. *Wake*
      up, Kaeleigh. Come back to me right now!
      Sharp strikes against my cheeks.

Sudden tears. My eyes want to float open.
But I won't let them. Won't see him.

I Fall Again

This time, I land in a soft swirl
of lavender, like the ocean at sunset
just after downpour. Beautiful.

Can I stay here? Forever? Lapping
against the beach, playing with
the sand. Frothing against the shore.

Footsteps again. They slap tile.
Running away from me.
Good-bye feet. Good-bye.

I am sinking. I can end it here.
But if I'm going to drown, I have
to go fast. Before the feet come back.

I Let Out All My Breath

Concentrate on sinking

deeper and deeper and . . .

oh, but what's poised below?

What monsters of the deep

might decide to chew on me?

Will it hurt, the final release?

Is there pain when the spirit

pries itself free of the flesh?

Why worry about that now?

I can feel the excavation, and

it's painless so far. My lungs

fill with water. Silt. Mud. Now

it hurts to breathe. So I won't.

I'll settle deep into darkness.

And I won't say good-bye.

Damn Footsteps

Won't let me sleep. And voices.
One belongs to Daddy.

> *Oh my God. Her face is blue.*

The other belongs to a woman. Mom?
No, not Mom. Softer. Younger.

> *Kaeleigh, wake up now.*

Melodic. Angelic. Angel?
That means I'm . . .

A sudden burst of air floods my
lungs. Pressure on my chest. Air.

Pressure. Air. Pressure. Air.
I'm breathing. Not drowning.

> *Atta girl. She's coming around.*

My stomach roils, like I gulped
lavender seawater. I lean over

the side of my bed, jet a big stream
of opiate-laced Wild Turkey.

> *Good girl. Get it all out.*

And now I'm in Daddy's arms.
I squirm, but he won't let me go.

Limp. Fall limp. My eyes wander
past his face, to the face of my angel.

Hannah. Of course. Who else?
Her hand is cool against my face.

What did you take, Kaeleigh?

Tell? Don't tell? Who cares?
"Percodan." No need to mention

Daddy's OxyContin. The Wild
Turkey, they can smell. Hannah sighs.

How many?

Her voice, sugared, irritates
me now. If heaven's host sounds

like her multiplied, I'll stay
home. "N-not sure. A dozen?"

Hannah points to the gross
disgustingness next to the bed.

She should be okay, but . . .

Oops, Too Late

She said the magic word: okay.
Daddy gulps in air like it might
disappear any second. Like I might.

> He gushes, *Are you sure?*

>> Hannah has been fussing over
>> me, as any good nurse would.

>> *Her vitals are good, considering. . . .*

> Good enough for Daddy.
> *Thank you so much, Hannah.*

>> But Hannah's not quite finished.
>> *She needs to go in for monitoring.*

I won't be monitored, won't answer
questions. I just want to be left alone.

> Daddy's got that covered. *I don't*
> *think that's necessary. And I know*
> *you know how important it is to keep*
> *this right here in this room.*

>> If she doesn't know, she definitely
>> understands Daddy's directive.
>> But she dares question him.
>> *May I speak to you for a minute?*

They Move into the Hallway

But I'm not really sure why.
I can hear every word,
despite their lowered voices.
Hannah is worried about me.

*A dozen painkillers, washed
down with whiskey. That
wasn't an accidental overdose,
Ray. Your daughter needs help.*

Duh. Serious help. But Daddy
won't admit it. *I think we
can handle this in-house.
I'll make some calls.*

But Hannah isn't satisfied.
*Look, I know this isn't something
you want spread in the tabloids.
But I'm just not sure . . .*

Daddy can be very persuasive.
*I appreciate your concern.
You wouldn't be a good nurse
otherwise. But leave this to me.*

She has to give it one last shot.
*Please think seriously about
getting some help for her.
Your daughter is disturbed.*

Yep. Disturbed semiregularly,
by her pervert father, a part
of the story she'll never know.
And even if she should find out,

Daddy apparently holds a trump
card. *I promise to think about it.*
Oh, and your problem with your
ex? Consider it solved.

I have no idea what the problem
could be, but Daddy's reach
is long. Almost as long as
the silent pause right before

Hannah acquiesces. *Okay,*
I'll back off. But please keep
an eye on her. If she follows
through, I'll never forgive myself.

Following Through

Isn't something I can think
about right now. I'll put it
on my back burner checklist
of things to think about

later.

My head hurts, far beyond
the dizzy left inside it. It hurts,
like my heart does. When I do
let myself think about tonight,

I'll remember

a whiteout of emotions.
A rush of anger, at my mom,
my dad, my screwed-up life.
A blush of love for Ian. Oh,

how

I wish that I could give him
what Daddy takes so easily from
me. But it would be a tainted gift.
Sadness now, and I wonder how

it feels

to live without a constant fog
of sorrow, a breeze of loneliness.
Complacent, I wait for my daddy
to come and punish me for trying

to die.

Raeanne
I Can't Believe

Kaeleigh had enough ambition
to down those pills, take dead
aim at whatever might come after.
If Daddy had found her much

later,

he'd have discovered an empty
shell. Seeing her slip down
that long, dark tunnel toward
permanent peace is something

I'll remember

the rest of my life. It didn't look
so difficult. Still, I'm not quite
ready to let her go. Needy,
shaky, I lie in bed with her.

How

long it's been since I've felt
this close to her. Her breaths
are shallow, raspy with exhaustion.
"Stupid shit," I whisper, and

it feels

like not enough. "If you're strong
enough to look death in the eye,
you're strong enough to fight
him. Please. I don't want you

to die."

Don't Know

If she heard any of that.
She's so weighted into oblivion,

she looks as if she did die.
The weirdest thing is,

Daddy has not come to
check on her. You'd think

he'd want to know if she
is still breathing. I'm guessing

he went straight for the Wild
Turkey. Hopefully Kaeleigh

left enough for him to drown
his guilt. Does he feel guilt?

          Does he feel

     anything

at all?

I Think

Maybe that's what he's looking for.

> A way to feel.
> Something.
> Anything.

Even if that something is pain.

> Remorse.
> Humiliation.
> Self-loathing.

What has brought him to this place?

> Loneliness?
> Greed?
> Genetics?

What redemption can there be for him?

> Penance?
> Prison?
> Demise?

It's Morning Before He Comes

To check on her. Kaeleigh feigns
sleep, but Daddy's determined.
He shakes her until she opens
her eyes, stares silently past him.

> *Good to see you're still with us.*
> His voice is about as warm as
> day-old oatmeal. *Don't you ever,*
> *ever do anything like that again.*

Anger fills her eyes. Anger,
and knife-edged hatred. So
much to say, no way to say
it. "I . . . I . . . I won't, Daddy."

> *I think it's best no one outside*
> *this room hears about this incident.*
> *Your mother would be very hurt.*
> He straightens, waits for an answer.

The tears in Kaeleigh's eyes
reflect denial, but she doesn't
dare let it spill. "Whatever you
say." She turns her head away.

> *You need to get up now and*
> *clean up this mess.* He gestures
> toward last night's vomit. *And I*
> *will be waiting for your apology.*

Almost a Week

Since Kaeleigh tried to off herself,
and believe it or not, she did apologize
to Daddy. She stood, head tilted toward

the floor, shoulders stooped like an old
woman. "Sorry, Daddy. I was stupid."

She cleaned up the floor, washed herself,
her clothes, her sheets. But she couldn't
wash away the indelible stench of Daddy.

She wore it to school. To play rehearsal.
To stolen moments with Ian. I watched

as she tried to put "the incident" behind
her. But anyone who ever noticed her
has to have noticed a change inside her.

She's no longer afraid to die. What she's
afraid of is living, accepting the status quo.

Daddy Acts

Like it never happened. It's how
he deals with any trauma in his life.
The accident. The incident.
Mom's winning the election.
Daddy simply moves forward. One
day, one night at a time.

Hannah has stopped by
several times to check up on Kaeleigh.
She always says the same thing:
Your daughter needs help, Ray.
The reasons behind the attempt are still
there. It could happen again.

Daddy's answer is the same:
It was just the stress of the election.
Now it's over, she'll be fine.

Then he'll change the subject,
to one he finds much more appealing.
You've had some time to
think things over. I hope
you've reconsidered. Kay and I
are married in name only.

Hannah remains steadfast.
You're still married. It was a mistake
to get involved. I'm sorry, Ray.

The Last Time

She dropped by, Daddy wasn't
home yet. But Kaeleigh was.
I listened in best I could.

> Hannah pounced. *Kaeleigh, I don't*
> *know what's going on in your life*
> *to make you decide it isn't worth*
> *living. But I'm pretty sure it has*
>
> *nothing to do with the election. If*
> *it had something to do with your*
> *father and me, that's all over, and*
> *I'm sorry. I never meant to hurt—*

"No. It wasn't that, so quit blaming
yourself, if that's what you're doing."

Then she made up a half lie. "There's
this boy who I like, but I know it won't
work out, no matter how much I want
it to. But I'm over that now. I'm okay."

Just then Daddy arrived. I vanished
as he stormed into Kaeleigh's room.
But I could hear every word.

> *Hello again, Hannah. As you can see,*
> *my daughter is doing well. I'd appreciate*
> *it if you wouldn't drop by unannounced.*
> *Kaeleigh, please go start dinner.*

He Is a Cold-Hearted Bastard

That's for sure. And suddenly
I desperately need to know why.
Did he not see Kaeleigh, screaming
for help, the only way she could—
wordlessly, helplessly, no one to hear?

I don't know how to get hold of my
grandmother, and considering
the reception she got from me
last time, I sincerely doubt she'll
call back any time soon.

But somewhere, buried deep in
Kaeleigh's journal, is an address
for Theodore Gardella. Grandpa
Teddy. (Pu-lease!) He lives less
than two hours south, in Calabasas.

I think it's time his granddaughter
paid him a visit. But first she
has to find a ride. I easily think
of exactly one person and pick up
the phone. "Hello? Is Brittany there?"

Operative Word: Easy

Brittany is quite simply the most
easy-to-manipulate person ever.

She had planned to see a movie
with Joel, but when I told her my

grandpa was really sick, she softened.
And when I threw in the part about

filling her gas tank and buying lunch,
I almost had her right there.

> *Okay, but only if Joel can come
> too. We're a thing now, you know.*

Yeah, and if she isn't careful, there will
be a little thing growing inside her.

If I can persuade her this easily, her steady
"thing" should have no trouble talking

her into whatever. But hey, that's not
my problem. And now I've got my ride.

I MapQuest directions, extract eighty
bucks from my private stash, pop

a single Oxy to steady my nerves,
go to meet Brittany and Joel.

Between Brittany's Driving

And a traffic accident jam, the hundred-
mile trip takes us over two hours.
Two plus hours of hip-hop, Brittany
giggling, and Joel's immature, totally
not sexy innuendos. Aaagh!

I'm mostly silent, filling with dread.
What if he won't see me, let alone
tell me the things I need to know?
Not like we've ever done anything
but exchange a letter or two.

> *So what kind of sick is your grandpa?* asks
> Joel. *We won't catch something, will we?*

"Well, I don't think you want to come
inside. You can drop me off, go have
lunch—on me, remember?—and come
pick me up. I don't have to stay that long,
just make sure he's got his medicine."

> *Hey, I know what I want for lunch,*
> sneers Joel. *Tuna! Got any, Britt?*

OMG! What a disgusting loser.
I can't believe Brittany actually
shrieks with laughter. This is why
I don't maintain friendships. Friends
tell friends what they *really* think.

We Find the House

Arrange a meeting time, and I give
Brittany forty dollars. "But don't
leave until he answers the door."
Last thing I need is to sit here
on his doorstep for two hours.

Brittany waits patiently while
I idle slowly up the walk, noting
his yard is neat but not pretty.
I swallow one more pill for good
measure, steel up my courage.
Reach for the doorbell. Push.

I hear footsteps immediately.
The door cracks, leaking warm air.

> *Yes? Who is it?* The voice
> crackles. *What do you want?*

"Um. Sorry to disturb you. But
I'm your . . . your granddaughter."
The door opens wider and Brittany
starts her car. I want to shout, "Wait."

But I don't. For the first time,
I look my grandfather in the eye.
"I think it's time we talked."

> *Long past time, young lady.*
> *But come on inside.*

The House Is Small

Gloomy, and like his yard, tidy
but not pretty. No adornments
anywhere. Serviceable furniture,
lacking comfort. Still, I accept
his offer to perch on the hard sofa.

> Almost to himself, he says,
> *I wondered if you'd ever come.*

In lieu of small talk, we sit
and stare at each other for
several skeptical minutes.
My grandfather is shorter than
Daddy, and much darker,

with weathered California skin
and gunmetal eyes. Oh, Daddy
got his eyes from his father,
whose own searching eyes slice
into me now. I swear, it hurts,

like he's dissecting me without
benefit of anesthesia. Someone
has to break the awful silence.
But I can't think of a single
icebreaker. Luckily, he does.

> *So what can I do for you after all
> these years? You have questions.*

It's a statement, as well it should
be. I could tiptoe around the real
reason I'm here. But why waste
time? "I want to know why Daddy
won't have anything to do with you."

                    Well, that's very direct, isn't it?
                    Why is it important now?

I could lie, tell him I want to
know him, learn all about my
roots. But I suspect he'd know
it was a fabrication. "I need to know
why Daddy is like he is. Why I am . . . "

                    Who you are, he finishes. Hesitates.
                    I'm not sure where to begin.

Oh, I can help him there.
"I don't need to hear any
happy stuff, if there is any
to tell. I need to hear about
when everything went to shit."

He Winces Slightly

But agrees. *I don't know you from
Adam, but someone should hear this
story. Your father would carry it to
his grave. How much do you know
about Charlotte, your grandmother?*

"Only that she walked out when
Daddy was a boy. Something
about your messing around?"

*A nice way to put it. Yes, I cheated.
I was lonely. Charlotte shared most
of her time with a whiskey bottle,
and so devoted little to your father
or me. When she left, it was a relief,*

*or would have been, except I had to
work long hours. Your father was still
young, so I placed him in the care of
a neighbor, a woman I had known,
or thought I did, for many years.*

*Turned out I didn't know her at all.
One day I came home early and
went to pick up Raymond. I knocked
but no one answered, so I went
around back, where I heard voices. . . .*

He pauses, clearly unsure
whether to tell me the rest.
"Please. Don't stop now."

> I found your father, on a swing
> with a young girl, about his age.
> They were naked, playing with each
> other. Miranda was directing them,
> and her boyfriend was taking pictures.

His voice breaks a little, and
his eyes—Daddy's eyes—spill
the tears of this horrible truth.

> Your father gained his manhood,
> if you could call it that, at the age
> of ten. His photographs appeared
> in magazines, for the pleasure of
> pedophiles. And he blames me.

Bam, Sledgehammer

His words don't so much sink
in as they are pounded in, down
through my skull, into my brain.

So much explained. So much
insight gained, in the space of ten
minutes of ugly monologue.

My grandfather's voice quivers.
He wasn't hurt, not physically.
But emotionally, he was scarred.

I tried to tell him how sorry I was,
but he wouldn't listen. Wouldn't
forgive me. For eight years, we

barely spoke. And after he left
for college, I never heard another
word from him. I followed his career

as best I could. Was happy that he
did well for himself. I kept thinking
with time, he'd come around. . . .

Oh, no. Not Daddy. Once you're
on his shit list, forget it. But one
burning question remains.

"Why did you call about your
ex-wife coming back? Did you
really think she wanted money?"

He crumples like a candy wrapper.
I didn't know what she wanted.
She'd been gone so long, I wasn't

even sure she was still alive
until she knocked on my door,
wanting to know about you.

I thought—hoped—it might
be a way back into Raymond's
life. Your life. I'm . . . all alone.

A Half-Assed Honk

Signals my ride home is curbside.
Better not leave them waiting
too long, or I might get stuck
watching Joel fish for tuna.
Did *I* just think that? Fuck!

"I have to go. My ride is waiting."
I consider what else to say.
I'll start with a hug. Grandpa
. . . um . . . weird . . . stiffens a bit
at my touch. "Thank you."

No, thank you. For giving me
the chance to maybe get to know
you. I don't want to die without
family knowing or caring I'm gone.
Please stay in touch. Please?

"I'll do my best. But Daddy
won't like it if he finds out."
We exchange phone numbers,
and he walks me to the door.
I turn. "Can I call you Grandpa?"

His smile is weak, weary.
I'd be grateful if you did. Tell
your ride to drive carefully.
I'd hate to lose you now.
The door closes behind me.

Ugly Little Movies

Replay themselves over and over
in my head on the ride home.

Thankfully the return trip is faster
than the outbound was. If I hear

one more frigging giggle, I'm
going to blow it completely.

I down yet another painkiller, chase it
with a swig of the Turkey stashed in my bag.

We drop over the top of the mountain,
where the hills bump and grind toward

the valley. I've admired this view
hundreds of times, but today it's different.

Today the hills are haunting,
vague as spirits fooled into being,

each blurring into the next in cool
bronze succession. Indistinct.

Yet somehow not quite meaningless.
Like information gleaned, but not

completely absorbed. Like ugly little
movies, in semiconstant replay.

I Should Go Home

My cell has four voice mails,
        three from Daddy:

Where are you?

*Where the hell are you?
Why did you leave without
telling me where you were
going?*

*Where the fuck are you?
When will you be home?
Are you okay? Do I have
to come looking for you?*

I have to call him, but first
I pick up the fourth message.
Can't believe it, but it's Ty:

*Hey. Sorry I took so long
to return your call. Been
away at a seminar. When
can I see you? Call me.*

Major Dilemma

If I call Daddy, he'll want me
to come home, and who knows
what kind of mood he'll be in?
(I've got a pretty good idea.)

But seeing Ty—and getting
wasted—is way up on my
priority list. If I get high
enough, I can deal with Daddy,

as long as he doesn't actually
come looking and find me.
He wouldn't come looking,
would he? And if he did,

could he find me way out
in the boonies at Ty's place?
Nope. No way. First I call
Ty. He answers, second ring.

"Hey. I'm in town. Can you
pick me up?" He agrees,
so I have Brittany drop me
at the park. "Thanks for

the ride. See you." Off they go.
I chance a one-sided call to Daddy.
"Hi. I'm fine. I'm with friends.
Be home in a while." *Click.*

I'm Living Dangerously

And I def know it. I power down
the phone. I'll have to deal with
whatever consequences Daddy

decides to deal me. But meanwhile,
I won't have my evening disturbed
by the incessant interruption of a cell.

It takes Ty forty minutes to get to
me, too much time with nothing
to do but think about today.

And that means thinking about Daddy.
No wonder he didn't want Kaeleigh
and me to have a childhood. He didn't.

I have no idea how I'll feel when he's
punishing me, but right this moment,
I can't help but feel sorry for him.

Finally the BMW cruises into view.
I wave and Ty pulls against the curb.
I give him my hottest smile. "Hey."

> *Hey. Great to see you again. Get*
> *in.* He opens the door for me, not
> quite a gentleman. *My place okay?*

His Place

Is exactly what I have in mind.
The top is down on the Beamer,
the sun low in the sky, and it's
cold outside. So why am I hot?

Feverish? Maybe. But I'm not
going to tell him that and maybe,
just maybe, the fever is hunger,
not sickness. I'm starving.

Starving for a high, a place to
hang out inside my own head.
Starving for touch. Pain, even.
A way to feel. I need to feel.

Funny how when your life is
mostly bullshit, you turn off
feeling. Sometimes it's hard
to turn it back on again.

Last time I let myself feel was
up on the mountain with Ian.
When he turned away, I flipped
the feeling off switch.

But now, just imagining what
Ty has in mind for me, for us,
I flip it back on again. Good
or bad, I'm ready to feel.

Ty's House

Is the perfect place to hang out
inside my own head. The first
thing he does is disappear

>   up the hall, toward his bedroom.
>   He comes back with a party in a box.
>   *You want to get buzzed, right?*

I nod and next thing I know,
we're smoking black African
bud. It's not really black, but

it's definitely purple, the buds
big around as my fist. And it
tastes like absolute heaven.

Almost immediately, my eyes
grow heavy and my tongue thick.
"Incredible," I manage, sounding

more like "increthible." We both
laugh, and I slide into a comfort
zone. Part of me keeps shouting

a warning. The other part tells
the first to shut up, quit trying
to fuck up my high. I realize

Ty is a dangerous man. But I
so want to walk that razor's edge,
take feeling to a whole new level.

He senses my eagerness.
His breath warms my ear
and my heart double-times.

How far will you go with me?
He kisses my mouth. My throat.
Will you let me draw blood?

He bites my neck, and a moan
escapes my mouth, unbidden.
How high will you let me take you?

For once, I want to relinquish
control. For once, I want to
completely let go. "You decide."

His grin is pure evil. *That's my
girl.* He yanks my blouse over
my head, spills me from my bra.

He kisses, bites. I'm already lost,
but hungry for more. He pulls
me to my feet, hands all over me. . . .

And the Doorbell Rings

Not just once, but three times,
in quick succession. Fuck!
Did Daddy find me after all?

> *Who the fuck is it?* Ty yells.

No answer, but another ring.
And another. I try to tug on
my shirt, and am halfway there

> when Ty opens the door. I stare
> at the face framed there, eyes
> wide with anger and hurt. Ian.

> He pushes past Ty. *Kaeleigh.*
> *What are you doing here, with*
> *him? You promised me . . .*

Promised? What did I promise?
I shake my head. Kaeleigh promised,
not me. "N-not Kaeleigh."

> Ty takes Ian's arm. *Get the fuck*
> *out of here.* He tries to muscle him
> toward the door,

> but Ian yanks away, comes over,
> puts his hands on my shoulders, looks
> into my eyes. *Who are you, then?*

I'm . . . I look at him, so full
of love for me. Me. Am I Kaeleigh?
No. Goddammit. I'm, "Raeanne."

      No, no, no! His head twists
      from side to side, until I'm sure
      it will spin off his neck. *Raeanne*

      *is dead, Kaeleigh. She died
      in the accident, remember?
      Listen to me, Kaeleigh.*

What is he talking about?
I'm not dead. I'm right here,
and I'm . . . too fucking stoned

to deal with this now. "What
are you talking about, Ian?
Can't you see I'm not Kaeleigh?"

      Ian's eyes are wild. Scared.
      Confused, like an animal
      in a trap. *Please, Kaeleigh.*

Why does he keep calling
me that? I'm not Kaeleigh, I'm . . .
Wait . . . What did he say

about an accident? Yes, yes,
there *was* an accident. Daddy
was driving and they took . . .

Mom and Raeanne Away

Not me. Didn't
        take me away.
Raeanne. My sister.
        My identical twin.
I called out to her.
        She didn't answer.
Mom came back.
        Raeanne didn't.

                Ty turns vicious.
                Ty? Who's he?
                Look, she said she's not
                this Kaeleigh person, so . . .

        But I *am* Kaeleigh.
Wait. Who am I?
        Who am I? The room
begins to spin.
        Goddammit. Too much
fucking good bud.
        Is that the problem?
Don't think so. Afraid
        that's not the problem.

                Ian turns toward Ty,
                and his look stops the
                bigger man's approach.

*Something's wrong
with her, but she is
Kaeleigh, and her twin,
Raeanne, was killed
in an accident years ago....*

"Stop saying that!
I'm not dead...."

Yes, you are.

"...can't be dead.
I'm standing right here."

Someone is, but
not you.

"I don't want
to be dead...."

I Think I'm Dead

Voices. Arms around me.
Hands, familiar. Ian's hands?
They don't belong to me.
They belong to Kaeleigh.
Kaeleigh isn't

dead.

I am. Lights. Floating.
Motion. Noise. Ian, beside
me. *Come on, Kaeleigh.*
Everything's okay. I'm here
for you always. He says

I'm not dead,

but he still thinks I'm her.
Am I her? If I'm her, where
is me? I can't go away, not
all the way away. Kaeleigh
is weak, no match for Daddy.

If I die,

she'll die too. I'll always
be right here. Ian doesn't
have to know. Daddy
doesn't have to know. Even

she won't

know I'm still here. I'll
have to hide better, always
be Kaeleigh. It's a new game,
but necessary for me to

survive.

Kaeleigh
I Wish I Were Dead

I'm sick. Confused. Hot.
My muscles ache, twitch.
They tell me it's withdrawal
from OxyContin. I smell

dead,

sweating death from my pores.
Three days now, and nothing
feels better. I keep puking . . .
did I once puke on purpose?
Is that part of me dead if

I'm not dead,

and if it is, am I half-dead?
I don't understand. I don't
understand. Big blocks
of my life are lost to me.
Big blocks of time, spent . . .

If I die,

will I remember them then?
Will I be condemned for them?
Was it really me doing them?
Or is Raeanne living inside me?

She won't

talk to me, though I've tried.
Searched for her. Screamed
for her. She was the better part
of me. Without her, how can I

survive?

Fragments   Shards

That's what I am now.

Incomplete.

They keep asking for

truths.

I'm afraid to give them

answers.

I keep hiding behind

dreams.

Except maybe they're

realities.

They keep asking for

reasons.

I give them lame

excuses.

I want to live in my

fantasies.

Except maybe they're

nightmares.

They keep asking for

explanations.

I keep telling them

I don't have them.

At First

They don't allow visitors.
Only nurses. Doctors. One
is a shrink. Dr. Carol Shore.

> *Call me Carol. I'm*
> *a psychotherapist.*
> *And I'm here to help.*

"Help what?" I ask,
pretending like I don't
need help. Never have.

> *Help you face whatever*
> *it is that you keep trying*
> *to escape from.*

"Why would I want
to do that?" My stomach
heaves, but it's empty.

> *Because only by confronting*
> *your demons can you ever*
> *hope to conquer them.*

What she doesn't seem
to understand is, I have
to go home to my demon.

I Tell Her I'll Think About It

Anything to get her off my back.
They give me something to calm
the withdrawal, help me sleep.
As I slip toward lovely nothingness,

> I hear a voice behind the door.
> *She's my daughter, goddammit.*
> *I have every right to see her.*

No. Don't want to see him. Ever.
Then snippets. Ugly movies.
Please! Go away. Let me sleep!
Relax . . . can't . . . he's here.

The door opens, but I refuse
to open my eyes. Maybe the drug
will kick in, push me all the way
down into unconsciousness.

> Footsteps. His. One, two. Stop!
> *Kaeleigh, girl. Wake up. It's Daddy.*
> *I'm right here beside you.*

> His hand, cold, strokes my cheek.
> His head tilts against my chest.
> *I wish I could take it all back. . . .*

When I Wake Up

I'm alone. In the dark.

Where am I again?

Who am I again?

I'm hot. So hot.

I was hot in a car.

A BMW? With . . .

More ugly movies.

Only Daddy's not

in them. I am.

Oh my God. What

have I done? Who

have I been with?

A collage of faces.

Ty. Ty? Who is he?

There was a party. . . .

I went there with

Mick. Mick? And

Madison was there.

Madison. She was

at Lawler's house.

Lawler? Mr. Lawler?

I told him I like

older men. Older,

like . . . Daddy. Daddy?

No . . . No . . . No!

But he said, *I wish*

I could take it all back.

Take It All Back

Okay, maybe I do need help.
I can't even remember what "all"
is. Only bits and pieces. And why
would I want to remember more?

Only by confronting your demons . . .

Confront him? How could I ever?
And how could I ever let anyone
know what my father has done
to me? Who would understand?

You've got some powerful demons. . . .

Greta! Oh, maybe I could tell Greta.
I need to see her, need to know
if she ever confronted her demon.
Can't believe it happened to her, too.

I met evil when I was very young. . . .

But you wouldn't know it to look
at her now. She's strong. Strong
enough to fight Nazis. Strong enough
to invite Lars back into her life.

Could not imagine sharing a bed . . .

Sharing a bed with a man
she loved. A man she trusted.
Instead she sent him away.
Out of her life. Such loneliness!

Please trust me enough to tell . . .

Ian. My amazing Ian. My best
and only true friend. If I told
you, you'd turn your back on
filthy me. If you haven't already.

I Stare at the Night Sky

Outside
the window.
The stars shine, as
they always do. Same
stars. Same sky. Only I am
different. Am I different? Will

my life change now? Better or worse? Will Mom come back,
save me? She can't. She has work to do, far away
from home. Will she take me with her?
Do I want to go? And a bigger

question. Will she listen now?
Memory jabs. I accidentally

told once. Didn't mean to make her
jealous. I was taking a shower. The soap stung
and when I said "Ow," Mom asked what hurt. I told her,
"Where Daddy touched me." She looked and her face grew red.

But she said, *I don't see a thing.*
I guessed Daddy was right.
She got mad, closed
her eyes. Like I
need to do
now.

I'm Still Tired

When sunlight wakes me.
I feel a little better, though,
and that's bad. They'll make
me go home soon. Unless I tell.

> A voice inside me whispers,
> "Can't tell. They'll be jealous."

Shut up. You're dead.

> "Am I? Guess you'll just
> have to wait and see."

When they finally bring breakfast,
I ask the nurse, "Am I allowed
visitors yet? Has anyone tried
to see me?" Anyone being Ian.

> The nurse shakes her head, and
> the voice agrees, "He ran like
> the wind. You're crazy, you know."

I wait for the nurse to leave,
so she doesn't think I'm crazy.
Then I tell the voice again,
Shut up. You're fucking dead.

> "If you say so."

When Carol Comes

I'm ready to talk. "Is there such
a thing as a split personality?"

                Her eyes measure me up and down.
                Dissociative identity disorder
                is extremely rare, but yes, it's real.

"Do the different identities
know about each other?"

                Sometimes. Usually not. Sometimes
                one does, but the others don't.
                There are no definites with DID.

"Could you split into someone
you know—or used to know?"

                The jury's still out on how the alters
                develop. But I suppose you could take
                on aspects of someone familiar.

"Will one—what did you call it?
Alter?—do stuff another one won't?"

                My questions have definitely piqued
                her interest. *Often that's the case, yes.*
                Why? Do you know someone like that?

Well, duh. Why would I ask?
"I think so. What causes it?"

Usually a childhood trauma. An illness,
or an accident. Most often it's related
to sexual abuse in the formative years.

"Does it mean the person
is crazy? Can you fix it?"

"Crazy" is hardly a clinical term.
It's a form of mental illness, and yes,
it can be cured, or at least regulated.

It doesn't happen overnight, though.
It takes years of treatment, and the guts
to dig down and extract the truth.

Guts? Do I have the guts? I smile.
"Guts? Is that a clinical term?"

That's All I'm Ready to Give Today

She provided a lot of answers,
though, and I'm more grounded.
So I get a jolt when she says,

> *Kaeleigh, if we've been talking
> about you, I want to get you
> the help you need. The nearest
> residential treatment center
> is in Ventura. . . .*

Residential treatment center?
"No. I don't want to go there.
I mean I . . . why can't I stay here?
Why can't you be my therapist?"

> *This is a regular hospital. There
> are no beds available for psychiatric
> patients. I could treat you, but only
> on an outpatient basis. You'll have
> to go home, and all things considered . . .*

"When? When are they going
to release me?" How long do
I have to make up my mind?

> *Your withdrawal symptoms have
> mostly subsided and your vitals
> are good. Probably tomorrow.*

Tomorrow Isn't Far Enough Away

"Have you talked to my mother?
Does she know what happened?"
Why haven't I heard from her?

Your father said he'd take care
of it. Hasn't she called you?

Well, of course he'd say that.
"My father is a liar." Whoa.
"I'll call her. Where's my cell?"

She goes to the closet, digs
through my things. Um, it
doesn't seem to be here.
You can use mine if you want.

It was in my pocket when all this
shit went down. Where is it?
One answer: Daddy. No wonder
I haven't heard from anyone.

Carol brings me her cell. I start
to dial and suddenly remember
Mom's *I don't see a thing.*
"Will you talk to her? Please?"

Of course. Carol waits, and
when Mom answers, the good
doctor pulls no punches.

535

Mom Promises

To get on a plane as soon as
she can. I don't know whether to feel
relieved or not. Totally weird
to think this, but I've never been so
fucking scared in my life.

I've always believed, of the two
of my parents, she was the one I could
count on. But I had completely
forgotten that bath scene. Who is my
mother? Who the fuck am I?

Am I one person? Two?
Maybe even more? Oh, great. Maybe
there are a dozen of me,
doing drugs and sleeping around
all up and down the state.

Speaking of drugs, I could
use a big fatty right about now.
How will I ever score after
I get out of here? And which one
of me is the loadie, anyway?

I'm sure getting high
isn't good for my "condition,"
but how can I not, if I have
to go home? I can't imagine living
there any other way.

I Suppose I Got the Addictive Gene

From my wonderful father. Something
else to thank him for. Bastard.

> "Thank him for giving you life."

Fuck that. All he did was have sex
with Mom. Probably just one time.

> "Have you noticed you're cussing?"

Now that you mention it, yeah.
That, I'm pretty sure, I got from you.

> "That, and a great sex education."

Sex is disgusting. And I really,
really wish you'd quit talking to me.

> "No can do. You need to hear me."

Well, if you're so smart, what do
I do about Daddy? I need to tell.

> "He'll go to prison for a long time."

So what? He deserves it. Daddies
shouldn't touch their daughters.

> "Not totally his fault. Remember . . ."

Yeah, yeah. So what, am I supposed
to just say okay, it's not your fault?

"You could have a little sympathy."

So I just go on home, wait for him
to go on a bender, drop in for a little?

"Maybe you should confront him."

Confront him? You mean like tell
him to his face that he's a sick man?

"The direct approach might work."

No damn way. He'd deny. He'd
blow up. He'd blame me.

"Face it. You're a chickenshit."

Damn straight. But I can't take this
any longer. And I can't rely on you.

"You always have before."

Sorry. I don't want to be pieces of me
anymore. I have to take care of myself.

"Seeing, my dear, is believing."

I'm Deep into Conversation

With one of me when Daddy walks
through the door. He looks around.

>   *Who are you talking to?*

"Uh. No one. Myself, I guess."
My belly starts cartwheeling.

>   *People will think you're crazy.*

Fuck, Daddy. I *am* crazy.
"I know. I'm sorry, Daddy."

>   *I just got a call from your mother.*

I'm going to throw up.
"I thought she should know."

>   *I told her we can handle this.*

No! No! No! "I want her
here, Daddy. I need her."

>   *You're not three, Kaeleigh.*

"No. I'll never be a little girl again.
You took that away from me."

>   *I'm sure I don't know what you mean.*

Wow, Ballsy

I can't believe I found the nerve
to say that much. But I can't
believe he told Mom not to come.

> *They're releasing you tomorrow.*
> *I'll take the day off to bring you home.*
> *Then we'll have to discuss our options.*

"Options?" What options? Back
to school, back to work, back to . . .
Oh my God. How can I go back?

> *I can't have you getting stoned*
> *and running around like a tramp. Your*
> *reputation may be trashed, but . . .*

"My reputation? *That's* what you're
worried about? What the fuck is wrong
with you, Daddy? You need help."

> *Don't you dare talk to me like that.*
> *He stalks over to the bed, raises*
> *his arm, and just as it starts to fall . . .*

> *I wouldn't do that if I were you,*
> *sir.* Carol. *I'm afraid I'd have*
> *to report you for child abuse.*

Daddy spins to face her, anger
leaking from his pores like sweat.
I know the law. Don't recite it to me.

Artfully, Carol maneuvers between
Daddy and me. *I'm afraid your blood
work indicated a problem, Kaeleigh.*

*We'll need to keep you an extra day
or two, to run a few tests. Sorry.
I know you wanted to go home.*

Daddy backs up a few steps.
*Problem? What kind of problem?
She isn't pregnant, is she?*

Carol's grin is sardonic. *Funny
place for you to go first. No, we've
found an electrolyte imbalance.*

*It's probably from all the vomiting
she's been doing, but we want to
test her for kidney disease.*

Phew. Saved by possible kidney
disease. At least for a couple of days.
Hey, wait. Kidney disease?

Turns Out

The electrolyte imbalance is real,
the result of not only puking
from Oxy withdrawal, but also

the binge-and-purge cycle
that my alter and I seem to have shared.
Speaking of bingeing, I'm starving.

> "You eat. I'll throw it up. You'd be
> a regular oinker if not for me."

They weren't really worried about
kidney disease. Carol just used
that as an excuse to keep me here.

> "She's a real pal. What she's really
> after is dissecting our psyche."

If I let her into my head, maybe she
can make you frigging disappear.
I'm sick of listening to you.

> "Well, then, you go away and let me out.
> I want to play. And I need to get high."

I want so much to talk to Carol.
But I'm not even sure where to begin.
Drug abuse. Alcohol. Bulimia . . .

"Don't forget that lovely bit about
shaving until you slice yourself open."

And that's the easy stuff. Promiscuity.
Dissociative identity disorder. And
the granddaddy of all—fucking Daddy.

"More accurately, letting Daddy
fuck you and keeping it to yourself."

Even if I tell her every bit of it,
there's no guarantee she can fix me.
Suicide sounds better and better.

"Yeah, but you'd have to get it right.
Or maybe, just leave that to me."

What Do I Have to Live For?

Can't think of a single thing.

> Mom? A long-distance mother
> focused completely on herself.

> Friends? Not a single one I've
> allowed myself to get close to.

> School? Can't stomach the thought
> of seeing Old Man Lawler again.

> Drama? Oh well, that's what
> understudies are for, right?

> Boyfriend? Don't make me
> laugh. I'd much rather cry.

> > "Hey, you can't really blame him."

I Can't Blame Ian at All

He's solid.

        "You're fractured."

He's hopeful.

        "You're hopeless."

He's always there.

        "You're half there."

He's faithful.

        "You're so not."

He's giving.

        "You're afraid to give."

He's honest.

        "You lie all the time."

He's loving.

        "You don't know how to love."

But I Do Know What Love Is

And all because of Ian.
I'm still not sure how
to give it, but I've tasted
it. Maybe that's enough.

Maybe that's more than
some people ever get.
Maybe I really need
to taste it right now.

I haven't let myself break
down and weep in a very
long time. Could never see
much use in it, really.

Tears impress no one. But,
oh yeah, there's no one
here to impress. So I go
ahead and let tears fall.

Rain. Storm. Flood. My
pillow soaks with the salt
of regret, and I rest my
head against it, until . . .

Someone's in My Room

I wake, certain of it. It's early
evening, and the room is pale
and the soft perfume of roses
drifts from the nightstand.

Hey. How are you feeling?

I think it can't be, but when
I turn my head, it's Ian's face
I see. The tears start up again
immediately. "Better now."

I should have come sooner, but . . .

He stands, comes over, sits
on the bed, gently brushes
the moisture from my cheeks.
"It's okay." He's here now.

No. I should have been here for you.

He opens his arms and I drop
into their circle. "Oh God,
Ian, I'm so sorry. I don't know
what to tell you, where to begin. . . ."

Don't. Not now. Just let me hold you.

Must Be a Dream

But if it is, I need to stay
locked inside it forever.
I can't believe he's here.
I can't believe he still loves
me, but my heart says he does.

"Oh, Ian. I love you so much.
I'm so sorry I ever hurt you.
If you give me time, help me
get well and strong, I promise
to make everything up to you."

He's quiet for a long time.
Finally he says, *I don't know
exactly what's wrong with you,
or with your life. It would be
easier to walk away, put you*

*and your pain behind me. I've had
days to think it over, and at first
that's what I decided to do.
But I love you so much, the idea
of life without you in it is scarier*

*than trying to deal with this. I've
talked with Dr. Shore, who tells me
you've got a long road to recovery.
I don't know if we can get
through this, but I want to try.*

Okay, One Thing to Live For

And right now, one thing is enough.

I have to believe we can make it.

Without that, I have nothing at all.

One thing to live for. One day at a time.

It will not be easy to let him all the way in.

But if I can open up to anyone, it's Ian.

Okay, maybe to Carol—Dr. Shore—first.

Then she can show me how to let him in.

One thing to live for. One day at a time.

Daddy will try to stand in the way.

So I have to push Daddy out of my way.

To do that, I need Ian's strength behind me.

One thing to live for. One day at a time.

Daddy Comes to Pick Me Up

And all the courage I gathered overnight
dissipates like smoke in winter wind.

> He hands me a paper bag. *Clean clothes.*
> *The ones you have here stink to high heaven.*

Dutifully I go into the bathroom, slip into soft
blue velour. It should feel comforting. But . . .

> When I emerge, Daddy is looking at Ian's roses.
> *I hope he has enough sense to stay away.*

Wrong! "Ian is the only good thing in my life.
Don't you dare try to keep him away from me!"

> Daddy's stare is iron. *I guess we're lucky*
> *you* aren't *pregnant, aren't we?*

"Shut up! Ian and I never . . . Don't you get
that love doesn't have to be about sex?"

> He stays in control, in case Carol is near.
> *Don't you ever tell me to shut up again.*

"Or what, Daddy? I won't let you hurt me
anymore. I swear to God I'll tell everything."

> He comes closer, lowers his voice. *Go ahead.*
> *Your word against mine. No one will believe you.*

I will. The voice precedes a woman—
not quite familiar—through the door.

Daddy's jaw drops. *Mother! Dear God.
How did . . . what are you doing here?*

Grandma Charlotte. Yes, I can almost
remember her face. Only it's thinner,

her gray eyes clearer. And she smells
of expensive perfume. Not whiskey.

She draws near, reaches out one hand, but
doesn't touch me. *Kaeleigh. How pretty you*

*are. So like your mother. Forgive my long
absence. And, please, forgive my silence.*

Six Months

Since my grandmother re-entered
my life. Six months of relative
safety. Ha-ha. Forgive the pun.

I live with her now, in my parents'
postcard-pretty dwelling, coiffed
and manicured from curb to chimney.

Like me, it's perfect on the outside.
But behind the Norman Rockwell facade,
I'm slowly coming to terms with our secrets.

> That day in the hospital, Grandma
> Charlotte confessed hers: *I was too*
> *young to be a mother, only sixteen.*
>
> *Ted was not a bad man. When I got*
> *pregnant, he did the right thing*
> *and married me. But we came from*
>
> *different places. I was a child of privilege,*
> *he a sweet blue-collar man. He was my*
> *rebellion. And when he couldn't give*
>
> *me the life I was used to, I fell into*
> *addictions. Whiskey. Cigarettes. And,*
> *to fight my depression, Prozac.*

He cheated, yes, but that's not why
I left. I left from utter boredom.
And I left your poor father behind.

Daddy winced, but continued to
listen. I wanted to know more.
I wanted to know everything.

Alcoholism is not a pretty thing,
and I was an ugly alcoholic.
I moved in with a string of men.

None wanted to deal with a drunk,
and eventually all of them showed
me the door. One time, I decided

I needed to find Ray, see how he
was doing. I tracked him to Santa
Barbara, a couple of years before

the accident. Your mother and he
seemed happy enough. Happy to
have two beautiful daughters.

I wanted to be part of your family,
even managed to clean up my act
so they'd let me spend time with you.

"So it *was* you who used to babysit
us. I remember we used to play
Monopoly and checkers, didn't we?"

> She nodded. *It was a wonderful*
> *time of my life. But then . . .*
> *then the accident happened.*
>
> *When Raeanne died, I only knew*
> *one way to cope. I'm sorry,*
> *Kaeleigh. You needed me.*
>
> *But I needed Dewar's to get me*
> *through the funeral. Once I started*
> *drinking again, I couldn't stop.*

I noticed Daddy's fingers,
drumming the arm of his chair.
"But why did you go away?"

> Grandma Charlotte glanced at
> Daddy, whose drumming quickened.
> *We can talk about that later.*

Turned Out

That part of the story helped
me make some major decisions.
That part of the story went like this:

> *I wanted to stay in your life, knew*
> *you might need me. Your mother*
> *was broken, your father cold as*
> *the death of his daughter—the death*
> *he most certainly caused. The death*
> *none of us could really accept.*
>
> *One day I came over and walked*
> *in unannounced. I heard noise*
> *in the bathroom, so stumbled back*
> *to investigate, about three sheets*
> *in the wind. I was drunk but not too*
> *drunk to take in what was going on.*
>
> *Your mother was gone, and your*
> *father was washing you. Only the way*
> *he was washing you was all wrong.*
> *He was touching you in a sexual*
> *way, Kaeleigh. I confronted him,*
> *but he just laughed in my face.*
>
> *"I'm a respected judge and you are*
> *nothing more than a disgusting*
> *drunk. Who would people believe?*

I could take you down, Mother.
Will *take you down. You made me
what I am. You and my father."*

He ordered me to leave, and I did.
In fact, I ran. Forgive me, Kaeleigh.
I should have kept you safe.
Instead I drank even more to forget.
I drank until one day I looked in
the mirror and saw death.

Getting sober once and for all
wasn't easy. But I didn't want
to die until I knew you were okay.
And I didn't want to come back
into your life, needing Dewar's
to cope with what I found.

I Forgave Her

She got sober for me. Besides,
Daddy played the same card
with me, and I believed him, too.

Anyway, Carol says the only way
to get past all this is to forgive
who I can. Confront, and forgive.

Easier said than done. I want to
forgive Mom. But how can I when
she won't say she's sorry, or even

admit her role in this melodrama?
I did confront her. I asked how
she could have closed her eyes,

pretended nothing was wrong. She
turned it back on me. *Why didn't
you tell? Why didn't you get help?*

I hated her for a while. Now
I kind of feel sorry for her. When
Raeanne died, it emptied

every ounce of love from Mom's
heart. Why couldn't she save
just a spoonful—for me?

Drained Dry

Of love, she's surviving fine
in DC. Comes home once in a while,

more because it's expected of her
than to spend time with me.

I think I scare her. I mean, how
can she be certain which one

of me she's spending time with?
Dissociative identity disorder

wasn't even in her dictionary,
let alone on her radar.

Now that it's on mine, I suppose
I'll always do a double take

whenever I happen to pass
by a mirror.

Except for Ian

No one at school knows
        about the two sides of me.
                Ian swore himself to secrecy.

Everyone else thinks I had
        a mild case of viral meningitis.
                Well, DID is a brain thing, after all.

I missed some school, but not
        much, made it up quickly, so
                I'm not really behind. At Carol's

urging, I apologized to Mr. Lawler,
        who gave me an A for the semester.
                In fact, I managed a 3.5 GPA. All As.

Except PE. Can't have everything.
        Drama? The play went perfectly.
                We brought 'em to their feet.

I still hate Madison, avoid her
        when I can. But I don't get in her
                face. The game has lost its appeal.

I Cringe

If I see Ty or Mick, who I guess
walked until he found his truck
and never said a word to anyone.

Ty is the only other person who
might suspect DID. But there are
lots of reasons for him to keep quiet.

Carol has helped me understand
why I pushed myself into such explicit
sexual behavior. It was programmed

into me when I was very small.
Part of me hated it. Part of me
couldn't help but enjoy it. Part.

I'm taking driver's training.
When I'm ready, Grandma
Charlotte will sign for my license.

One cool thing. She and Grandpa
Ted are talking again. Not like they're
dating, but at least they're cordial.

I still work at the old folks' home,
but only one day a week, mostly
just to stay in touch with Greta.

She Is My Real Angel

And the only one who understands
the depth of Daddy's deceptions.
Not even Carol knows firsthand
how it feels to be hurt in such a way
by someone who's supposed to protect you.

> Greta is the one who convinced me
> I had to confront Daddy with every
> ugly truth, had to force him out of my
> life. *If you don't, you will never
> begin to heal. And you can heal.*

I didn't want him to go to prison.
He probably would have pulled
strings to avoid it, anyway. I didn't
want to see him locked up. But
more, I didn't want to testify.

Didn't want the world to hear all
the dirty details. Daddy checked
himself into a pricey rehab,
promised to get his head fixed.
Not sure that's possible.

When he gets out, he'll move
into an apartment in Santa Barbara.
Thirty miles away. Not far enough.
But it is what it is. I have not
forgiven him. Not sure I ever will.

Ian Still Doesn't Know

About Daddy. I just can't bring
myself to tell him. He thinks

the stuff that happened is because
of the accident. Childhood trauma.

Oh yes, one of many. But he doesn't
need to know the worst of them.

Maybe one day I'll be able to let
him that far in. But not yet.

For now, it's enough to have him
in my life, to see him every day.

Grandma lets him come over,
is good with us dating. Maybe

she knows we still don't have sex.
Not ready yet. And he knows it.

We've come close. Lots of times.
Can't help but get turned on by him.

I'm not a frigging saint. But when
we do, I want it to be for all the right

reasons, and I won't know it's right
until I get beyond all the wrongs.

I'd Like to Say

I'm over my addictions.
Not sure I ever will be completely.
It's good that Grandma

is in the twelve-step program.
She doesn't keep alcohol in the house.
And, of course, the Oxy is gone.

I'll never do that stuff again.
The withdrawal is killer. Never again.
But I have to admit, I've smoked

a little bud. Not that much.
I'd probably do more, but it's expensive.
And now it's cash-and-carry.

I still use food for comfort.
I still purge when I get too comfortable.
And once in a while, when

memory intrudes, I still
enjoy a good, deep shave. Oh, come on.
I never said I was perfect.

When I Do Those Things

When I use or purge or cut,
I'm still not myself. Maybe
I just use her as an excuse
to do them, but I feel as if

she

takes over then. The only
difference is, I'm aware
of her. I never used to be.
I'm not sure if I

will

remember everything I did
as Raeanne. I'm not sure
I want to, though Carol thinks
I need to try. And hey, I could

always

blame Daddy. He's my forever
scapegoat, really. Okay, that's not
so healthy. But totally healthy
is something I might not ever

be.

One thing for sure. I will break
the abuse cycle. It stops with me.
My children will not live in fear.
I will create a home of nurture
and love, and raise them safely

there.

Raeanne
And I'll Be Watching

Watching her. Watching out
for her. And if the time comes
she needs complete escape,

I

will walk for her. Talk for her.
Take punishment in her place.
Some things don't need to be
remembered. And I

will

hold on to those things for her.
Carol believes she can make
me go away, and I'll pretend
to let her do her job. But I will

always

be the strongest part of Kaeleigh,
so I can't let her dispose of me.
I'll stay quiet, no more than a dark
shadow inside. That's what I'll

be.

A silhouette, rarely seen, and yet
believed in. Kaeleigh wants to
believe in me. I am her twin,
forever alive inside her. And
when she needs me, I am always

here.

Be sure to read

Ellen Hopkins's

PERFECT

Perfect is the story of four high school seniors, all of whom have friends, siblings, and a drive to attain "perfection." They each have very different goals, and very different ways of achieving them. Meet Cara, whose parents' unrealistic expectations have already sent her twin brother spiraling toward suicide; Kendra, a pageant girl who stops at nothing in her pursuit of runway modeling; Sean, who uses whatever means necessary to win a baseball scholarship; and Andre, whose real talent seems destined to languish. Just how far does someone have to go to be *perfect*?

Cara Sierra Sykes
Perfect?

How

    do you define a word without
    concrete meaning? To each
    his own, the saying goes, so

why

    push to attain an ideal
    state of being that no two
    random people will agree is

where

    you want to be? Faultless.
    Finished. Incomparable. People
    can never be these, and anyway,

when

    did creating a flawless facade
    become a more vital goal
    than learning to love the person

who

    lives inside your skin?
    The outside belongs to others.
    Only you should decide for you—

what

    is perfect.

Perfection

I've lived with the pretense
of perfection for seventeen
years. Give my room a cursory
inspection, you'd think I have OCD.

But it's only habit and not
obsession that keeps it all orderly.
Of course, I don't want to give
the impression that it's all up to me.

Most of the heavy labor is done by
our housekeeper, Gwen. She's an
imposing woman, not at all the type
that most men would find attractive.

Not even Conner, which is the point.
My twin has a taste for older
women. Before he got himself
locked away, he chased after more

than one. I should have told sooner
about the one he caught, the one
I happened to overhear him with,
having a little afternoon fun.

Okay, I know a psychologist
would say, strictly speaking,
he was prey, not predator.
And, in a way, I can't really

blame him. Emily is simply
stunning. Conner wasn't the only
one who used to watch her go
running by our house every

morning. But, hello, she was
his *teacher*. That fact alone
should have been enough warning
that things would not turn out well.

I never would have expected
Conner to attempt the coward's way
out, though. Some consider suicide
an act of honor. I seriously don't agree.

But even if it were, you'd have to
get it right. All Conner did was
stain Mom's new white Berber
carpet. They're replacing it now.

Kendra Melody Mathieson
Pretty

That's what I am, I guess.
I mean, people have been telling
me that's what I am since
I was two. Maybe younger.

                                        Pretty

as a picture. (Who wants
to be a cliché?) Pretty as
an angel. (Can you see them?)
Pretty as a butterfly. (But

                                        isn't

that really just a glam bug?)
Cliché, invisible, or insectlike,
I grew up knowing I was
pretty and believing everything

                                        good

about me had to do with how
I looked. The mirror was my best
friend. Until it started telling
me I wasn't really pretty

                                        enough.

Pale Beauty

That's what my mom calls the gift
                    she gave me, through genetics.

We are Scandinavian willows,
                    with vanilla hair and glacier blue

eyes and bone china skin. Two
                    hours in the sun turns me the color

of ripe watermelon. When I lead
                    cheers at football games, it is wearing

SPF 60 sunblock. Gross. Basketball
                    season is better, but I'll be glad

when it's over. Between dance lessons
                    and vocal training and helping out

at the food bank (all grooming for Miss
                    Teen Nevada), I barely have time for

homework, let alone fun. At least
                    staying busy mostly keeps my mind

off Conner. I wish I could forget
        about him, but that's not possible.

I tumbled hard for that guy. Gave him
        all of me. I thought we had something

special. He even let me see the scared
        little boy inside him, the one not many

other people ever catch a glimpse of.
        I wonder if he showed that boy to

the ambulance drivers who took him to
        the hospital, or to the doctors and nurses

who dug the bullet out of his chest. Sewed
        him up. Saved his life. I want to see him, but

Cara says he can't have visitors. Bet he doesn't
        want them—scared he might look helpless.

Sean Terrence O'Connell
Buff

Don't like that word.
Not tough enough to describe
a weight-sculpted body.

"Built"

is better. Like a builder
frames a house,
constructing its skeleton
two-by-four

by

two-by-four, a real
athlete shapes himself
muscle group by muscle
group, ignoring the

pain.

Focused completely on
the gain. It can't happen
overnight. It takes hours
every single day

and

no one can force you to
do it. Becoming the best
takes a shitload of inborn

drive.

Drive

That's what it takes to reach
            the top, and that is where
                        I've set my sights. Second
            best means you lose. Period.
I will be the best damn first

baseman *ever* in the league.
            My dad was a total baseball
                        freak (weird, considering
            he coached football), and
when I was a kid, he went

on and on about McGwire
            being the first base king.
                        I grew up wanting to be
            first base royalty. T-ball,
then years of Little League,

gave me the skills I need.
            But earning that crown
                        demands more than skill.
            What it requires are arms
like Mark McGwire's.

I Play Football, Too

Kind of a tribute to Dad.
　　　　　But, while I'm an okay
　　　　　　　　　safety, my real talent
　　　　　is at the bat. I'll use
it to get into Stanford.

The school's got a great
　　　　　program. But even if
　　　　　　　　　it didn't, it would be
　　　　　at the top of my university
wish list because Cara will

go there, I'm sure. She says
　　　　　it isn't a lock, but that's bull.
　　　　　　　　　Her parents are both alumni,
　　　　　and her father has plenty of
pull. Money. And connections.

Uncle Jeff has connections, too,
　　　　　and there will be Stanford
　　　　　　　　　scouts at some random (or
　　　　　maybe not so) game. I have
to play brilliantly every time.

Andre Marcus Kane III
Bomb

Give most girls a way
to describe me, that's what
they'd say—that Andre
Marcus Kane the third is

                           bomb.

I struggle daily to maintain
the pretense. Why must it be
expected—no, demanded—of

                           me

to surpass my ancestors'
achievements? Why
can't I just be a regular
seventeen-year-old, trying to

                           make

sense of life? But my path
has been preordained,
without anyone even asking

                           me

what I want. Nobody seems
to care that with every push
to live up to their expectations,
my own dreams

                           vaporize.

Don't Get Me Wrong

I do understand my parents wanting only
the best for me.
Am one hundred percent tuned to the concept

that life is a hell of a lot more enjoyable
fun with a fast-
flowing stream of money carrying you

along. I like driving a pricey car, wearing
clothes that feel
like they want to be next to my skin.

I love not having to be a living, breathing
stereotype because
of my color. Anytime I happen to think

about it, I am grateful to my grandparents
for their vision.
Grateful to my mom for her smarts,

to my father for his bald ambition,
and, yes, greed.
Not to mention unreal intuition.

My Grandfather

Andre Marcus Kane Sr. embraced
the color of his skin,
refused to let it straitjacket

him. He grew up in the urban
California nightmare
called Oakland, with its rutted

asphalt and crumbling cement
and frozen dreams,
all within sight of hillside mansions.

I'd look up at those houses, he told
me more than once,
and think to myself, no reason why

that can't be me, living up there.
No reason at all,
except getting sucked down into

the swamp. Meaning welfare or the drug
trade or even the cliché
idea that sports were the only way out.

𝒜 true story
of escaping abuse
in a small town
only to find more
in the big city
and the way
one girl overcomes
them both.

A MEMOIR

smile for the camera

kelle james

Bigger, Faster, Stronger*

*achieved through harder workouts, longer runs . . . and steroids

EBOOK EDITION ALSO AVAILABLE

ATHENEUM BOOKS FOR YOUNG READERS

TEEN.SimonandSchuster.com